Hell's Hundred Acres

Andrew Serra

Tudor City Press

Copyright © 2025 by Andrew Serra

All rights reserved.

No portion of this book may be reproduced in any form without written permission from the publisher or author, except as permitted by U.S. copyright law.

This is a work of fiction. Certain real events, places, and institutions are mentioned, but all of the characters and events in this book are either products of the author's imagination or are used fictitiously. Any resemblance to actual persons or events, living or dead, is purely coincidental.

ISBN: 978-1-7322380-8-4 (hardcover)

ISBN: 978-1-7322380-7-7 (paperback)

Library of Congress Control Number: 2024923268

Cover art & interior illustrations by Chris Burke

Cover design by John (Viet-Triet) Hoa Nguyen

Newspaper and magazine article templates used with permission from Canva

Tudor City Press, New York, NY

"Hell's Hundred Acres is the name aptly given, by Fire Commissioner Edward F. Cavanagh, Jr., to the area in lower Manhattan, roughly bounded by Chambers Street on the south, Bowery on the east, 14th Street on the north, and Avenue of the Americas and West Broadway on the west. An area of old and deteriorating loft buildings, it is probably the worst fire hazard area in the city, and has been described in some quarters as an industrial and commercial slum..."

With New York Firemen, 1961

Prologue

The Progressive Era was a time of upheaval. Toiling under the hardships and misery industrialization had brought, workers began pushing back. There was coalescence and there was action. Unions were rising but were not yet at their peak. But it was a golden age for private detectives. If a robber baron needed a strike broken up, he'd call Pinkerton, the country's largest detective agency. Some jobs, however, required special measures. And for these they called Max Schlansky. Private detectives would rough-up picketers, with mixed results. Schlansky wasn't afraid to take it one step further. He was a violent, but careful man, and that's what made him so effective. The rich and powerful paid him well to take care of their problems.

He stood along the wall of a tenement, just out of the light of a streetlamp, with the rim of his Bowler hat low and his collar up. Inside his coat was a heavy wooden club. He would avoid a repeat of last time, where despite doing his job well, the result had been opposite the clients' intentions. Instead of intimidating the victim, he'd turned her into a martyr—one who inspired thousands. This time he'd be more careful. The chilly air kept most people off the street. He waited in the shadows and watched out for his target. Sooner or later, she'd be coming home.

Part One

1

1911

ESTHER GREENBERG WOKE SUDDENLY with a terrible dread. Her heart was racing and she sat up to see the moonlight arching softly across the bed she shared with her sister. It was the same dream—always similar but each time slightly different—that had frightened her from her sleep. Esther was running beside a moving train. Gunshots cracked from somewhere behind. On the step of the rolling train car was her mother, father, and sister. They reached out and called her name. Esther tried for their hands but could not grab hold. They were just out of reach. "*Tate!*" she called out. Dad! He gazed at her with those loving brown eyes and stretched further. He was right there. She remembered feeling strange in the dream, as if suddenly realizing she'd been mistaken all along. *See, he's not gone. He's right there. He's alive and he's right there.* There were more gunshots and Esther ran so hard her chest hurt. She reached again but the train car kept getting further away. "*Tateshi!*" she cried. Daddy!

That's when she'd woken up. She looked over at Rachel. Her sister was sound asleep, breathing softly. Esther put her head back on the pillow and tried to fall back asleep. It would be a long day at the factory tomorrow if she didn't.

Esther was sleeping heavily when Rachel tapped her shoulder and went out into the public hall to use the toilet. The next thing Esther knew, Rachel was frantic.

"We're going to be late!"

"Huh."

"Get up, get up, get up."

Esther opened her eyes and saw Rachel seated on the edge of their bed tying her brown leather ankle boots. "Ugh, the sole is falling off," she complained while looping the laces. "The front is flapping down." She flattened the pleat of her skirt, which was just above the boot tops.

"What time is it?" Esther asked.

Rachel went through the doorway deeper into the railroad flat and called out across the apartment: "Six twenty-five."

Esther shot up and pulled her night gown over her head. She quickly grabbed her long skirt from the chair and stepped in, pulling it up over her slip. She took her shirtwaist next and put her arms in and then frantically began buttoning. Rachel returned, bundled in an overcoat.

"Ready?"

"Where's my shoes?"

"Est, come on!" The panic in Rachel's voice was growing. Just last week, their friend Francine had arrived four minutes late and the foreman sent her home without pay. She had to schlep all the way back home to Brooklyn minus a day's wages.

They were at the apartment door and Esther was pulling her arms through her coat when their mother crossed the room with a small skillet. It contained two slices of rye bread sizzling in schmaltz, or chicken fat. "*Es! Es!*" she said in Yiddish. Eat! Eat! Esther and Rachel each grabbed a slice.

They were practically running up Essex Street, still chewing the rye bread. When they got to Houston Street they turned left and headed west. They held hands and weaved between a train of vegetable-laden push carts. When an old man yelled at them in Italian, they began laughing and almost had to stop because it was hard to catch a breath between giggles. Hand in hand, they jumped over manure piles and swerved around puddles. It was a cool, damp winter morning. Esther was pretty sure they'd make it on time. They needed to stop at the grocer to buy lunch, but that wouldn't take long. Above all, she wanted to go pee. If she had to run straight to her sewing machine for the starting bell, she'd have to hold it till lunch.

When they arrived at the corner of Greene Street and Washington Place, the line of workers outside the service entrance was hundreds deep, all waiting to be brought by elevator to the ninth floor in groups of fifteen. Esther stood in line, dancing and praying she would make it to the toilet. When they finally boarded the service elevator, a young man wearing a bell cap held the accordion gate open and called out: "Step aboard ladies. Step aboard."

Esther and Rachel stepped past the young man, while he smiled and said softly: "Good morning, Miss Rachel." Esther had wondered if this young man—Gaspar was his name—would be there this morning. He usually operated one of the two passenger elevators. But every so often he would man the service elevator. He always tried to speak to Rachel.

Rachel said good morning and looked down at the floor trying not to smile. Esther elbowed her sister in the ribs, but she did not react. "He *loves* you," whispered Esther as thirteen other girls and young women packed in around them. Gaspar closed the gate and pushed a brass handle forward. Up they went. The elevator was little more than a cage—and Esther could see right into every floor they passed on the way. It stopped and Gaspar opened the accordion gate. Out poured the workers, mostly all seamstresses. Cutters and foremen were allowed to use the passenger elevators at the front entrance. Esther looked over to Rachel.

"See you later, Gaspar," said Rachel, not too loudly.

Esther giggled but instead of further teasing her sister she ran around the crowd headed for the coat room. She had to get to the toilet. She came out just ahead of the starting bell and scrambled to her seat. The ninth floor was a big open space with over 270 sewing machines, arranged on eight long tables. Esther's place was opposite the coat room and she had to circle the perimeter. Rachel, who had yet to be promoted from trainee, sat opposite and there was a trough in between for finished pieces.

Esther and Rachel were both "body makers", which is to say they only sewed the torso portion of the shirtwaist, or blouse. Esther sat and picked up the piece she had left half-finished on her machine at closing the day before. She stepped on a pedal and her machine buzzed to life. The pace was intense. Esther's foreman was paid by the number of shirtwaists his team produced, and each garment was rigidly checked by inspectors for size uniformity and craftsmanship. When the foreman, Mr. Craven, wasn't yelling at the seamstresses about their speed, he was reprimanding them for their quality. "Rejected shirtwaists earn nothing," he liked to say. Esther concentrated on her seam but couldn't help glancing up at her sister. Rachel caught her gaze and they exchanged smiles. While Esther was again looking down at the thin silk material she fed under the needle, Rachel spoke.

"Francine and Ida are going to the dance at the Manhattan Lyceum Saturday night."

Esther looked across to the young woman beside Rachel. Ida glanced up and smiled without slowing her work. Esther continued stitching, expecting Rachel to say more. After a moment's silence, she glanced at her sister again. Rachel was staring at her—she raised her eyebrows. Esther returned her focus to the sewing machine but heard her sister whisper to Ida: "We'll see you there."

Esther smiled.

2

CHARLES FRANCIS PENDERGRASS SAT in the dark kitchen drinking a cup of black coffee. It wasn't as sweet as he would have liked it—the sugar jar was empty. He could hear his mother stirring in the bedroom. He stood to put the cup in the sink when she walked in.

"Up bright and early," she said.

"Yeah, well... can't be late my first day." His tone betrayed a hint of bitterness.

"Ach—enough of that," she answered while taking the coffee pot from the top of the stove. She went to the shelf for a cup and poured.

"We're out of sugar," he said.

She made a face but kept pouring. "This job will be the best thing for you. What would'ya have done... Tie up boats on the docks for the rest of your life?"

"I could've learned the trade—the riggers all liked me."

"Ach—sure. You did all their dirty work for two years. Now you'll have a profession."

Charlie was quiet for a moment while he bent down and tied his shoes. "I just wish it wasn't always him—always him giving me something. I'm my own man."

"And what did he ever give you that it wasn't his God-sworn duty as a man to give? Answer that. Your father died working for *him*. So he paid our rent for six months—and he let you sweep the floor in his hoity-toity saloon when you was a boy. Is that so much more than the Lord would have asked of the man?"

"There were thirty men with me at the Fire College. All of them were assigned to the new battalions in the Bronx and in Queens. I was the only man sent here to Downtown. You don't think *he* had a hand in that?"

"So what if he did? He kept you close to home is all."

"He'll be wanting something in return."

"It was me who asked *him*," she rebutted as she sat and sipped her coffee. "Ach—damned sugar. It was me who asked him to find something for you, something where you could make a proper living. If he's got any idea in his head, it's only 'cause I was the one who put it there. But you're right, Charlie. You *are* your own man. Give this a try is all I asked you when you started, and it's all I ask you now. If it's not the job for you, I'm sure they'll take you back at the docks."

CHARLIE WALKED OUT THE front door of his tenement onto East 20th Street. The breeze from the East River was strong and he looked left to see the sun rising over the massive, circular gas tanks dominating the skyline of the Gas House District. It wasn't long after sunrise, but this was his first day and the instructors at the Fire College had stressed the importance of being early. Over one shoulder hung a duffle bag and draped off the other was his long rubber slicker coat. He held a brand-new fire helmet. It was shiny black leather, delivered from the Cairns Brothers Company to the Fire College just last week. He slipped the helmet onto his head, and it looked so odd without the angular company number front piece affixed that it might have been mistaken for a top hat.

Overnight rain had left the unpaved 20th Street with little surface besides puddles and mud. He moved quickly to First Avenue where the cobble stones shone brightly from their rinsing. Charlie smelled only damp winter air, but he knew the stones would be littered with manure soon enough. For now, he walked down the center of the avenue without a carriage in sight, or an automobile for that matter. He guessed it would be about a half-hour's walk to Mercer Street, where Hook and Ladder Company 20 was quartered.

He passed a closed food market and thought about buying some sugar for his mother. He would be at the firehouse for the next ten days, but he'd be leaving with a week's pay. His mother had had a hard life, worked long hours and raised him by herself. She was right to feel that her husband's cousin owed them something. And Charlie couldn't blame her for wanting a better life for him. But this was not the life he'd envisioned for himself. He may have resented his father's cousin, but he also admired him. He too had started out on the docks and he'd saved money to buy a saloon. From bartender to local political organizer, he worked his way up. Sweeping the floor as a boy, Charlie was amazed at how lucrative such a place could be for its owner. When he was eighteen, instead of asking his cousin to be promoted to bartender, he quit and started working on the docks. If he could have made rigger, he would have been able to save enough to buy a saloon—and then a whole string of saloons. He had no intention of getting drawn into politics like his cousin. He just wanted to get rich.

But then there was his mother. She'd sacrificed so much to take care of him. She really wanted him to join the fire department. The other men in the Gas House District—the policemen and firemen—all made steady livings. Their wives always had money for groceries. Their rent was always paid. One man, Martin Donleavy, even made police captain and moved his family to Middle Village, Queens. But the other policemen and firemen were all working class. They would never be rich, but more importantly, they'd never be poor. Charlie knew that his mother—more than anything else in life—wanted that kind of security for her son. He owed it to her to try this.

The firehouse was three-stories tall with two bay doors—one of which was open. He stepped inside and his nostrils filled with the smell of horse hair and manure. Up front, along the wall was the housewatch, where a massive, cast-iron radiator painted silver was jutting out from the wall. Butted up against it was a square pinewood desk with a lamp and ledger book. Framed by a dark wood border, the wall beside the desk had a blackboard crammed with chalk numbers. In the center was two silver bell housings mounted flat on the wall with a telegraph switch between them, and also a telephone box consisting of two smaller bells and a handheld receiver hung on the front and attached by a chord. A fireman sat upright and proper, a badged uniform cap on his head, writing in the thick ledger. Steam rose from a cup of coffee resting atop the radiator. Charlie stepped inside and the fireman looked up. He stood and stepped from the desk to Charlie. He was tall—six foot three maybe—and brawny.

"You Pendergrass?" he asked brusquely. His eyes were light-colored, blue or even gray, Charlie thought, and he stared-down Charlie hard.

Charlie placed the duffle bag and slicker coat on the ground and stepped closer with his hand extended. "Yes, Charlie Pendergrass."

There was an awkward moment and Charlie wasn't sure if he should take his hand back. At last, the man shook hands. "Andrew Ott," he said and gave a big smile.

"How did you know my name?"

"Chief Worth got the special orders from division yesterday. You're the first probationary fireman here, since—well, me. Almost three years ago. It's all the men are talkin' about."

"Oh," offered Charlie weakly. "I see."

"Bring your stuff over here," Ott said as he grabbed his coffee and walked toward the back of the spacious apparatus floor. A glimmering brass pole came down through a man-sized oculus in the ceiling and stood fixed in the cement floor along the wall behind the housewatch desk. Charlie looked up into the hole and wondered what was going on in the mysterious world above. After the pole was a work bench and Ott instructed him to leave his things there.

    Charlie did as told. He was beside a long ladder truck—longest truck he'd ever seen. There was a steering wheel up top on the back of the truck, and then a sectioned wooden ladder affixed to a massive crank of some kind. The front had a leather riding bench up top, and out front was a cross bar with three sets of wooden shafts each preassembled to a hitch. Each hitch, a horse's harness consisting of a leather backband and backstrap, was hanging empty from a rope tied to the ceiling, as if fitted over an invisible horse. The wooden body of the truck was painted bright red, with the initials F.D.N.Y. emblazoned in gold leaf on either side. It sure was a beautiful rig.

    "Tallest ladder in the city," Ott said.

    Charlie turned. "Sure is big."

    "We need 'em—both of 'em." Ott motioned with his head to the identical truck resting parallel, adjacent the other bay door. "Tallest buildings in the city are all down here. We're a double company here, Twenty Truck. We do more fire duty—hours wise—than any company in the city. When the first section here is at an alarm, the second section takes in the runs."

    "Runs?"

    "Yeah—Runs! Ya know... Alarms... Fires! Jeeze, didn't they teach you anything at that fancy new Fire College?"

    "They taught us scaling ladders, and life nets... And how to pack a hose bed."

    Ott laughed. "Well, you won't be packin' much hose here on the truck. Runs is what we call any alarm we respond to. From the old days, before horse-drawn engines, when the firemen pulled the pumpers and ran on foot." Ott grabbed Charlie's new helmet from the bench. He took off his uniform cap and placed the helmet on his head. It didn't fit and Ott looked ridiculous with the helmet teetering atop his bulging temples. "Shiny," he said dryly. "You'll break it in soon enough."

Behind the truck was a narrow swing door and out walked a stern looking man with a newspaper folded under one armpit and a cup of coffee in his hand. He was tall, with silver-streaked hair neatly combed. Charlie thought the man looked very neat in his necktie, so early in the morning.

"Mr. Ott," the man bellowed. The subway tiles carried his voice across the long apparatus floor with perfect acoustics. "Why is the housewatch unattended?"

"Sorry Capt'n," uttered Ott.

"Foreman, Mr. Ott. How many times must I remind you you're not in the navy anymore?"

"Yes, skipper," answered Ott.

The man stopped directly in front of them and Charlie wasn't sure if he was going to rip into Ott for being a smart Aleck, or bite off his (Charlie's) head for some unforeseen reason. "You must be Pendergrass," he said simply, but not without a hint of kindness. The man offered his hand and Charlie shook it.

"John Jennings, I'll be your foreman. Mr. Woll is upstairs. He's your assistant foreman. Mr. Ott here will show you around..." He paused and looked at Ott. "*After* he gets relieved on the housewatch. Once you get settled, come up to my office and I'll go over some things."

"Yes skip... I mean sir," Charlie answered timidly.

Jennings shot a dirty look at Ott and then said sharply: "Where's your uniform cap, Housewatchman?"

Ott quickly reached for his cap, and Jennings went to the back of the apparatus floor to climb a huge, wrought-iron spiral staircase.

"That's Foreman Jennings. He's not so bad. He's a stickler for discipline but he looks out for us." While Ott was speaking, Charlie turned his attention to the line of stalls at the rear of the apparatus floor. Seven horses stood neatly—all of them chewing.

"You'll meet them soon enough," Ott said softly as he leaned closer to Charlie's ear and laughed. "Hope you like shovellin' horse shit!"

The door swung again and out charged a Dalmatian—straight to Charlie. He jumped up and pawed Charlie's chest, trying to sniff his face. Charlie laughed and petted the dog behind the ears. Two men followed. "Smokey—down boy," one yelled.

"Pendergrass, huh," said the other. "You don't look six feet!"

Confused, Charlie said nothing.

The man went to the ladder truck and pulled off a tool. It was a wooden pole with an iron point and hook mounted on one end. "Stand next to this six-foot hook here. Let's just see how you measure up."

"Floyd," Ott broke in. "I think he's good."

"Quiet, Johnny," the man answered. "Let's go, Pendergrass. Stand upstraight."

Johnny, Charlie thought. *I thought Ott's first name was Andrew.* Floyd held the six-foot hook straight up while the other man grabbed Charlie's shoulders, spun him and put his back against the tool.

"Ehhhh... Not quite there!" Floyd announced, holding his hand atop Charlie's head.

"How tall did you say you are?" the other man said.

I didn't say anything, thought Charlie. "Five-eleven," he answered.

"See," said Floyd. "I knew that chief was full of shit. Only men over six foot two he promised."

"Who are you kid?" the other man asked. "The mayor's nephew or somethin'?"

A quick bolt of fear shot through Charlie, but he said nothing. He looked at the three men: Ott, Floyd something, and the other man. They were all taller than him. The Dalmatian suddenly barked and charged at the open door up front.

"Smokey..." Floyd called after him. The two men went after the dog, leaving only Ott with Charlie.

"That's Floyd Mance and Fred Schley. My first year here I just kept my mouth shut and did what they told me to. They'll come around to ya' eventually."

"What did they mean about the chief's promise?"

"Oh yeah, that. There's a Deputy Chief, uh Kenlon. He looks at all assignments here in Twenty Truck and makes sure only tall men are assigned. It's the loft buildings, ya see! The ceilings are high and its harder for short guys to open them up—plus there's the iron shutters on the factory windows. Tall guys can reach 'em from the ladder and unlatch them."

Now two dogs were barking, and Charlie saw a bushy black dog charging at him. He jumped up on the step of the ladder truck and the dog ran past, followed quickly by Smokey the Dalmatian barking after him. Floyd Mance and Fred Schley were chasing the two dogs and shouting. The black dog circled the rig and went out the front door. Ott had positioned himself by the front of the truck and grabbed Smokey. They all laughed until the squeaking hinges and clanking of a swinging gate could be heard overhead. Ott, Mance, and Schley fell silent immediately. From the hole in ceiling at the top of the brass pole boomed a stern voice: "Wouldn't happen if there was a man on the watch!"

Charlie gave a small chuckle seeing the hulking Ott run to the housewatch like a chastened schoolboy.

THE WORKDAY BEGAN WITH a whirlwind of activity and a lot of new faces. Charlie didn't think he'd ever remember all the names. There was his foreman, Jennings, his assistant foreman, Woll, and of course Andrew Ott—those he knew. But there were six other firemen working in Hook and Ladder 20 with him. Then there was Hook and Ladder 20's second section with another six firemen on duty. There was also a chief—the chief of the Third Battalion. His office was upstairs, and he had an aide as well. And to add to the confusion, the third floor of this spacious firehouse was the dispatch office for the borough of Manhattan. All telegraph alarm signals went there, where anywhere from two to four men received and transmitted the signals. Every way Charlie turned, there was a new face. But they all knew who he was—the probationary fireman, or probie.

It was a strange feeling for Charlie. He was essentially moving into this new home. He would be on duty continuously for the next ten days. The men lived and slept in quarters. Foreman Jennings explained that had he been married, Charlie would have been permitted to sign out every evening to go home for dinner. But since he was a bachelor, Charlie would eat in the firehouse with the men. The second floor of the firehouse featured two rows of beds. The walls were lined with wooden lockers. The back wall had tall windows facing the rear yard and at the front end were the offices. Charlie went from bed to bed. Ott had explained the system. The men continuing on-duty left their beds unmade when they woke. It was now Charlie's job to remake those beds. Of course, his first attempt was considered unsatisfactory, and Ott showed him how to tuck the coarse wool blanket tightly over the white sheets, with exactly nine inches of sheet showing at the top. "Just like in the navy," Ott said. The men going into their day off stripped their beds and put the blanket, pillowcase, and sheets in the tin can outside the bathroom. These beds got fresh sheets and blankets from the wooden cabinet near the stairs.

From there, Ott brought Charlie to the stalls. The first horse of the row was Snowball. He was ten years old, fast, and very smart, Ott explained. White, with a gray silky mane, the horse made no reaction to Charlie's hand as he petted the animal's neck. Ott walked him forward and left him, untied, behind the second section apparatus.

"First, we shovel all the shit into one of the cans," Ott said as he dragged a tin can over and removed the lid. He handed Charlie the shovel. "Get all the hay up too," he added. "It's full of piss and we put down fresh hay every morning and night. Twice a week we pull all the horses out together and we rinse the floor with the hose and scrub it good."

As Charlie scooped up the manure, a series of loud bells echoed across the apparatus floor:

Ding... Ding... Ding...

A brief pause. Charlie looked at Ott, who stood motionless intent on counting.

Ding...

Another brief pause.

Ding... Ding... Ding... Ding... Ding...Ding... Ding... Ding... Ding...

"Box Three-One-Nine," Ott said. "Let's go. You take Snowball, and I'll take Apollo and Jack.

Charlie reached his trembling hand for Snowball's neck and wondered how he'd get him to the front of the truck. But the horse walked confidently with no directing at all. Charlie marveled at how the animal knew its way around the rig and into the hanging hitch. Once the horse was under the harness, a man tapped Charlie's shoulder.

"I'll get this, kid. Go put your coat and boots on."

Charlie hurried past the housewatch where one of the firemen whose name he couldn't remember was writing on a chalkboard beside the bells. "Box Three-One-Nine," the man yelled. "Spring Street and Mulberry. Turn out Twenty Truck!" Charlie went to the side of the ladder truck. His long rubber slicker coat and helmet rested on top of a mounted portable ladder. He kicked off his shoes and stepped into the pull-up boots. He put the helmet on his head and swung the coat on and buckled furiously. He stepped onto a side rail and grabbed the top of the mounted ladder to hold on. Then, nothing happened.

Charlie looked around. Two men were still fastening the horses' harnesses. He could see over the top of the rig that Foreman Jennings was climbing up to the front seat. The driver was Floyd Mance. He was already up in the driver's seat holding reins. Ott came around near Charlie and stepped into his own pull-up boots. He put on his helmet and coat, but instead of a long rubber slicker coat, he wore a shorter denim work coat—almost like what the welders in the shipyard wore, Charlie thought. Ott stepped up onto the rail beside Charlie and also grabbed hold of the ladder.

Mance made a clicking sound with his tongue and shook the reins, and then the rig rolled forward. Smokey barked as he ran from the back of the apparatus floor, past Charlie, and out the front door ahead of the horses.

Charlie squinted as they came out the bay doors and sunlight hit his face. The horses—three abreast—swung evenly into the turn as they headed south on Mercer Street. He looked back to see Fred Schley sitting up top at the very end of the long truck furiously working the steering wheel as the rig straightened out. He turned again to look ahead. Foreman Jennings rang the bell and they picked up speed through the intersection at Prince Street. He could hear Smokey barking as he ran just ahead of the team of horses. Down Mercer Street, Charlie could see men hurrying to move push carts to the side of the road. People gathered on the sidewalk and stopped to watch the truck go by. He gripped the top rail of the ladder tightly as they turned left onto Spring Street. His heart raced as he peered ahead, looking for smoke.

What he did see was a team of horses galloping around the corner pulling a steam engine. Behind was another team pulling a hose wagon. They stopped and several firemen dismounted but nobody seemed to be going anywhere. Hook and Ladder 20 was still two blocks away, but as they drew closer Charlie didn't see any kind of fire. When they finally stopped, Charlie took a six-foot hook, just like he had been told, and ran around the truck to be next to Foreman Jennings. He looked around the intersection, up and down each block, but saw no fire.

Foreman Jennings spoke to the foreman of Engine Company 55, the steam engine on scene, then motioned to Charlie. On the corner was a cast-iron column, painted red, with the initials *F.D. N.Y.* stenciled in gold. The front-top section was a handle attached to a hinged door. *Fire Alarm Telegraph Station 319* was printed on the door. The handle was hanging down and Foreman Jennings opened the door. "Come closer, Charlie," he said. "See this here?"

"Yes, sir."

"Well, that's a telegraph key—you tap down the button here to send a message to the dispatcher. The chief's aide uses it to transmit a second alarm and so forth. Now, I'll tap in a false alarm signal."

Charlie was familiar with telegraphs but knew nothing of Morse Code or any signals. When the foreman was done, he pointed to a handle above the telegraph key. "This here is how we reset the box's lever, so it's ready for the next time someone transmits an alarm—it'll automatically telegraph the box number to the dispatcher." He spun the lever handle around until it stopped moving, then closed the door and spun the outer handle upward. "We'll go over telegraph signals later." Jennings added.

The men of Hook and Ladder 20 began mounting the ladder truck again, so Charlie did likewise. He laid the six-foot hook in its bracket and stepped onto the running board. He held on tight as the truck rolled forward. Two children stood at the corner—boys, brothers perhaps, not more than ten years old. They looked at Charlie with big smiles and waved. Charlie waved back and this excited the boys.

Charlie felt excited also.

Once back outside the firehouse, the men—minus Fred Schley at the back wheel—dismounted and unhitched the horses. Floyd Mance and Foreman Jennings stood off to the side holding Snowball, Apollo, and Jack, while the rest of the company pushed the ladder truck backwards into the firehouse. Schley worked the rear steering wheel with one hand while his body was spun to look behind him. Charlie was holding a side rail and pushing the rig, which to his surprise rolled fairly easily. The horses were walked back to the stalls and Ott brought over a pail of soapy water and a brush. He told Charlie to scrub the truck's wheels after every run.

Charlie was working the brush around each spoke when Foreman Jennings approached. "I forgot to give you this earlier," he said, holding something out to Charlie.

Charlie grabbed it: a red, leather helmet front piece. The top was pointed, like a knight's shield, and the number *20* was stitched in white leather in the center. It felt heavy.

"You represent Hook and Ladder Company 20 when you wear this—don't ever forget it," said Jennings.

"I won't, sir."

"There should be some white paint and a fine brush around. Paint your badge number here along the bottom." The foreman added. "And make sure it's neat—if you need to, ask Mr. Mance. He's quite the artist."

"Yes, sir," Charlie repeated, thinking how little he wanted to ask Floyd Mance anything.

LATER THAT NIGHT—AFTER A dinner of pot roast and potatoes—Charlie was sweeping the apparatus floor. It was after 11pm and many of the men had gone up to the bunk room, though a handful were still in the kitchen at the rear of the apparatus floor. The phone rang and Charlie heard Bill Murphy, the housewatchman, answer. Murphy walked back to the kitchen and swung the door inward. "Mr. Woll, sir—there's a telephone call," he announced.

A moment later, Assistant Foreman Woll came out and took the call. Charlie swept, straining to hear the conversation.

"I see..." said Woll. "What was that address? I see. Yes, thank you Sergeant."

Woll walked over to Charlie. "There's a red lantern here somewhere, Pendergrass. Have you seen it?"

Charlie froze. He had no idea.

"Under the workbench—here Mr. Woll," said Murphy.

Woll grabbed the lantern and handed it to Charlie. "Make sure it's filled with oil. I need you to go down to Spring Street—right here on Mercer. There's a dead horse lying in the road. You need to put the red light on it, so the sanitation men know to come take the animal away.

Murphy slid open one of the two bay doors, and Charlie headed out lantern in hand. Halfway down the block, he turned back to see Assistant Foreman Woll, Bill Murphy, Floyd Mance, and Fred Schley out front of the firehouse watching him. Woll waved his hand forward, urging Charlie on.

There was a saloon on the corner of Prince Street and Mercer, and barroom banter as well as tobacco smoke poured out the front door each time a patron opened it. Further down the block, however, was desolate. The street was lined with factory lofts—all closed for the night. It was dark at the corner of Mercer and Spring—the lantern's red glow the only light. He circled the intersection twice and even looked under an abandoned pushcart. There was no dead horse. He didn't know what to do. Would the assistant foreman be angry if Charlie failed to put the lantern on a horse corpse? He stood on the corner, stuck in indecision, when—seemingly out of nowhere—a policeman approached.

"Whatcha got there, Sonny? A red light?" the policeman asked.

"Uh... Yes, sir. I'm looking for a dead horse."

"A dead horse? Huh—is that the term nowadays?" He stepped closer and tapped the tip of his nightstick on Charlie's chest. "I know what you're up to, boy! This isn't my first night on the beat. You'll find no prostitutes tonight."

The words landed on Charlie like hammer over the head. "No—you see. I'm a fireman. There's a dead horse, and I..."

"Dead horse my arse, boy. You're coming with me." The policeman blew a whistle, and suddenly a horse-drawn wagon headed down Spring Street from Broadway. The policeman grabbed the lantern and then he and another took hold of Charlie's arms and put him in the back of the wagon, locking him in behind a gate with iron bars.

"You don't understand," Charlie yelled but it was to no avail, the policemen mounted the wagon and they rolled down Spring Street. Charlie was hoping they'd pass the front of the firehouse so he could call out for help, but they circled up Greene Street instead.

He spent two hours at the precinct in a jail cell before the desk sergeant opened the gate and told him to scram. Charlie walked back to the firehouse, wondering if Foreman Jennings would fire him. It was his first night in the company and he had gotten arrested and disappeared for two hours. Would anyone understand?

He knocked on the bay door and, to his chagrin, Fred Schley was now on housewatch. With a smirk on his face, Fred stepped aside to let him in. "We thought you had enough of us and ran off," he quipped.

"No I..." Charlie began, then thought better of telling the story too many times. "Is Mr. Woll upstairs?"

Fred nodded toward the kitchen door. "He's back there."

Charlie walked around the ladder truck. The clock over the housewatch desk said quarter after one and he considered himself lucky the assistant foreman was still up. He would have hated to wake him. He pushed the swing door in and was hit with a wall of tobacco smoke. A round of applause went up, followed by laughter.

Mr. Woll, Floyd Mance, Andrew Ott, and three other men whose names Charlie couldn't quite remember at the moment were all sitting around the table cheering. They held cigarettes and hands of playing cards. Mr. Woll was smoking a pipe. Seated at the end of the table, holding a hand of cards himself was the policeman who had arrested him, laughing as well.

"Did you find the horse, Pendergrass?" asked Woll.

"No, sir—there was no horse," Charlie replied.

"Ah well," the assistant foreman said. "Must have been a false report. These things happen."

3

Lunch break at the factory was just a half-hour. Some workers brought food from home, wrapped in newspaper, and kept in coat pockets. Esther and Rachel usually bought sandwiches from the grocer on Washington Place and Broadway—five cents each. But this morning they bought only dried cake for two cents. They were saving money for the dance Saturday night. They ate at their stations. In warm weather, some of the workers sat on the fire escape. But it was narrow and uncomfortable for more than a handful of people. Besides, often a foreman or worse, the factory manager Mr. Bernstein, would yell and make them come back inside. Esther knew she could enjoy the most of her brief lunch break if she didn't waste time traveling anywhere.

As Esther was finishing her dried cake, she watched a group of men exit a passenger elevator on the other side of the room. Leading them was Mr. Bernstein. He was a short but powerful looking man. Esther did her best to avoid him. They crossed the room and walked over to the inspector's table near the stairwell. Esther's foreman, Mr. Craven was there, and she heard Mr. Bernstein ask him: "Do any of your girls speak Russian, or Yiddish? My Jewish cutter is off today and the other cutters and girls downstairs only speak Italian."

The foreman pointed in the direction of Esther and Rachel's station and walked over with Mr. Bernstein. "Can you speak Yiddish?" he asked, and Esther hesitantly nodded.

"Go with them, please."

Mr. Bernstein was stern, but usually polite. For all her fear of the manager, and the stories she'd heard of him firing people, she'd never heard him raise his voice. He explained to Esther that one of the owners, Mr. Harris, had two cousins visiting America and they wanted a tour of the factory. So that was how she would spend the last ten minutes of her lunch break. Translating. She followed the group to the passenger elevators and Mr. Bernstein rang the bell. There was a heavy door beside the elevator bank and one of the cousins went over and turned the doorknob. The door was locked and didn't budge.

"That's a set of stairs," said Mr. Bernstein. "But no one is allowed to use them."

Esther translated.

"Everyone exits through the Greene Street stairs over there," he pointed across the spacious floor. "We funnel them into the partition and check each worker. We've essentially eliminated the petty thefts that other factories must endure."

The cousins stood expressionless while Esther put Bernstein's words into Yiddish, then they nodded, and one whispered something to the other as they looked over toward the Greene Street stairwell partition. One of the passenger elevators arrived and the door slid open. Esther had never ridden the passenger elevators before. The hoistway doors were finished in dark wood. Behind them was the car's accordion-style steel gate. The operator pulled the gate open. He was a handsome young man with slick, dark hair covered on top by a rounded uniform bell cap. "Take us up to ten, Joe," said Mr. Bernstein.

Joe pulled the hoistway doors closed and with them the car's gate. He smiled at Esther as he stepped back to the control levers. The car moved and Esther could see the ninth-floor ceiling roll past and the tenth floor hoistway doors come into view. When Esther stepped out onto the tenth floor, she was struck by how fancy the reception area was. A thick, colorful carpet led to the secretary's desk. Mr. Bernstein waved the cousins closer and pointed to a contraption next to the telephone.

"In addition to the telephone, we have the telautograph machine here. It can transmit a written page," he explained. When Esther finished translating, they both gasped in wonder and reached out to touch the mysterious device. The group moved along, and Mr. Bernstein showed them the owners' offices, belonging to Mr. Harris and Mr. Blanck, then the showroom and fitting room, the pressing department, and the packing and shipping workstations. "We'll take the stairs down," he announced when they were across the floor on the Greene Street side.

Mr. Bernstein reached for the door and pulled it open. "The stairwell is narrow," he explained. "The doors open inward, so as not to block the stairs." Esther was between Mr. Bernstein and the two cousins. She didn't bother to translate this last bit as the group descended to the ninth floor. He pushed the door into the ninth floor, where it hit against something. There was a partition wall blocking it. "This is the inspection area I told you about before, every worker is searched." The cousins voiced their approval when Esther finished speaking. "As you'll see," Bernstein continued. "Here on Nine we have our main production line. There are two hundred seventy-eight machines arranged on eight long tables, all connected to power turbines under the tables. Over there is the inspection table, and on the far wall is the girls' coat room and toilet."

It seemed to Esther that even Mr. Bernstein was growing impatient with the tour, and he herded the group back behind the partition and into the stairwell. Once on the eighth floor, he began speaking before the cousins were even out of the stairs: "There are five more sewing tables here, but more importantly, the eighth floor is where we do all the cutting." Esther quickly translated and then hurried to stay beside Bernstein. She'd never been on the eighth floor and was herself curious about the operation. It certainly was a wonder to behold. Across the ceiling dozens of cords were strung. Hanging from each were template garment designs for each component of the shirtwaist blouse. The template consisted of a thin piece of fabric in the necessary size and shape which was bordered with a thin metal frame to keep the fabric shape taut. Heavy bolts of fabric were stacked all around the room. At the long cutters' tables, assistants meticulously stacked layers of fabric and Esther watched in wonder as a cutter effortlessly worked a huge pair of scissors through the stack, cutting all layers evenly with one stroke.

"You'll see how skilled our cutters are here," said Bernstein. "They measure and cut perfectly, leaving a bare minimum of left-over scraps." He paused to give Esther a moment to put it in Yiddish, then continued: "A few inches of wasted fabric on every bolt adds up to hundreds of dollars a month." The scraps were indeed small, and Esther watched the assistant slide them across the table directly into a bin underneath.

Bernstein led the group back to the passenger elevators and rang the call bell. For a moment it was just Esther and him while the two cousins looked around some more. "What is your name?" he asked.

Esther felt her hands tingle with fear. "Esther Greenberg."

"Well, Esther, Thank you for your assistance today. I don't know what I would have done with those two," he motioned his head toward the cousins. "I'll have the elevator drop you off on Nine. Had you finished your lunch? I can have Mr. Craven give you a few minutes."

Esther had not expected such kindness and did not have a response ready. She awkwardly shook her head and muttered: "Oh, thank you, Mr. Bernstein, but I'd already finished."

Bernstein smiled and then pressed the call button again.

She should ask him now, she thought—the question she'd been wanting to ask for a couple of months. Mr. Craven, had said it was a terrible idea. In truth, Esther thought it should have been the foreman who approached Bernstein, but he was a coward. Why should he fear asking for a simple mistake to be fixed? "Complain, and you and your sister will be out of a job," Craven told her. Esther wasn't sure if he'd meant Bernstein was likely to fire them for bringing up the matter, or that he, Mr. Craven, would fire them for making him look bad. But Mr. Bernstein seemed to be in a good mood at the moment and was treating Esther with kindness. Then the elevator door opened. It was not the same elevator as before. This time it was Gaspar operating.

Bernstein looked over at the cousins, now over by the Washington Place windows pointing at something out in the distance. "Ugh," he grunted. "Gaspar—take Esther up to the ninth floor and then come back for me, please."

Esther stepped in and Gaspar pulled the doors and gate shut. He pulled up on the control lever and then turned his head and smiled at Esther. "Your Miss Rachel's sister, ain't ya?"

"I am. Esther's my name."

"It's my favorite thing 'bout workin' here. When Frank is out and they have me man the service elevator in the morning—gettin' to see Miss Rachel."

It was the most Esther had ever heard him say, and she was struck by just how young he was. "How old are you, Gaspar?" she asked as the elevator stopped on the ninth floor.

"Seventeen."

"Do you like dancing, Gaspar?"

"Oh, yes. Very much."

"There is a dance this Saturday evening at the Manhattan Lyceum. I'm sure Rachel wouldn't mind a dance or two if you asked her."

Gaspar's boyish face turned beet red and he smiled. "Then I'll be there!"

THE CLOSING BELL RANG and the power cut off to the machines before Esther had even taken her foot off the pedal. The churning buzz that had bounced off concrete pillars and tall windows for nine hours was silenced. The floorboards shook as hundreds of workers stood and slid their chairs backward. The chair legs dragged across the wood floorboards, releasing a loud groan. Esther and Rachel retrieved their coats and joined the line of seamstresses stretching across the back of the floor. One by one they filed through the wooden partition before the stairwell door, where an inspector checked inside the women's coats and handbags. Once checked, the women exited via the stairs.

Now outside, Esther and Rachel headed east toward Broadway. Esther looked up to the ninth-floor windows. Even against the darkened sky, the building towered over Washington Place—a modern wonder of concrete and steel. The lower floors were handsomely fitted with masonry designs. The upper floors contained tight rows of high windows for well-lit and ventilated factory floors. The corner of the building, where Washington Place met Greene Street was fitted with large placards detailing the business names of each floor's occupant. The eighth-floor sign stood atop the row. It was still visible in the night sky: *Triangle Waist Company*.

They'd only made it a short way down Washington Place, but Rachel seemed about to burst with anticipation. "So? Est—what happened?"

"What do you mean?"

"With Mr. Bernstein. What happened?"

"I translated for him while he showed some people around."

"That's it?"

"That's it."

"Did you ask him?"

"No—the time wasn't right."

"Uh! Est—if Craven won't ask him, what am I going to do?" Rachel did not sound angry, just disappointed.

Esther hated disappointing her sister. Rachel had worked at Triangle for four months now. Usually, seamstresses were considered trainees for the first six months and paid just five dollars per week. Although Rachel was only sixteen years old, she'd spent years doing button work as a child in their father's factory and, most recently, worked a sewing machine for their uncle. Other girls at Triangle, with similar experience, had started with the regular starting pay for a seamstress, ten dollars per week. Esther was now certain Mr. Bernstein would correct the oversight if he knew. But what to do about Mr. Craven?

"I'll think of something," Esther said, but Rachel's expression remained glum. "But I did talk to Gaspar."

Now Rachel's cheeks reddened, and a hint of a smile appeared.

"I told him to come to the dance Saturday night."

Rachel's eyes bulged. "No!"

"I did. And I told him you'd be happy to dance with him if he asked you."

"Ahh!" Rachel squealed. "Est!" She slapped Esther's shoulder. "I can't believe you did that."

"He said he'll be there."

Rachel smiled. "He did not!"

"He did."

ESTHER AND RACHEL REACHED the front steps of their tenement on Essex Street just as a young woman was coming out.

"Clara!" called Esther.

The woman's face lit up. "There you are," she said. "Your mother told me you'd be home soon. I was going to wait for you here."

"How've you been?" asked Esther. "I haven't seen you since… Well, I don't think since the strike ended."

"Yeah—I've been very busy indeed. Local Twenty-five has thousands of new members. Even Triangle has a dozen or so!"

"I know," Esther answered sheepishly. "Julia Rosenthal approached me about joining up. It's just—after what happened to you during the strike... I was worried. Especially now that my sister is working there." She turned and put her hand on Rachel's shoulder. "This is my sister, Rachel. Rachel, this is Clara—the one I told you about."

Clara held out a hand and Rachel shook. "Clara Lemlich," she said.

"Esther told me all about you," Rachel replied. "How you organized the strike and got the factory owners to cave."

Clara laughed. "Well, some caved, some didn't. Your men Harris and Blanck held out most of all."

"Things are better now with the fifty-two-hour week," said Esther.

"Until they send'ya home for a month when it gets slow. My cousin Lena just started at Triangle."

"Oh—I'll have to find her."

"Don't worry," Clara added. "I didn't come to badger you again about joining the union. It's something else. There's a meeting, end of the month. A man from the state legislature and the fire chief are going to be there. It's about fire safety in the garment factories. I want you to talk about the Triangle."

"I don't know," Esther replied. "What if someone finds out. I'll be fired."

"You don't have to say your name. I'll vouch for you—they'll believe me when I say you work in the Triangle factory—and I'll tell them you don't want to give your name. It's not a trial or anything. The state legislature man is just looking for the facts. I'd ask Lena, but she's too new. We need someone who's been there a while—who was there for the strike. Someone who knows about the safety of the girls, especially if a fire breaks out."

Esther looked over to Rachel, who grinned and nodded. Esther had complained to Rachel before about the line at the stairwell door to exit. Just six months before there had been a small fire in a waste basket. Two of the foremen put it out quickly, but there was a great deal of smoke. One of the cutters—a tall muscular fellow who always wore a wool cap, even in summer—came up from the eighth floor and made sure the inspector checked each worker's bag before letting them leave. By the time Esther got to the stairs, the smoke had cleared out the windows and everyone was told to get back to their machines.

She looked at Clara's raised eyebrows and nodded.

4

1884

Edward Croker had grown up a quiet boy, some may have mistaken him for shy. From his late teens he worked hard and became a brakeman at the New York Central Railroad. Still, he kept mostly to himself. Saturday was payday at the railroad, and he usually stopped at the pub on his way home—his only real social activity. One evening, Edward was belly up to the bar enjoying some friendly conversation with the bartender. An overserved man telling a story next to him swung his arms and knocked into Edward, spilling his beer. "Pay attention, sir," was all Edward said as he motioned to the bartender for another.

"To hell with you," the man shouted just as Edward was sipping his new beer. The man pushed Edward's shoulder, lurching him forward and nearly spilling the glass again. Edward calmly placed his beer on the bar and began rolling up his sleeves. "Whatcha gonna do?" sneered the man.

Behind the bar was a shelf lined with whiskey bottles and above it a mirror. Edward watched himself methodically folding up his shirtsleeves as he answered without turning toward the belligerent patron.

"I'm going to throw you out of here and break your fucking neck."

It had only been a couple of hours since the policeman angrily slammed the bars shut on his cell. But now the same policeman was back, looking much friendlier. "Croker," he said through the bars. "You're free to go."

There was a round of laughs as Edward stepped outside the precinct house. A horse-drawn police wagon was parked out front, with a group of men standing beside it talking.

"Tis all off in a bottle of smoke, lads," Edward heard the unmistakable voice of his uncle say. "But that's the last time he'll be hidin' in a thorn bush without his britches!"

The small group again erupted in laughter. There were three policemen in uniform—one looked high-ranking—and a man in a suit surrounding Edward's uncle, Richard Croker. The elder Croker puffed a cigar and slapped one of the policemen on the back before noticing Edward.

"They say you took on three men," Richard told Edward, then he looked to the group. "My nephew must have gone soft, the poor lad. When I was his age, I could've easily taken six."

"One of them broke a barstool across my back—caught me by surprise," Edward answered defiantly.

"The owner of the establishment is ward boss. He sent for Captain O'Brien here at the station when the fight broke out." Richard put his hand on the captain's shoulder. "O'Brien, however, sent for me when the officers told him your name."

"Ahh, Uncle," Edward replied, "I should have known Tammany Hall would somehow be tangled up in this."

"There is no *this*, lad. It's all been swept under the rug." Richard shook hands with the group and started walking. "Thank you, gentlemen," he said, then took a long draw of his cigar and turned to his nephew. "Are you coming?"

A chestnut-colored horse was hitched to the police wagon, and an elderly groom ran a brush across the animal's back while singing an Irish folk song. The words were in Gaelic and Edward did not understand. He almost asked his uncle what they meant, but Richard spoke first.

"Do you enjoy working at the railroad?"

"It's as fine a job as any other I suppose."

"You know—now that I'm fire commissioner, I'm well placed to be of service to you, lad. You should take advantage."

Edward was thoughtful and did not rush to answer. "And what would you get out of it?"

"Hah! Always with your guard up. Just like your father. Let me ask you, lad. What is wrong with a commissioner hiring a good man for a job he is well-suited for? Where is the scandal in such an arrangement?"

Edward had never thought of being a fireman. Perhaps he had heard too many stories of his uncle's days in the volunteer force. But the new paid department had come a long way. And there was an element of excitement to it all: the burly men with their shiny steam engines speeding down the street with bells ringing.

"Think about it, lad," Richard added. "We could get you started right away."

EDWARD TOOK TO FIREFIGHTING quite well. He didn't mind climbing ladders and despite his lean youthful build, he handled the punishing hoselines with ease. He had been in the firehouse barely two months when his foreman came down the stairs holding a letter.

"Well, Croker," the foreman sneered. "That didn't take long."

Edward took hold and read the letter. Seeing his foreman was expecting a reaction, he managed only to mumble: "I don't understand. How?"

Edward hopped off the trolley car at the corner of Beaver Street and South William. As the car rolled away, he stared across at Delmonico's Restaurant—the epicenter of New York's political power. Nicknamed the Citadel, its façade resembled a medieval castle. Edward approached the sharp-angled corner entrance and glanced up in awe of the eight stories looming above. The doorway was flanked by stone columns and covered with a circular portico. Edward Croker marched up the steps and through the door with the letter in hand, determined to give his uncle a piece of his mind and pretty sure he'd find him here, holding court as usual. Bypassing the host at the front desk, he went directly to the back corner. Blue cigar smoke wafted across the dark wood ceiling and Richard Croker was seated in the back of a large round table. A round of laughter filled the room as Edward approached.

"Have you lost your mind, Uncle?" Edward shouted, holding up the letter.

Richard lowered his cigar. "Oh, laddie. You've gone and worked yourself up into a dither now, haven't you?"

"Assistant foreman!" cried Edward, again he waved the letter. "How can I be an assistant foreman? I've only worked there two months!"

Richard turned to the man beside him—a balding, gray-haired man with a bushy mustache. "You'll have to excuse my nephew, Governor. He's experiencing some growing pains with his new profession." As if to keep Edward from embarrassing himself any further, he held up a hand and said: "Edward, may I introduce Governor Cleveland."

Edward was dumbstruck. Grover Cleveland was the Democratic Party's nominee for president. The election was less than three months away. "Pleasure to meet you, Governor," he said after a moment's pause.

"Will you excuse me, gentlemen?" said Richard as he stood and walked around the table. He pulled Edward aside by the arm.

Edward was staring back at Cleveland. "I thought the governor was at odds with Boss Kelly—says so every chance he gets in the papers," he said quietly to his uncle.

"Nevertheless, lad... He will be president. It is important to have contingency plans, I say. And about this promotion, what is the issue? I thought you'd be pleased."

"Pleased?" Edward's voice rose higher, and Richard held his hand up to signal him to keep it down. "You have made a mockery of me. How can I lead men who don't respect me?"

"They will respect your rank."

"I disagree, Uncle." Edward was having a difficult time keeping his emotions in check and feared tears would form. He held his words to keep from getting more upset.

"It will all be fine. In a year's time you will thank me," said Richard plainly while turning to go back to the table.

"Uncle," called Edward, and Richard turned back to face him. "I do thank you—for offering me the position of fireman. It is a job I have come to admire and respect. I have much to learn, and it is my intention to apply myself greatly in that endeavor. But you have burdened me with this unearned promotion. And now that it is done, I have no choice but to go forward. I *will* go forward. But, please—no more favors. I will accept no more undeserved honors."

Richard put the cigar to his lips and answered simply: "Suit yourself, lad."

5

1899

Deputy Chief Edward Croker sat at his desk reviewing a fire report from last month's third alarm blaze in a West Side hotel. He meticulously noted pumping pressures for every engine company on scene. He was mapping out the distances each water main was expected to deliver the required pressure to each hydrant. The politicians made a show of purchasing shiny new fire engines for their local company, Edward thought. But what was really needed was more water pressure. Buildings were getting taller and the pressure in the city's main system was struggling to keep up. There was a knock at the door and Croker called out to enter.

"Chief, there's a reporter downstairs," a young fireman announced. "He's asking to speak with you."

"Yes, Frazier—you may send him up. Thank you."

A moment later a skinny, baby-faced man came in. His fedora did not make him look older—but rather as a child pretending in his father's hat. "Chief Croker?" he asked while reaching out for a handshake.

Croker stood and shook his hand. "Yes," he said simply.

"William Gunn Shepherd—I write for the *World*."

"Is Joseph Pulitzer hiring children now?" said Croker with a small laugh.

"Well sir," Shepherd answered nervously. "I'm fairly new, not even on the payroll yet. But I sold them two stories."

"And now you're looking for a third. Is that it?"

"Well—Chief, I was just wondering if you'd heard the news. Chief Bonner is retiring."

Taken by surprise, Edward sat and motioned to a chair for Shepherd. "I hadn't heard. Hugh Bonner is a good man—and a damn fine chief of department."

"Well, I have it on good authority that Commissioner Scannell will name you as his successor," said Shepherd with a hint of triumph in his voice.

"What—oh hogwash! Where would you hear such a thing?"

"From a trusted source, Chief."

"Well, I don't believe it."

"Would you care to comment?" asked Shepherd as he took a small note pad out of his coat pocket."

"Not at all."

"Well, I also heard that Chief Bonner is not happy about it all. Thinks your uncle had something to do with the appointment."

Croker stood and grabbed young William Gunn Shepherd by the arm, pushing him across the office and out to the hall, then down the spiral staircase, past the steam engine on the apparatus floor and past the seated housewatchman, who looked on in amazement. Shoving the reporter out the open bay door and onto the sidewalk, the chief yelled: "The next time I see your bony ass, I'm going to kick it so hard you'll taste my shoe."

EDWARD CROKER *WAS* NAMED acting chief of department that spring. The new Civil Service Commission weighed in on the appointment and insisted on a competitive test for the position. Croker earned top score and was officially promoted to chief of department in December. In addition to overseeing the deployment of resources across the newly consolidated five borough city, the chief of department was required to respond to all fires, citywide, of three alarms or greater. Never one to sit still, Croker usually responded to all fires in the immediate area of his lower Manhattan quarters—much to the annoyance of many battalion chiefs. Rumors of nepotism shadowed the new chief wherever he went.

Afterall, Richard Croker had just pulled off the impossible. Now the boss of Tammany Hall, "Squire" Richard, as he was called, had gotten his candidate elected to mayor in 1897, and gotten the leaders of Brooklyn, Long Island City, Bronx and Richmond counties, as well as the New York State legislature, to go along with his plan to create the five-borough metropolis of Greater New York. He was at the zenith of political power. Sure, the new governor, Theodore Roosevelt, was no friend of Tammany Hall. But Squire Richard had a plan for that problem as well. President McKinley was up for reelection next year. With the right persuasion, the Republicans could be convinced to nominate the "Hero of San Juan Hill" for vice president.

All of this meant a tough time for Edward Croker as chief of department those first few months. It didn't matter that Edward had outscored the other deputy chiefs on the test. All anyone saw when his buggy showed up at a fire was Squire Richard's nephew. Then, one cold night at a stubborn warehouse fire, Chief Croker silenced all his critics.

THE WAREHOUSE STOOD AT the corner of West Street and Hubert Street. Engine Company 31 arrived with their foreman, Joseph B. Martin. The fire was in the basement. Thick black smoke completely filled the cellar, and all floors above. It was extremely difficult to get the hoselines down the stairs, through the choking smoke, through the intense heat, and near the seat of the fire for extinguishment. Chief Croker arrived just before the third alarm was transmitted and was informed by the battalion chief on scene that conditions were so punishing the men of Engine 31 had been forced to fight the fire in shifts. The nozzleman would lay on his belly, sucking whatever little air might have been along the floor, operating the powerful hose and advancing however far he could crawl, before being overcome by smoke and passing out. He would then be dragged outside, while another member of the company took over the nozzle. Still, the fire raged.

Croker looked on for several minutes. Three men from Engine 31 lay unconscious on the ground. The iron sidewalk shutters that led to the cellar were open and thick smoke pumped out forcefully. The thick two-and-a-half-inch hoseline went into the front door, which also pumped thick black smoke.

"How long since they stretched-in?" Croker asked the battalion chief.

"A quarter of an hour, perhaps."

"I don't like it," said Croker. "I want all of our men out of the building."

The battalion chief turned to his aide, who ran ahead to the doorway. Edward watched as the aide tapped a fireman on the shoulder and yelled something. The fireman had been kneeling, about three feet inside the door, feeding hose into the building. He got down on his belly and disappeared into the smoke. Edward turned to his aide.

"What's the time, Oswald? Tell me when three minutes passes."

Croker watched as the men of Engine 31 crawled out the doorway. Eventually five came out. With the three already lying on the ground, that made eight. Once he counted the members of 31, he approached one of the firemen. His face was black with soot and smoke and the man coughed forcefully, but Croker did not wait.

"Who is your officer today? Where is he?" the chief demanded.

"It's Foreman Martin," the man answered between coughs. "He ordered us out. He took hold of the nozzle and told me to come out."

Edward turned and waved his aide and the battalion chief over. "Joseph Martin has not come out yet," he told them.

"Truck Five is on West Street," the aide, Oswald, said. "They're forcing open a garage door. I'll have them put a ladder down this sidewalk hole."

Oswald ran off. "There isn't time," Croker told the battalion chief. "Have Engine 24 stretch-in also. We may need it for back-up." The battalion chief nodded, and Edward turned toward the front door of the warehouse. He ran in and made it perhaps ten feet before the smoke knocked him to the ground. His eyes teared. He grabbed the hoseline and crawled ahead following the line about twenty feet to the top of a stairway. He could see nothing and only discovered the stairs as his hand slid off the top step while pushing it over the hose. Edward turned, with his face toward the stairs, and shuffled down the steps backwards with both hands grasping the hose. Once at the bottom, he crawled on his belly, following the line. Intense heat pushed down around the rim of his helmet, burning his ears.

The further along he went, the louder the flowing water of the nozzle became. Eventually, he bumped up against the prone form of Martin's body. Edward climbed atop him, but to his surprise, he was not unconscious. Martin coughed and said: "Everybody out damn-it. I have the nozzle." He coughed again, then added. "It's just a little ahead."

Coughing himself, Croker managed to yell: "Damn-you... Martin... Outside now!"

There was no answer. Edward heard the stream of the nozzle beginning to thrash wildly, up and down, back and forth. Martin had lost consciousness. He spun him around and locked his hand around Martin's wrist. Following the hose with one hand, he dragged Martin to the stairs. He sat him up and was reaching under his armpits to lift when Martin coughed forcefully.

"Mr. Martin," he called out. "Can you get up?"

Martin nodded, still coughing, and began crawling up the stairs. Croker followed behind. They continued along the route of the hoseline all the way out to the street. Once outside, Martin began another coughing fit. Croker stood and helped him to his feet.

When the foreman turned and saw that his rescuer had been none other than Chief of Department Croker, he was dumbstruck. He kept trying to speak but seemed he could not find the words. Croker smiled and said: "Hold that thought!"

He took Martin by the arm and walked him over to a small group of reporters across the street. He patted the foreman's shoulder and wiped some soot away from under his eyes. "Gentlemen," Croker announced. "This is Smokey Joe Martin, and by the gods, he certainly does love it."

No fireman ever criticized Edward Croker's appointment again.

6

1911

CHARLIE STOOD IN FRONT of the firehouse holding a six-foot hook. There was a brisk chill in the air, and he buttoned his rubber slicker up to his chin. Battalion Chief Edward Worth, commander of the Third Battalion, had informed Foreman Jennings that morning that he wanted a full review of Hook and Ladder Company 20's life saving equipment. Floyd Mance had said they would roll the ladder truck out of quarters by hand instead of taking the horses out in the cold. But Foreman Jennings thought it a good idea to review hitching the horses with Charlie. Jennings used a chained pocket watch to time the men, and Charlie was tasked with strapping the beasts into the harnesses.

Once the truck was centered in front of the firehouse, Mance placed a thick wool blanket over each horse. Chief Worth stood before the company in a navy-blue wool coat and uniform cap. Though not exceptionally short, his stature stood out among the tall men of Hook and Ladder 20—he was a good four or five inches shorter than any of them. His commanding presence, however, was no less imposing. Streaks of silver ran through the sideburns and mustache he kept neatly trimmed.

"I know she's a heavy stick, boys," said the chief, pointing at the bedded aerial ladder atop the truck. "She's a good ten feet longer than any other ladder. But there's a reason you men have this. Look around you!"

Charlie was the only one to take the chief literally and he craned his neck to see all the high loft buildings filling the neighborhood sky.

"When we need her, we need her fast," the chief added.

"Men of Twenty Truck," shouted Jennings. "Let's get 'er up."

Floyd Mance and Fred Schley each ran to one of the two front wheels and began cranking a lever. On each side of the truck a stabilizer winded downward and diagonally outward. They cranked until the arms rested securely against the cobble-stoned pavement. Charlie followed Andrew Ott, John Stafford, and Martin O'Connor up atop the truck's platform. Each side of the ladder's connecting hinges had large crank handles protruding. Ott reached for one and Charlie grabbed hold as well. "Heave," yelled Stafford and they began cranking. The four men strained, and the ladder rose out of its bed slowly. With a worried eye, Charlie watched the cable and pulleys yanking the wooden behemoth upward. Surely they would snap! It took a couple of minutes but eventually the ladder was securely upright and Stafford began working a separate crank. The ladder, which was actually three separate ladder sections laid one atop the other, began telescoping outward. The top ladder section slid forward, ever higher. O'Connor now worked another crank and the platform spun, moving the extending ladder toward the firehouse's façade. At Ott's direction, Charlie worked the crank some more. He looked upward to admire the ladder's tip landing smoothly against the building's parapet.

"Pendergrass," shouted Jennings. "Get up there, probie!"

Charlie looked at the foreman and then to the tip of the ladder. The firehouse was three stories tall; Charlie had completed higher climbs at the Fire College. He placed his hands on the rails and raised a foot. Ott pulled him back.

"Where's your tool?"

Charlie's heart dropped. He looked around frantically, trying to remember what he'd done with the six-foot hook. Fred Schley picked up the hook from the ground and handed it up to Charlie. Steadily, he began his climb. Every few rungs, he had to stop, take hold of the hook, and reach up to hang it on a higher rung. Otherwise, he strived to maintain a two-handed grip on the ladder rails. The ladder's angle was about forty-five degrees, and Charlie was bent forward as he climbed. Consequently, his rubber slicker coat hung below his knees and made his movements clumsy. Slowly he continued upward.

"Get up there, Johnny!" Floyd Mance yelled.

There it is again, Charlie thought. *Johnny!* He reached the tip and threw the six-foot hook down onto the roof. He reached around and gripped the underside of the ladder by a rung and stepped onto the lip of the parapet. Again, the slicker caught his legs, but he managed to dismount the ladder and land safely on the roof. He retrieved the six-foot hook and found the bulkhead stairs. Back out in the street, he found the men lowering the ladder. He leaned the hook against the truck and was climbing the pedestal to help, but Foreman Jennings stopped him.

"Pendergrass, pull down the life net, please," he said.

Strapped to a running board was a semicircular frame of piping and canvas. Charlie was well-acquainted with life nets, the Fire College instructors seemed obsessed with the contraption. Every morning began first with group calisthenics, then with teams of eight unfolding the life net and holding the round landing net while other trainees jumped into it.

Charlie unlatched the straps and lowered the net to the ground. The aerial ladder was now fully bedded, and the men came over to help Charlie unfold the life net. They opened it to form a full circle and laid the net on the sidewalk. No sooner was it on the ground than Charlie heard barking coming from inside the firehouse. He looked to see Smokey run across the apparatus floor and jump right onto the net. The men lifted and Fred and Floyd pulled the handles up quickly, like a spatula flipping an egg, and the dog was heaved several feet in the air. Smokey yelped, landed on the net, and the men yanked it up again. Another loud yelp. They all laughed and lowered the net to the ground. Smokey's tail was wagging, and Schley petted his head and pushed him off.

"Mr. Ott—go to the window in the chief's office, please," said Jennings.

Ott appeared at the second-floor window and climbed out onto the sill. During training, Charlie had both held the life net and even jumped into it. But here on the sidewalk in front of the firehouse, with the men of Hook and Ladder 20 all watching him, he felt his hands shaking and worried the rail would slip from his grip.

With no warning, Ott hurled his body outward and kicked his legs up. A split-second later he hit the center of the net, landing in a seated position. Charlie felt Ott's weight and momentum lurch the life net downward and it took considerable effort to resist the force pulling Charlie's own body forward and down.

"And that's only from the second floor, Pendergrass. Imagine a body coming down from the fifth floor," said Battalion Chief Worth.

The Fire College was new, it had been the brainchild of Chief of Department Croker—the fruit of years of planning and fundraising. Charlie was the only man present who had attended. Consequently, he had received extensive training on the life net. But he said nothing. He was new, but already had a sense that telling the chief, or the foreman, or any of the men "I know" would be a mistake. Besides, Charlie was quite sure these men had real-world experiences well beyond the books at the Fire College. Charlie nodded at Worth. "Yes, Chief."

CHARLIE HAD HAD TROUBLE sleeping the first few nights in the firehouse, but eventually he grew tired enough to overcome his apprehension. He was told to make sure he was the last to lay down. If some of the men were still awake, whether tending to the horses or playing cards in the kitchen, then Charlie needed to be up and working. If the horses were cared for, then he swept. He worked his way across the apparatus floor, and then started again at the other side. It was better to be seen pushing a broom than loafing around. Ott had showed him how to work the housewatch. It was not as simple as it looked, between answering the bells with a telegraph message, recording the run, alerting the company, and shouting out the address. Charlie was getting the hang of it, but Foreman Jennings had said that for the first month, he would not be assigned housewatch duty after midnight. So, by the third or fourth night, once the other men—besides the housewatchman—had all gone to bed, Charlie went upstairs and laid down as well.

It was the tenth night, after Charlie had drifted off into a deep sleep, that he was baptized by fire. He had been dreaming, but of what he could not recall once the bells began ringing out across the bunkroom:

Ding... Ding... Ding...

Charlie's eyes shot open and he sat up. Through the dark bunkroom, he could see one or two other men sitting up as well. When the bells paused after the third bell, the rest of the men sat up. Had the bells continued to six or seven, they all would have laid back down knowing the box was outside of Hook and Ladder 20's first alarm response area. But three bells meant a 300 box, the heart of Twenty Truck's district.

Ding...

The firemen stepped into pants bunched up around shoes on the floor. Charlie dressed quickly and went to the gate along the wall and swung the arm outward. He reached out and wrapped his arms around the brass pole and then his legs. He dropped down through the hole in the floor and slid the pole all the way down to the apparatus floor.

Ding... Ding... Ding... Ding... Ding...Ding... Ding... Ding...

Charlie went quickly to his pull-up boots and kicked off his shoes.

"Box Three One Eight," Ott called out from the housewatch. "Elizabeth Street and Spring. Second Due—Second Due!"

Other men slid down the pole in quick succession. Charlie went to the stalls and took hold of Snowball. He walked beside the horse as he went on his own to the front of the ladder truck and stepped into the hitch. Charlie fastened the harness straps, helped Ott slide the bay doors open, then returned to the side running board where his slicker coat and helmet rested on the rail. Once his gear was donned, he stepped up and held on. Smokey stood by the housewatch and let out a single bark once he thought the company was ready to roll. Floyd Mance clicked his tongue and jerked the reins. The team stepped off and out went Twenty Truck.

Smokey barked while he ran, and Assistant Foreman Woll rang the bell from the front seat—neither being necessary as Mercer Street was deserted. *Second Due,* Ott had yelled. Charlie knew that meant another Hook and Ladder Company was due to arrive first. The truck swerved around the corner and onto Spring Street, the team of horses were now in full gallop. Charlie held on tightly and in his mind went over the duties of a second due hook and ladder company. He had been taught at the Fire College that it was the job of the engine company to secure a water source, usually the nearest hydrant, connect to their steam pumper, and then stretch hoselines into the building to extinguish the fire. Hook and ladder companies operated differently. It was their job to access the fire if gates and doors were locked, rescue trapped occupants, and then overhaul the structure. They carried ladders, obviously for rescues, and hooks—long wooden poles of varying lengths with an iron pointed hook at the tip—for opening ceilings and walls to expose hidden fire. Hence the name—Hook and Ladder. Since their apparatus was not a steam pumper, but a long ladder truck, many firemen referred to hook and ladder companies simply as trucks. The first due truck company (hook and ladder) operated on the floor of the building where the fire was located. The second due hook and ladder company operated on all floors above the fire.

As they approached the block, Charlie smelled smoke. A ladder rig was already set up in front of the building and four men were raising the aerial ladder. Floyd Mance stood and yanked the reins and the truck slowed and then stopped behind the first ladder truck. Charlie jumped off the step and grabbed a six-foot hook from the bracket. He ran around the horses to catch up to Assistant Foreman Woll, who was charging toward the front door of a six-story brick tenement building. Charlie glanced up for just a second to see flames blowing out two windows on the fourth floor. There must have been a dozen people scrambling down the fire escape—all of them below the fire. He couldn't see anyone above, but he didn't look for long. He was terrified of getting separated from Woll. *Stay right up the skipper's ass,* Ott had told him. There was a hoseline already laid out into the front doorway and up the stairs. A thin spray of water jetted out from between brass couplings and Charlie stepped over the hose to follow Woll. The inside of his pant legs got wet, and he remembered that he hadn't pulled up his boots. *Too late now,* he thought while taking two steps at a time. The hose wound around each newel post and across each hall landing up to the next floor.

At the fourth-floor landing Woll paused. The hallway was banked down to the floor with thick gray smoke. Woll crouched on the floor with a hand on the hose. Charlie kneeled behind him.

"Truck 9..." Woll yelled into the smoke. "Truck 9."

"Ho!" a voice called back from the abyss.

"Truck 20 going above."

"Good!"

Woll turned and looked Charlie in the eye. "Stay right up my ass," he barked. "Got it?"

Charlie nodded.

"Ott..." said Woll.

"Here skipper," Ott answered, and only then did Charlie realize Andrew had been behind him the whole way up. He placed one hand on Charlie's shoulder and Charlie saw he was carrying a claw tool, a three-foot long pry bar. Woll crawled forward and Charlie followed. His eyes immediately burned and began tearing. He wanted to cough but did his best to stifle it because neither Ott nor Woll were coughing. They turned around a newel post and climbed the next flight of stairs. Charlie could see nothing. He kept reaching forward to touch the back of Woll's coat. The assistant foreman stopped, reached up for something, then called back: "Ott, pop this door!"

Though he saw nothing, Charlie felt Ott climb over him and begin working his claw tool—three big swings. He heard wood smash apart and the door swing inward. The men entered the apartment and Woll closed the door. The smoke was still thick and Charlie kept reaching for Woll's coat as they made their way deeper into the flat. He touched the wall, then Woll's coat, all the while dragging his six-foot hook and getting it caught on things: first shoes by the front door, then the legs of a small table. It seemed like they were crawling for a very long time. Unable to control himself any longer, Charlie began a coughing fit. Over his head he heard glass shatter. Ott pulled Charlie up with one hand while he cleared glass shards from the window with the tool. He then leaned out the window, pulling Charlie forward as well. "Catch a breath," he said. Smoke was now pouring out the broken window, but Charlie gasped greedily at the fresh air.

"Mr. Ott," called Woll from the dark smoke.

"Here skip."

"Get that window fully cleared."

Ott stood upright and knocked the wooden sash and upper panes out, then cleared all shards. The smoke cleared enough for Charlie to see Woll dragging a limp body toward the window.

Ott called out the window to the men of Hook and Ladder 9 who were manning the truck pedestal. He waved his arms and yelled. "They're moving the ladder," he said.

"Not that big a fellow, luckily," said Woll. "Pendergrass, help me sit him upright and onto the windowsill."

They got him up and waited, the ladder was in place rather quickly, Charlie thought. Two men from 9 Truck climbed the aerial ladder and Charlie and Ott passed the unconscious man out to them. No sooner was he out than Assistant Foreman Woll grabbed Charlie's arm and said: "Get the rest of these windows open. Don't just slide them up—the smoke won't lift unless the top pane is out, and we can't be sure we found everyone till the smoke lifts."

Charlie ran his hand along the wall and found a window. He swung his six-foot hook and smashed the top pane. He then worked the tool around clearing out all the shards. "Get that sash out," Ott yelled from somewhere behind. "You can't bail out a window with a sash across the middle!" Charlie used the weight of the hook to snap the wooden sash and pulled it away. Little by little the smoke cleared out of the apartment. Woll came back.

"No other occupants here. The hallway's clearing up too—they finally got the bulkhead door open. Ott, go check the two apartments upstairs, make sure everyone got out."

"Aye-aye, sir," said Ott as he headed out.

Woll turned back to Charlie. "You see, Pendergrass—this is always the most seriously exposed apartment, the one right above the fire apartment. Smoke builds up fast here. People get overcome quickly. Fire also extends here first." He waved his arm and Charlie went over. They stood in the front parlor room of the railroad-flat apartment, so called because each room led straight to another room with no hall. "The fire was right below us. Do you hear the hose stream, still hitting it from below?"

Charlie did hear and feel the water hitting the ceiling below. He looked around and was shocked by how small the apartment was. When crawling in, he would have sworn they'd crawled a hundred feet. The room they stood in was ten feet wide. The whole apartment was maybe thirty feet long, three rooms in a row.

"Let's open up the baseboards—see what we got," Woll said.

Charlie spun his six-foot hook and held it like a spear. He drove the pointed tip into the plaster wall a few inches above the floor under the front window. "Really open it up," the assistant foreman instructed. Charlie opened a small hole and then spun the handle so the hook grabbed onto the strips of wooden lath behind the plaster. He yanked the hook back and pulled out a ten-inch section of wall. The inner bay was exposed, and Charlie saw flames flickering—almost dancing—up a wooden stud.

"We need a hoseline," said Charlie anxiously.

Woll peeked out the window and said: "The chief is way ahead of you. Looks like the second due engine is stretching-in as we speak. They should be up here shortly. Keep opening this wall, I'll go get them."

※

CHARLIE UNBUCKLED HIS SLICKER and hung the coat on the side of the truck. "How can you crawl in that thing?" said Ott. Charlie looked up and saw Andrew unbuttoning his denim work coat. "Most of us truck men prefer these," he said, pointing to his coat. "I just keep my slicker for when I get detailed to an engine company."

"Do you think Mr. Jennings would mind if I wore one as well?" Charlie asked.

"Don't see why he would, he wears one."

Charlie thought about going to the supply store on Avenue A the next day. It was his day off and he would have his first week's pay as well. Floyd Mance stepped between Charlie and Ott and began winding up the stabilizer on the side of the rig. "That fella you guys handed out was still kickin' when they brought him down. Worth had Samson take him over to Bellevue in the chief's carriage," Floyd announced.

"Good news," said Ott.

Charlie didn't know if he should say anything and remained quiet. "Help me fold up the blankets," Mance said. Charlie followed him to the front of the truck and pulled a wool blanket off Jack. He held it up and folded, all the while Smokey lay across the driver's seat with his head on his paws watching Charlie, until Assistant Foreman Woll climbed up and kicked him out of the seat.

"Whadd'ya think, Pendergrass?" Woll called down from top of the truck. "Is this what you signed up for?"

Smokey hopped down from the rig and went over and rubbed his shoulder into Charlie's leg. Charlie bent down and rubbed the dog's neck. Smokey gave his approval with a soft, murmuring, growl.

"Yes sir," Charlie said, looking up at Woll. "I believe it is."

7

1906

ESTHER GREENBERG WAS 14 years old and living in Bialystok, Poland, which was at that time part of the Russian Empire. Her father owned a small textile factory. Her mother kept the books and Esther and her sister Rachel, 11, helped out on the floor. Esther had become a skilled seamstress and Rachel sewed buttons. There was a large Jewish community in Bialystok and many were employed in the textile industry because other professions were forbidden to Jews. Across Russian territories, there had been a rise in violence against Jewish communities since the assassination of Czar Alexander II in 1881 by a group of revolutionaries—for which blame was laid on the Jewish population. Many Jews fled the violence to America. Though his brother had emigrated to New York, Esther's father chose to stay. So much of the family's struggles and limited wealth had been poured into his factory and he didn't want to lose it.

A series of pogroms had broken out across the empire that spring and rumors of potential violence circulated in Bialystok. The city was a powder keg waiting for a spark, and the moment came during a Christian parade. A bomb was detonated, killing a priest. Though several anarchist groups were suspected, the angry Christians of the town blamed the Jews. A mob stormed the Jewish quarter of the city, set fire to homes, and dragged people outside to bludgeon them in the street or simply threw them out upper-floor windows.

The Greenberg's apartment was just two blocks from the factory, which was closed for Sabbath. Esther's parents could hear the violent mob moving across the quarter: breaking glass, shouts and cries, gunshots. Esther's father looked out the window.

"The factory is burning," he said simply. Esther's mother ran to the window.

"*Meydlekh,*" he called out in Yiddish. Girls. Put on your shoes and coats.

"*Tateshi,*" said Rachel. Daddy. "It's warm outside."

"I said put on your coats," he answered impatiently. He turned to Esther's mother. "You too, Dear—please hurry. And put all of your jewelry in your pockets."

Esther tied her shoes with shaking fingers and watched her father slip on his coat and then retrieve a bunch of papers from the desk drawer in the hall. He turned and said: "Let's go—Now!"

They, along with hundreds of other Jewish residents—ran toward the train station. Their best hope to flee would be a train out of town, but more importantly, a contingent of soldiers was garrisoned at the station. Surely, they would protect the Jewish men, women, and children escaping the angry mob. Esther saw a train pulling into the station. The panicked residents bypassed the ticket window and rushed the platform. The rioters were in close pursuit.

Esther and her family were packed in a mass of people as the train doors opened and some passengers tried to get off. Shrieks of pure terror arose from the outskirts of the crowd, but all Esther could see was her father's chest as he pulled her in close. Her mother held Rachel in her arms. With rifles in hand, soldiers pushed their way through the crowd and entered the train. A moment later, Esther turned to see two soldiers dragging a man down the train steps.

"*Żyd,*" one of the soldiers announced in Polish. Jew.

The man struggled and shouted, and Esther cried out in horror when one of the soldiers crashed the butt of his rifle down on the side of his head. Some screamed—while others, farther back, cheered. Esther turned back toward her father and hugged him tightly.

The train conductor must have decided to cut the stop short, and the car started to roll forward. "We need to get on," Esther's father said. He grabbed Esther with one hand and her mother's arm with the other. People were pushing from behind. Gunshots rang out. Before they could get to the car door, the train increased speed. They weren't going to make it.

Esther's father picked her up in his arms and pushed forward. More gunshots rang out and people began to flee the platform. Esther's parents, each carrying a child, pushed ahead. They caught up to the train car door and Esther's father pushed her mother and Rachel upward and helped them onto the moving step. Then, running alongside the train, he handed Esther to her mother. Esther put her feet down and turned. Still running, her father grabbed a handrail and began to pull himself up.

A gunshot rang out.

Esther watched in horror as her father let go of the handrail and crashed down to the platform. She screamed as the train kept rolling. Soldiers and rioters surrounded her father and beat him with rifle butts and clubs. Her mother grabbed her arm and pulled her up into the car cabin. Esther screamed and ran to the window, but she saw her father no more.

Esther and Rachel arrived with their mother in New York and set out to find her uncle. He lived in a tenement on Essex Street and operated a textile company out of his apartment. There were four foot-pedal powered sewing machines in the parlor room.

Stacks of fabric were piled up in between. There was hardly any light and even less fresh air. The first month after their arrival, Esther, Rachel, and their mother slept on the kitchen floor of the apartment. Esther operated a sewing machine and her mother and Rachel sewed buttons. When another apartment upstairs opened up, they moved in. Esther settled into her new life, working in her uncle's "sweatshop"—the term that had been given to these small, tenement room, textile factories that had sprung up across the city.

To many Jewish textile factory owners and workers, Sabbath observance had become much less strict now that they were struggling so to make ends meet in America. Esther's uncle, however, remained devout, and the operation was shut down each Friday just before sunset. Unlike every other night of the week, where Esther worked until ten or eleven pm, on Friday nights she had a modicum of leisure. She attended English classes at the Lower East Side's Educational Alliance, a social services foundation for Jewish immigrants. Esther was a fast learner.

Her English instructor was a middle-aged woman from Lithuania who also encouraged Esther to express herself by writing. At the teacher's prompting, Esther submitted a composition to the *Journeyman*, a small English-language newspaper for immigrants on the Lower East Side. The paper had announced an open contest for "Old World Family Memories" and Esther wrote a brief but lovely description of the last Seder meal her family had spent together in Bialystok. She did not win, and her story was never printed in the *Journeyman*. But for the first time in her life, Esther felt passion. She had taken something that had previously only lived in her mind, and crafted it, shaped it, nurtured it into something tangible, something she could share with others.

It was also through the Educational Alliance that Esther heard about the Triangle Waist Company. They were always looking for skilled sewing machine operators. What's more, the factory occupied three upper floors of a spacious new loft building. There were high ceilings and large windows. There would be plenty of light and fresh air, unlike the sweatshops.

8

1911

NAMED FOR TAMANEND, CHIEF of the Lenape nation, the Society of St. Tammany formed in the late Eighteenth Century with the purpose of fostering alliances and political discussions among emerging political parties in the fledgling United States. By the middle of the Nineteenth Century, Tammany Hall had become the de facto headquarters of the Democratic Party in New York City. From the bottom up, the political machine controlled all levels of public and political life, especially in districts heavily populated by immigrants. Often arriving with nothing, immigrants were welcomed by Tammany representatives, given assistance finding housing, coal in winter, and—above all else—jobs. The only thing asked for in return was a loyal vote.

Tammany leaders, known as bosses, became all-powerful. Despite impressive records of public works and genuine improvements to the lives of immigrants, figures like William "Boss" Tweed and Richard "The Squire" Croker, deservedly, became symbols of greed and corruption.

The Squire may have brought forth the five-borough metropolis of Greater New York, but his hopes to rid his domain of the crusading Governor Roosevelt backfired when President William McKinley was assassinated, and Theodore Roosevelt assumed the highest office in the land. It wasn't long before Richard Croker's empire crumbled and he set sail for Ireland.

The stage was set for a new kind of boss at Tammany Hall. Charles Francis Murphy was in many ways the opposite of his predecessor. "Silent" Charlie's rise coincided with the rise of the Progressive Era and the astute Murphy decided on a much less conspicuous way of doing business. Whereas prior bosses had few qualms about skimming public funds and shortchanging the government on contracted works, Murphy quietly moved Tammany Hall towards a system of so called "honest graft." The bidding for public contracts was as corrupt as ever and therefore still monopolized by Tammany-friendly businesses. But the work involved and goods purchased were faithfully carried out and delivered. The newly-united boroughs of New York City were undergoing massive expansion and numerous infrastructure projects. These "honest graft" schemes were the greatest source of power, and money, for the Tammany Boss. This was especially true with the rise of civil service reform. Doling out jobs for patronage became much more difficult.

Silent Charlie was still able to take care of his cousin, however. The boy's father had died many years ago and Murphy had always felt responsible for his young cousin, tried to look out for him. He steered him toward a civil service appointment as probationary fireman. Truth be told, the young man had been appointed on his own merits. The new, Albany-based, Civil Service Commission was notoriously obstinate to Tammany influence, so Murphy was glad the young man didn't require any "special consideration" for the appointment. Once the appointment had been made, however, Silent Charlie was able to ensure that his hand-picked fire commissioner, Rhinelander Waldo, took good care of him. His company assignment was given much thought.

AFTER TEN DAYS ON continuous duty, Charlie Pendergrass left the firehouse both exhausted and exhilarated. With money in his pocket, he took the elevated train on the Bowery up to 14th Street. No sooner had he climbed the steps at Houston and Bowery than the train arrived, and he hopped on, laughing to himself at the irony. Weighed down by his gear on his first day of work, he'd been forced to walk to the firehouse. Now that he could afford the train, he wasn't carrying anything. It was late morning and his block on 20th Street was still coming to life. The vegetable cart by First Avenue was set up, and the German man who owned it, Mr. Schermerhorn, sat on a stool beside it waiting for the women of the block to come pick their cabbages, potatoes, and onions for the day's pot. For all of Charlie's life, Mr. Schermerhorn and his cart had been on that corner six days a week.

In front of Charlie's tenement, an open cabbed automobile was parked. A mustached man with a Bowler hat sat behind the wheel smoking a thinly rolled cigarette. Charlie made eye contact with him before turning to climb the short stoop.

"Pendergrass!" the man called.

Charlie turned, remaining on the stoop, and said nothing.

"He wants to see you."

"Now?"

The man reached over and opened the passenger door. There was an awkward moment where neither said anything or moved, but then Charlie went to the car and got in. They sped through intersections and around horse-drawn buggies. Charlie didn't have to ask where they were headed. The famous Delmonico's, once downtown Manhattan's Citadel, was now located at Fifth Avenue and 45th Street. They pulled up to the front and a doorman came out to open the car door. Charlie stepped down in his linen pants and simple wool coat. Seeking further permission to help this underdressed young man, the doorman looked at the driver, who tipped his Bowler.

"He's here for the boss, George. See him upstairs," said the driver.

The doorman nodded and motioned for Charlie to enter. He was led past the dining room entrance to an elevator, which stood ready on the first floor. The doorman took a pencil and small card from his pocket and scribbled something quickly. He handed the card to the elevator operator and motioned for Charlie to get in. They only went up one floor and the doors opened. The operator handed the card to a burly man at the landing who then grabbed Charlie's elbow and led him to a huge wooden door. He swung it open and pushed Charlie into the room.

Across the deep study, flanked by bookshelves and a glass-topped whiskey bar, was a long wooden desk. A broad-shouldered man sat behind it, sipping from a coffee cup. He wore narrow, rounded eyeglasses too small for his face. "Come sit, Charlie," he said. As Charlie moved to a chair opposite the desk, he added: "We're both named after the same man, my great-uncle Charles Francis Pendergrass, back in Ireland."

Only then did Charlie realize that his cousin, Charles Francis Murphy, was not speaking to him but another man in the room. He was surprised to see a silent, round-faced man, seated in the corner. A long coat was folded over one arm and a Bowler hat rested on his knee. Charlie wondered why he hadn't hung them on the coatrack by the door, but then remembered how he himself had been shoved in by the man outside and thought maybe he didn't have time before being ushered to a chair. Charlie sat and waited for an introduction. None came.

Instead, Silent Charlie Murphy began talking. "Charlie here is a fireman—stationed down by the factories. He can tell us firsthand if they are safe or not. After all, the factories themselves are a great improvement for the garment workers—better than the sweatshops in those rat-infested tenements. So, we need to convince the workers the factories are safe. And we need to convince Chief Croker that the workers *feel* safe." He paused and looked over at the man in the corner, who nodded. "Charlie," Murphy continued. "Is there anything you've seen in your profession, anything the factory owners should be forced to do?"

Charlie was flabbergasted. He'd been a fireman for less than two weeks. What did he know about factory safety? He'd never even seen the inside of a factory—the one fire he caught was in a tenement apartment. The two runs he'd responded to in loft factories turned out to be a false alarm and a smoldering trash-can that the workers had dragged outside before the firemen arrived. He didn't know how to answer, but Murphy and the other man were waiting. "Cousin, I... I..."

"You can't think of anything," Murphy filled-in. "I know—short of shutting the factories down and going out of business, what do the politicians want factory owners to do?" He smiled and winked at the seated man, who laughed in response. "The State Assembly is investigating factory safety. Al Smith is holding a meeting next week with the members of Local Twenty-five—the ones who went on strike last year." Murphy looked over at the other man. "We'd like you to be there Charlie—let them know that the fire department is well equipped to handle any fires that may break out in a factory."

Charlie looked over at the other fellow. His thick neck billowed out from a stiff, buttoned collar. His cheeks were full, but more muscular than fatty. He was bald, and stared at Charlie with beady eyes patiently waiting for an answer. Charlie scrambled thoughts for a quick excuse, then remembered. "Cousin, I'm back on duty tomorrow morning. My next day off is ten days after."

"Perfect," Murphy exclaimed as he took a last sip of coffee and stood. "The meeting is not far from your station. I'll see to it you are excused and send a car for you."

A new panic set over Charlie. He could not tell Foreman Jennings he was leaving for a union meeting—or worse, have someone from city hall telephone the foreman to inform him his probie was leaving for a meeting. And most of all, he could not have an automobile pull up out front to pick him up. "I... Cousin, I..."

Murphy was next to the other man who stood and shook hands. They walked together to the door. Murphy had a hand on his shoulder and was shuffling him along, but the man turned his head and nodded. "Nice to meet you, young man."

Murphy pushed the big door open. "Bring my cousin some coffee, please, "he said to someone outside. Charlie sat back and looked at the imposing desktop. Neatly folded newspapers were fanned across: *New York Times*, *World*, *New York Tribune*, and *Telegram*. Aside from the pack was an unfolded copy of the *New York Call*. Charlie new it well. The *Call* was a socialist daily popular among union organizers and many laborers. Many of the patrons at the saloon used to read it and discuss the articles loudly. The burly man from outside brought a cup of black coffee and left it on the desk in front of Charlie. Murphy waited at the door for the man to leave, then pulled it shut and came back to his seat. Charlie gingerly sipped the steaming cup.

"Who was that man?" he asked.

Murphy had picked up the *Call* as he was sitting back. He pushed his narrow glasses up on his nose. "A factory owner—one of the garment shops down there. He and his partner run one of the biggest operations. They were one of the few that held out the entire strike."

"Cousin—I can't speak at any meeting," Charlie said. He was not pleading. After the initial surprise and his trouble finding the right words, he now felt more confident. "I hardly know the first thing about fire safety in factories."

Murphy was skimming the paper. Without looking up he answered: "I don't need you to know everything. You just need to know more than a state assemblyman. Throw some fancy words in the mix and sound sure of yourself."

Charlie put the cup down and stood. "You and my mother put me up to this. I was happy at the dock. But here I am now. I agreed to be a fireman—not a politician."

Murphy laughed. "Politician! Little chance of that, my boy. You've not the right temperament for politics."

Charlie thought to feel offended but couldn't be sure why.

"I'm trying to do something new here as well," Murphy continued. "You see this here?" He held up the *Call*. "I read it every day—to know what's going on in the factories, to know what's going on with the Italians and the Jews. They're not like the Irish. They've got their own languages, their own customs, and their own ideas about how things should be. And they're organizing. Last year's strike was just the beginning. The Strike of Twenty Thousand they called it! The next one will be a hundred thousand. You'll see. Change is coming, and we here at Tammany can get with it or get left behind."

Charlie sat again. "So why not stand with the workers? Why are you cozying up to the factory owners?"

"Is that what'ya think I'm up to here? Is it? Cozying up."

"I know you, Cousin. You don't invite just anyone to your kingdom here. If that man was here, it was a special audience he was granted."

"Indeed, it was. And that is how I need him to feel—like he's been given something special. Other than your expertise, did you hear me promise him anything?"

Charlie shook his head.

"I listened to his complaints and spoke to him little. Most of the troubles of the world could be avoided if men opened their minds instead of their mouths, I like to say."

Speaking of which, Charlie couldn't remember ever hearing his older cousin say so much at one time. "So now he feels he has a friend in you. What do you get out of it?"

"I need the factory owners to stand down and let this State Assembly inquiry run its course. They could kill it if they feel threatened and band together. Let the Assembly have their meetings—a hearing in Albany maybe. Then we'll pass a new law. One that sounds grand but changes very little. The workers gain a victory. The owners stay in business. And both sides keep *us* in business."

"Will the factories be safer?"

"They already are. That's the point. The union leaders want to topple the system—but then where will their members work? When Chief Croker asked for high-pressure water pipes, I gave them to him."

With Tammany controlled contractors and their kickbacks, Charlie thought.

"The mayor didn't want it—but I made it happen. When the chief asked that all skyscrapers be outfitted with uniform standpipe outlets, so the firemen could use their own hose in all buildings, I gave that to him as well. I know as well as any man how important fire safety is."

Charlie was unaware of the history of these measures but could not disagree. The high-pressure water system and uniformed standpipe outlets were very important. He didn't need years of experience to see that. What's more, his cousin's concern for fire safety seemed genuine. "All the same, Cousin. I can't speak at that meeting."

Murphy removed his glasses and wiped them with a handkerchief. "Just be there. You'll not have to speak. Your presence will be enough reassurance."

As much as Charlie resented it, he did feel indebted to his cousin. It had been Silent Charlie, more than anyone else, who looked out for him and his mother after his father died. Attending the meeting, without speaking, seemed compromise enough. "All right. But no special requests for me or any car to pick me up. I'll get there on my own."

9

1890

Max Blanck was seventeen and had worked in the shop for over a year. The room was small, dark, and cramped with sewing machines and piles of fabric. It was the ground floor of a tenement on Orchard Street where the owner, Mr. Steiner, also lived with his wife and four children. There were four machines powered by the operators' feet. The operators were three middle-aged women and one fourteen-year-old girl, a trainee paid half the rate of the other three. Max had started as a runner, bringing bolts of cloth and baskets of fabric in, and finished pieces out, but was now acting as foreman because Mr. Steiner had set up another sweatshop in an apartment upstairs and couldn't directly supervise both. Max worked twelve, sometimes fourteen hours a day, six days a week. If the sewing machine operators had it the worst—with constant pedaling, strained eyesight, and aching fingers, hands, and backs—a foreman had it little better. Max was on his feet all day, circling the room, stepping over piles of cloth, keeping a close eye on the operators' work in terms of quality and speed. He hand-tested the seams of every finished piece. If an operator had a small child, she might bring the child in to hand her fresh cloth and crawl under the machine to change spools of thread. Otherwise, it was Max who went around handing the women fresh fabric and crawling under the machines each time a spool ran out or a belt slipped off the spinner.

The days were long and filled with darkness and dank, stuffy air. And for all this, he only barely made ends meet. He did not yet have a family to support, and was splitting rent with his cousin in a single-room apartment. After food and rent, there was hardly any money left each week. But he saved. A few pennies here. A half-dollar there.

Max stepped over a pile of fabric and nearly tripped. "Miss Horowitz," he said to the trainee operator. "There's no need to double stich the cuff on these. If the stitching is right, one pass will hold just fine."

He stood over the girl's shoulder while she put a line of stitching around the cuff. When she was done, he took the piece and tugged on the end of the cuff checking for any separation or irregularities. "This will do just fine," he said, handing the piece back. The girl remained silent and stitched the other cuff.

"Mr. Blanck," another operator called out. "Something is wrong with Yetta."

Max looked over to Yetta's machine. The woman had slumped forward with her head on top of the motor. He climbed over piles and went around the circle of machines. He put his hands on her shoulders and leaned her back. Saliva and mucus were running down her chin, and he kicked over a stack of cloth bolts and lay the woman on the floor. Gurgling noises arose from her throat. Max had no idea what to do. One of the other women knelt beside her to offer care, but nobody knew exactly what was wrong. For a moment, Max felt paralyzed. He'd just been thinking about cuff stitching. How did this happen? What should be done? He couldn't put thoughts together enough to come up with a plan. He stared at the saliva running down the poor woman's chin and felt a deep-seated panic emanate from his gut.

"Can we get her out to fresh air?" someone said. After a moment, Max agreed and he put his arms under the unconscious woman's armpits and strained to hold her up. Two other women each grabbed onto a leg. They took two steps toward the door and one of the leg holders tripped over a bolt of cloth, bringing Max and the other woman down as well, landing atop the poor unconscious operator. He struggled to lift her again and they worked their way through the room agonizingly slowly.

Max had to squint his eyes nearly closed when the bright sunlight smacked his face. He could not let go of the woman to shield his eyes and nearly tripped again. By the time they lay the unfortunate woman on the sidewalk, she had stopped breathing altogether.

There was no coroner investigation, or any questions asked, really. Mr. Steiner sent a message to the woman's apartment that she had died. When the woman's brother-in-law arrived, Steiner gave him her final week's pay and the man arranged for a funeral director to cart her away.

Max would eventually forget the dead woman's name. Later on, he would not be able to recall which operator had alerted him, or what time of year the incident occurred. But for the rest of his life, Max never forgot the feeling that came over him when he left that dead woman on the sidewalk and went back inside the darkness of that tenement sweatshop. He crossed the threshold and the world became black. In the few seconds it took for his eyes to readjust, a sick feeling washed over him. It was the darkness that killed her, he was certain.

10

1911

MAX WALKED OUT OF Delmonico's feeling very pleased with himself. Silent Charlie Murphy was the most important political figure in the state and a good man to have on your side. The strike of 1909-1910 had been bad for business, but he and his partner, Isaac Harris, had fared better than most of the other factory owners. The few concessions they'd made—a small wage increase and fifty-two-hour work week—hadn't made much difference in profits or operations, and most of the political will for further reforms had dissipated once the strike ended. But the terrible factory fire across the river in Newark that past November had caused a resurgence. If their company, the Triangle Waist Company, was going to continue to thrive, he needed to stay ahead of these currents. And thriving it was. The loft factory on Washington Place alone was the largest women's shirt-making operation in the city, with over 500 employees, and Blanck and Harris owned several others. They were known as the Shirtwaist Kings.

11

THE MANHATTAN LYCEUM STOOD on East 4th Street, just off Bowery. On Thursday, Friday, and Sunday evenings the theatre housed productions of the latest plays. That January, *Molly and Marvin* had finished a sold-out run of several months. On certain Saturdays each month, however, the theatre also held evening dances. Being a Saturday, and most importantly because it was not considered a busy season for Triangle, Esther and Rachel had gotten home from work just after five and immediately set to piecing together the nicest outfits they could. Esther had one dress, a hand-me-down from her aunt on which she had stitched a lace border around the neckline. Rachel wore a dress handed down from Esther.

The line was out the door and Esther could hear piano music while she waited. They each handed twenty-five cents to a woman at the table inside the doorway and went inside. There was a rolling coat rack in the entrance foyer and Rachel and Esther hung their coats. The song that had been playing ended and a new one began—the notes rang out and Rachel jumped and began clapping. "*Temptation Rag!*" she squealed. "Let's go Est." Rachel dragged Esther to the dance floor.

The room was not very large, as theatres go. There was a wooden stage at the front with an upright piano that an old man was playing. Most of the seats had been stacked in the rear to create the dance floor, where dozens of young men and women now danced to the year's most popular ragtime tune. Rachel hopped from foot to foot while clapping her hands and Esther laughed at how excited her sister was. The dances were perhaps Esther's favorite thing about America. She couldn't imagine any such gatherings being allowed in Bialystok. But living in New York, however dreary the weeks could seem with the long hours at the factory, she had dances to look forward to.

Over Rachel's shoulder, dancing among several young men, was a familiar face. Esther beamed a great big smile, then covered her mouth from embarrassment. Catching on, Rachel stepped closer. "What is it?" she asked, while still dancing.

"Look who's here," Esther said.

Rachel began to turn, but then shot her gaze right back at Esther once she saw his face. "Gaspar," she whispered. The two giggled, and Esther peaked over her sister's shoulder again. Gaspar hadn't noticed them. The song ended and the pianist played a bland interlude with one hand while he swapped out sheet music with the other.

Rachel grabbed Esther's sleeve and pointed to a table in the back of the room where refreshments were served. "Can we get Coca-Cola?" she asked with such enthusiasm that Esther's heart swelled. Rachel was working full time, earning her own money, grown-up some would say. But in many ways, she was still a child—just sixteen. Bottles of Coca-Cola were being sold for five cents each—a whole day's lunch for the sisters. But Esther didn't have the heart to say no.

They sat in a row of chairs along the wall enjoying their soda. They were lost in conversation when Gaspar approached. "Good evening, Miss Rachel," he said with a smile.

Esther waited for Rachel to answer but she was frozen, so she nudged her elbow into her side. "Hello, Gaspar," Rachel said at last.

"Would you like to dance?"

Rachel nodded eagerly. She handed the bottle to Esther and ran off, hand in hand with Gaspar. Esther smiled and took a sip of Coca-Cola. He really was a nice boy, always friendly. In Rachel's vacated chair, another young woman sat. "*Guten avent*," she said. Good evening.

"Hello, Ida. Is Francine here as well?"

"She's still out on the dance floor. I needed a break."

Ida wore a white shirtwaist with pleated sleeves and a long gray skirt. Her brown hair had a braided ponytail that was wrapped into a bun. "It's lovely to get out for an evening. I love dances, so," said Ida.

"Me too," Esther agreed.

"Since the fifty-two-hour rule came in, I haven't missed one."

Esther smiled. "I don't think we have either. Were there dances in the Bronx—when you first arrived?"

"Not at all," said Ida. "Not that I would have attended anyhow. I worked from six-thirty in the morning, even though we were supposed to start at seven, and didn't finish till near eleven most nights, except Sunday."

"It was a little better at my uncle's shop," Esther replied. "And we closed for Sabbath."

"I'd have liked that. I'd have liked havin' an uncle around also. Instead, there was only that weasel-faced Mr. Brinkley. They said he was some kind of soldier or something when he was young. He stared at me all the time. So much that I tried never to look his way, except when I brought him the coats when I was done. I'd bring him two coats. He pulled the sleeves inside-out and tugged at the seams I just stitched for the liner, then put them in the bin and gave me two more. And he'd always come over right before seven, when I was supposed to finish, and put a pile of coats that *had* to be done before morning. The weasel-face bastard would put his hand on my shoulder and tell me to hurry."

"How terrible—how on earth did you manage?"

"Every day was like a month. But I think the other women were worse than him. I was the youngest, fourteen when I started. That's how weasel-face Brinkley bullied me to work longer. And it was all piece-work. If Brinkley got more work out of me, he made more. If I sewed more coats, there were less for the other women to sew. But they paid me trainee wages, no matter how many coats I did. The other women hated me for sewing their coats for less money. They said the nastiest things about me and told me I was taking food out of their mouths. I'm so much happier now—and living down here with the Educational Alliance and the dances and all. It's just so fabulous."

Esther thought of her life in New York. How different it would be had there been no pogrom and they were still in Bialystok? She wouldn't have dances in the Manhattan Lyceum with handsome elevator operators to dance with. She wouldn't have classes where she learned English, discussed books, and wrote compositions. She would have worked long hours in her father's factory and married the son of one of his business associates or fellow synagogue members when the time was right. Her father would be alive.

"I think you deserve a Coca-Cola," Esther said and handed the bottle to Ida, who smiled and took a big gulp. The piano player beat into *Let Me Call You Sweetheart*. Esther stood and reached for Ida's hand. "This is my favorite, let's go." Ida handed the bottle back and Esther finished the last sip before leaving it empty on the chair.

They found Rachel and Gaspar on the dance floor. The two were face to face, her right hand locked in his left and held shoulder high. His right hand was on her hip, with her left hand on his shoulder. They swept the floor from side to side in a waltz-like motion. Esther saw her sister's smile and it filled her with happiness. She held her two hands up—shoulder-height—and locked them with Ida's. They laughed as they went back and forth with the music.

THE GUNSHOTS RANG OUT from all directions. There was screaming and crying and a loud train whistle. Esther was running beside the moving passenger car—the handrail just out of reach. She stretched her arm, her fingers brushed against it, but still she could not grab on. Her chest hurt from breathing heavy. Another gunshot. More screaming. Esther reached deep inside for every last bit of strength and lurched forward. She wrapped her exhausted fingers around the handrail and heaved herself up. Once on the step, she turned to see Rachel running as well. Esther reached out for her sister's hand. She gripped the railing tight and leaned her body out, desperately trying to grab hold of Rachel. Rachel was running as fast as she could. Tears streamed down her cheeks as she called out: "Est... Est.. Help me."

Esther's body was almost completely outside the train car—only one foot remained on the step and she held the rail with one hand. Rachel's fingers weaved into Esther's and they squeezed tightly. But Esther felt her sister slipping away. She cried out: "Hold on, Rachel! Hold on." But it was no use. She lost her grip and Rachel fell back. Esther screamed as the train sped away—Rachel getting smaller in the distance.

She woke when Rachel shoved her shoulder.

"You were talkin' in your sleep again," she said.

"Huh?" Esther was groggy, but slowly realized she'd been dreaming. Rachel rolled over back to her side of the bed and Esther lay on her back staring upward. A faint wisp of moonlight made its way in through the air-shaft window in their tiny bedroom. Sounds of a barking dog and a distant argument in some undecipherable language seeped in the window as well. Esther turned her head and looked at Rachel's back, heard her soft breathing.

12

1902

THE HORSELESS CARRIAGE WAS a new phenomenon. They were too expensive for most people, and even the wealthy still preferred their luxurious horse-drawn buggies and carriages. Edward Croker, however, saw the future—and it was motorized. He procured the department's first automobile, an open-top buggy with a tiny motor underneath, to be the chief of department's vehicle. When the bells sounded, Croker and his aide were speeding out the bay doors before Engine Company 33 had even finished hitching their horses.

One clear Sunday morning, bells rang, and out went the chief. Right out of quarters, two blocks. then right on Broadway. Croker drove. He wore his rubber slicker coat, buttoned up to his neck, with a tweed flat cap and a pair of goggles. His trusted aide, Oswald, was seated beside him wearing his navy-blue uniform coat, cap and badge. Two horse-drawn carriages rode side-by-side heading north. "Bugger!" Croker shouted as he stepped on the gas pedal and steered toward the sidewalk. The curb was not much higher than the road's paving stones, and the car jumped onto the sidewalk without slowing a bit. Oswald rang the mounted bell and shouted *Make way, Make way!* Pedestrians—women in Sunday dresses, fathers scooping up young children in their arms—jumped out of the way as the chief sped down the crowded path. At the corner Croker jumped the car off the sidewalk and steered back out to the middle of Broadway.

The car arrived at the corner of Broadway and 14th Street and Croker parked behind a steam pumper hooked up to a hydrant. The pumper supplied two thick hoselines, snaked out down the block toward a theatre with smoke pumping out the front door. Croker exited the car and took off his cap and goggles. Oswald handed him his leather fire helmet—panted white with a gold-leaf encrusted front piece. *Chief of Department* was printed across the front piece over the initials *F.D.N.Y.*

Edward placed the helmet on his head and stepped over the hoselines. In front of the theatre, conferring with an aide and an engine company foreman, was Battalion Chief Joseph Martin.

"Good morning, Mr. Martin," said Croker.

"Hello Chief—she's cookin' real good in the back of the building," Martin replied. "I don't think Engine Fourteen is hitting the main body of fire. I was just sending my aide here to the box to transmit a third alarm."

Edward looked up. The theatre was only one-story tall but the façade was high, probably the height of a three-story building. Two firemen were climbing a ladder to the roof. They were each carrying an axe. "Is there access in the rear of the building?" he asked Martin.

"I believe so—Engine Seventy-two is stretching to the back. I'm awaiting the next truck company to go in with them."

"Very well." Edward stepped back. Contrary to rumors, he was happy to let a battalion chief run a fire if he was doing it well. Across the street was a crowd of people watching the fire, including a batch of reporters. He recognized a face and walked over.

"Chief Croker... Chief Croker," called a reporter. "Does Smokey Joe Martin think the fire department will get a handle on this one?"

Croker smiled. "I do believe so, yes. Chief Martin has matters well in hand, boys."

Several reporters were scribbling in note pads and Edward called over the group to a man in the back: "William Gunn Shepherd!"

The reporters all turned to look at a skinny young man in the back. He wore a fedora with a tab in the ribbon that said *Press*. He stopped writing and looked up at Croker in shock.

"How could I forget a name like that?" said Croker.

Shepherd stepped forward. "Well Chief, our last encounter was quite memorable."

Croker laughed. "Indeed, it was." He patted Shepherd on the shoulder. "Still shaping for the *World?"*

"United Press, actually, sometimes it gets picked up for the *World.*"

"Good for you," Croker answered, then turned his attention to the group. "It's a fine day, boys, get some nice photographs. I think it'll be a fifth alarm before we're through here."

"What makes you say that, Chief?" a reporter asked.

"You see this theatre here—very high ceilings. I know it well. Inspected it myself when the mayor asked for a theatre survey. Luckily it was built with heavy roof timbers—she won't collapse right away. But it'll hold a lot of heat in those rafters until the men can chop holes in the roof."

<hr />

CROKER WAS PLEASANTLY SURPRISED not long after the transmission of a fourth alarm, when Battalion Chief Martin told him he was placing the fire "under control." Martin's aide went to the box to send a telegraph signal to the dispatcher. The fire had been contained to just the theatre and there had been no deaths or injuries.

Oswald went to the car and returned with a fedora, and Croker removed his leather helmet, handed it to his aide and donned the hat. His slicker coat was unbuttoned and he reached in his pocket and pulled out a cigar that had been burned half-way down. The butt was flatted from having been chewed and he put the stub in his mouth and struck a match on a dried-leather breeching strap attached to a steam pumper. The match sparked alive and he lit the cigar, puffing intently and then spitting to relieve the taste of stale smoke trapped from the previous burn out.

He patted Martin on the arm. "Smokey Joe does it again!" he bellowed with a laugh.

Martin smiled. "I'll never live that down, will I?"

"You love it. Don't pretend otherwise."

Martin smiled and turned to speak to his aide. Croker went back to the reporters across the street. "I need your help boys," he announced to the group. "You see these pumpers here, they can supply six hundred gallons of water per minute, assuming the hydrant pressure is adequate."

The reporters looked around at the scene. Three separate engine companies had attached their pumpers to hydrants on the Broadway side, and apparently there were more steam pumpers hooked up around the block.

"Trouble is, the hydrants don't always supply good pressure. Now, they work just fine if the fire is on the ground level, like today. But if we need to pump water up multiple stories—like the lofts or new skyscrapers—it becomes very difficult. The hydrants and pumpers just can't handle it."

"Isn't that what standpipes are for, Chief?" asked a reporter.

"Indeed—standpipes are a great help. But the roof-level water tanks can hold only so much water. The pipes must then be fed by engine companies at street level using hydrant water. And the water pressure is just not adequate."

"What's the answer, Chief?" one reporter asked.

"A high-pressure water system! I want to pump water, with massive turbines, from the Hudson River, across this swath of lower Manhattan where so many of these buildings are located."

A few reporters laughed. One whistled. "Do you think you'll secure the funding?" William Gunn Shepherd called out from the back.

"Well, that's where you fellas come in. I need you to write about it—put the pressure on the politicians. You see?"

"Chief, what about Mayor Low's announcement that he is endorsing all of the Civil Service Commission's proposals?" a reporter shouted, apparently uninterested in the high-pressure water system.

"What about it?" Croker replied.

"Do you support it?"

"Indeed, I do."

This released a flurry of simultaneous follow-ups. Edward held up a hand and spoke over them. "Who would know better than I the stain upon one's character that accompanies even the appearance of impropriety or favoritism?"

The reporters diligently took the quote down in notepads. "Mr. Shepherd," Croker said as he turned to leave. "Take a walk with me."

Shepherd and Croker walked toward the chief's car, stepping over leaking hoses and around puddles. "I often have dinner at Lyons's on Bowery—if the fire gods don't call me away," Edward told the young reporter as he buttoned his slicker. His cigar was now down to little more than a nub and he tossed it into a brown puddle beside a steam engine pumper.

"I know it well, Chief. That's Big Tim Sullivan's joint."

"It's Mike Lyons's joint, no matter which Tammany man frequents it. Fine place, it is. Come see me if you ever need a scoop."

"Thank you, Chief. I'll do that." Shepherd gave a cursory tip of his fedora and began walking away, then stopped. "Why me?"

Croker took off his own fedora and wiped his forehead on the rubber sleeve of his coat. He looked Shepherd in the eye and smiled. "You've got guts, and you do what you have to, to make your way in the world. Your uncle doesn't own a newspaper—you go out and hustle. I like that."

"Uncle, aye?" Shepherd began, then he switched topics abruptly. "I want to hear more about this high-pressure system."

Edward put the fedora in the car, donned his tweed flat cap, then climbed into the driver's seat. "Lyons's Restaurant, Mr. Shepherd." He then looked ahead to a group of firemen talking. "Oswald," he called out to his aide. "We're up."

"You're the only fire chief I've ever seen who doesn't let his aide drive," said Shepherd. "Granted, all the other chiefs have horse-drawn carriages. So, what is it chief?"

Edward placed his tweed flat cap on his head and donned his goggles. "Shepherd," he said. "One thing you'll learn about me, if you haven't already, is that when I want something done good and fast I do it myself."

"And what about your aide, Chief? What does he do?"

"Oswald?" Croker smiled and motioned his head toward his aide. "Well, he just holds on tight and prays!"

※

CROKER STEERED THE CAR onto Great Jones Street and pulled up in front of the firehouse. Both bay doors were open and a woman stood out front with three children and a suitcase. Edward shut off the motor, leaving the car parked outside. "Back her in for me will you, Oswald. Have the housewatchman help."

Edward removed his slicker coat and draped it over the back of the car, where his leather helmet and fedora both lay on a rack. He placed his tweed flat cap and goggles on top and stepped to the woman. "Hello, Dear," he said and kissed her on the cheek.

"I'm taking the children to Shinnecock Bay," she said while his lips were still pressed against her cheek.

"We agreed to wait till the school term ended. We can't change schools on them now." Edward looked down at his boys, Richard, thirteen, and Edward, five. They stood silently beside the suitcase. His daughter Edith, seven, held her mother's hand.

"I won't spend another minute in that apartment," she said. "It's better for the children to be out in the country."

"But Richard's studies? You heard what that officer said. If he's to be accepted in the Naval Academy, it's paramount that his grades for these years are flawless. How will he adjust to a new school? What if his grades suffer?"

Young Richard just stared at the ground and kicked pebbles. His mother answered for him: "He'll adjust like any clever boy would. Besides, that Academy business is your wish, not his."

A hot flash of anger rose to Edward's head, but he held his tongue. He could yell at an engine company officer for not making an aggressive push with a hoseline. He could yell at a policeman for not keeping the sidewalk clear at a third alarm fire. He could yell at politicians, and newspapermen, and the drivers of slow-moving carriages. But he couldn't yell at his wife in front of the children. He let a moment pass, then said calmly: "This is ridiculous. How will you get there?"

"We'll find a hansom cab on the Bowery here to take us to the ferry. Then make our way to the railroad station in Brooklyn."

Edward was thoughtful for a moment, then called to his aide. "Oswald, strap the suitcase to the rack, please."

"Sure thing, Chief."

"Climb up children," Edward announced. The children shouted with joy and jumped up into the seat immediately. "I'll drive you to the ferry. You'll have to squeeze in. I would take you over the bridge, but I don't think we ought to with the little ones piled on your lap."

"The ferry will do fine," she said with a wry smile.

Oswald handed Edward his slicker coat, tweed cap and goggles. He tied the suitcase to the rear running board and wedged

Edward's helmet and fedora between the suitcase and the seat. Edward got in behind the steering wheel with Richard between him and Mrs. Croker. Edith and Edward sat on her lap. The single seat-car was weighed down, but Edward was able to maneuver it down Delancey Street to the waterfront.

He waited at the dock until the ferry boat pushed off. Edith stood by the railing waving. Edward smiled and waved. He had already been a fireman when he married. It came as no surprise to his wife that he would be away from home most of the time. When the paid department was formed, many of the new professional firemen had been sailors. Years at sea accustomed them to long periods away from home. In those early years, married men were the exception, at least among the lower ranks. Chief officers were outfitted with a small suite in the firehouse—an office, a sleeping room, and bathroom. Many chiefs had their wives and perhaps a young child living with them in the firehouse. With three young ones, however, Edward knew that would not be practical. Not that his wife would have agreed to such an arrangement anyway. And as chief of department, he was often outside the firehouse for long periods—a fourth alarm in Brooklyn; a ceremony for a new firehouse opening in the Bronx; a funeral for a fallen fireman in Queens. He thought it a good thing to have his family in a nearby apartment, but Edward had grown weary of his wife's complaints and longing for the country. They bought a house on Long Island and he spent his vacation leave that year fixing it up for a move-in after the school year.

Watching the ferry chug over choppy water, making its way to Brooklyn, he put a fresh cigar in his mouth and struck a match on the ferry landing's railing. Puffing the cigar to life, he wondered when he'd make it out to Shinnecock Bay. A voice called out from behind.

"Chief Croker! Chief Croker!"

Edward turned to see Oswald running down from the roadway, waving his arms. Edward walked back to the car as his aide approached. "Second Alarm up in Yorkville—Tenth Battalion," Oswald said. Edward reached for his goggles and pulled his flat cap down tight over his head. He carefully knocked the ash off his cigar and lay it on an indentation between the seat and the rack.

"Well by all means, hurry up man!" Croker said as Oswald gasped for air and hopped in the car. "Give me some bells," he added as he sped away from the dock. Oswald duly rang the bell with one hand, squeezing the seat rail with the other. "We'll head up First Avenue," Edward said and accelerated around a line of horse carriages.

Once they were on a straight away, Oswald reached into his pocket. He opened a newspaper-wrapped sandwich of hard bread with cold, sliced ham. He ripped it in half and handed a piece to Croker. Edward shifted the car into the next gear and took hold of the sandwich—scarfing it down in two bites. He then put his hand back on the gear knob and shifted again.

∞

THE FIRE WAS OUT by the time Edward arrived. It had started on the first floor of a tenement building and extended rapidly, through open windows in the air shaft, up to the second and third floors. He was pleased to see that engine companies had quickly positioned three hoselines into the building—two up the interior stairs, and a third up the front fire escape into the third floor. Stretching hoselines up fire escapes was not easy, but it avoided clogging the interior stairs with a third line. It took discipline and prior preparation, two things Croker liked to see. He had parked down the block, donned his slicker coat and white helmet and was stepping over hoselines to find the battalion chief. He wanted to compliment him for his companies' efficiency. In the middle of the block was a parked hose wagon. The horses had been unharnessed and led down the street, and the wagon had a mess of hose pulled out the back. The hose was "uncharged", which is to say it wasn't filled with water—just flat, cotton jacketed hose piled in a tangled mess in the street. Sifting through the knot was a young fireman. He was frantically pulling bends of hose, but only making it worse.

"What goes here, young man?" Croker said.

"I just... I was..." the baby-faced fireman seemed unable to speak as he pulled more hose down. He looked up and, presumably seeing Edward's white helmet with the gold Chief of Department front piece, he froze.

"I say—you've made quite the mess of this," Edward said.

"Sir, I was... You see.... Foreman Johnson told me to charge our line. But our engineer, Willis, he moved the pumper—you see. He wasn't hooked up to the hydrant he had stopped at when we arrived. And I couldn't find him—there were so many engine companies arriving. And I didn't want my foreman to get mad at me—so I thought if I brought in another hoseline, I could have another engine feed it. You see?"

"Why didn't you just follow your company's line?" Edward asked. "From the building out, straight to the pumper, wherever it's parked."

The young man seemed stumped—that had not occurred to him and he panicked. Edward thought he might cry. "How long have you been a fireman?"

"This is my second day."

"All right, all right. Well, the fire is out now. What's your name, son?"

"Baker—Thomas Baker."

"Well, Baker—you're not going to fix this by pulling off more hose. Uncouple it there, at that fitting." Croker pointed to a brass coupling hanging off the hose bed. Baker screwed apart the two sections of hose. Edward sifted through the hose spaghetti at his feet and found another coupling. He began unscrewing it himself. "Find all the couplings and disconnect them."

When all the hose lengths were separated, Edward pulled on one end and walked it out, all fifty feet, and lay it flat on the street. "Lay all the lengths out," he told Baker. Noticing Oswald walking down the block, he called him over. "Give us hand," he told the aide.

Edward took off his slicker coat and helmet, lay them on the wagon's harness rails and rolled up the sleeves of his wool jacket. He climbed up onto the hose bed, straddled the neatly folded rows and grabbed the dangling male-ended brass coupling hanging over the edge. "Baker, hand me the female coupling there on that length." He pointed to a length. "Oswald, help Mr. Baker, the two of you feed it to me, keep it nice and flat. While I'm folding the top end in and laying it back, one of you couple the next fitting."

In his panic, Baker had pulled off ten lengths of hose. Edward meticulously packed it away in the hose wagon. He had always thought a neatly packed hose wagon showed pride in one's company. He lay it flat, straight to the backplate and then put a crisp fold and brought it forward diagonally to the outer edge, bent it over again and brought it straight back once more. Line after line, row after row. Baker and Oswald screwed couplings and fed the line flat and even.

"Did I ever tell you about my citation, Oswald?" Croker said while folding the last length.

"Most efficiently run engine company—when I was foreman."

"Baker!" a stern voice called out from up the block. The engine company foreman approached. His helmet was coated in plaster dust, his face covered in soot. Brown water dripped from his slicker coat. His salt and pepper mustache was wet. "Baker, what the hell happened with that line?" He yelled, stepping toward the young man. "I had to send Smitty out to get our line charged." The foreman noticed Edward atop his hose wagon. "Who's this?" he asked Baker. "Why is this man atop *our* hose bed?"

"Mr. Johnson, sir..." Baker was flustered. "I came out... and the steamer... I was..."

Edward climbed down and retrieved his slicker and helmet from the harness rail. He placed the helmet on his head and went to the foreman with his hand extended. The man oozed anger as he turned his attention from Baker to Croker. Edward would have liked a photographer to capture the shock on the foreman's face when he saw the white helmet and gold front piece.

"I, uh… Chief Croker, sir," he managed to squeak out. After a moment, he saw the chief's held-out hand and shook it. "Daniel Johnson."

Edward swung the slicker around his shoulders and slid his arms in. "Take a walk with me, Mr. Johnson," he said as he stepped away from the hose wagon. Once away from Oswald and Baker, Edward spoke to the foreman. "It's clear your new man there needs to be drilled in controlling a hose stretch, and I have no doubt you'll see to it."

"Well, yes, sir. Of course," Johnson answered quickly.

"But he's not the only one in need of instruction, now, is he?"

"Sir?"

"I don't know what you were thinking, but when I was foreman of an engine company, I would not have assigned a probationary fireman with two days' experience to control a hose stretch."

"Sir, I…" the foreman trailed off and wisely said no more.

Edward gave the man a stiff pat on the shoulder and stepped back to the hose wagon. "Let's go Oswald—that ham sandwich is wearing off." He began walking to the car, then turned. "And Baker…"

"Yes, Chief," Baker answered eagerly.

"You've entered a noble profession, son. Make me proud!"

For the first time, the panic left Baker's face and a smile emerged. "Yes, sir."

THEY RETURNED TO THE firehouse on Great Jones Street and a man in a black suit, long black wool coat and Derby hat stood outside smoking a pipe. His mustache was waxed and the ends curled up to a point. He stared at Edward as the chief's car came to a stop and it appeared he was waiting for Croker. "Well, this doesn't look like good news," Edward said quietly to Oswald.

"You're a popular man today, Chief," answered the aide.

"Chief Croker," the man called out as Edward was climbing out of the car.

"That would be me, sir."

The man stepped closer and offered his hand. "Alderman John Callaghan."

Edward shook his hand. "How may I help you, sir?"

"I was hoping for a moment of your time?"

"Well, yes, of course. We're just returning from a fire. Follow me upstairs and I'll take you to my office."

The man nodded and removed his hat. Edward turned toward Oswald and raised his eyebrows. His aide had been with him long enough to read his boss's face. This was a nuisance for Croker. "You'll back her in," Croker said, nodding to the car.

"Sure thing, Chief."

※

ALDERMAN CALLAGHAN SAT BACK in the chair and puffed his pipe. Edward remembered that his cigar was still on the car's dashboard but was in no mood to go back downstairs for it.

"Have you any word from your uncle at all?" the alderman began.

"None since he set sail almost two years ago."

"Pity, really. But fully predictable, once Teddy Boy took the reins. He never liked Richard. In his run for governor, I think he spoke more against your uncle than his Democratic opponent."

Edward fidgeted with his hands. He really wanted his cigar and he wanted Callaghan to get to the point. "Well—what's done is done. What can I do for you today?" he said, hoping to move things along.

"I'll get right to it. Joseph McWilliams is my friend, known him since we were boys. He would like to be assigned to the Eighth Battalion."

"Why are you here asking, instead of Battalion Chief McWilliams?"

"I feel this method is the better approach."

"You feel it is better for a politician to interfere with the administration of a department which has a chief officer sworn to run it to the best of his ability."

"You run your department as you see fit. All I'm asking for is a friendly accommodation."

"I've seen what comes of Tammany accommodations."

Callaghan gave a cheeky little smirk. "Firsthand, I'm told."

Edward stood and went to the door. He opened it and looked Callaghan—still seated—dead in the eye. "Get the hell out of here," he said through pursed lips. "And if you ever come back I'll throw you out and break your fucking neck."

Callaghan took another long draw from his pipe and took his time getting up. Edward waited at the door saying nothing. The alderman put his Derby cap atop his head and walked out without offering a handshake or salutation. As he turned around the newel post to go downstairs, Edward heard him mumble: "Pity, really."

ONE CENT

Evening Edition

SPECIAL EDITION

VOL. 10. THURSDAY, FEBRUARY 10, 1910 NO. 41.

WHAT THE 20,000 HAVE DONE

WILLIAM G. SHEPHERD

New York, NY., Feb. 10—Here are the ultimate results of the so-called Strike of the Twenty Thousand which has so abruptly concluded after many months of bitter struggle:

The textile workers of the shirtwaist factories will receive pay raises and shortened work weeks—generally 52 hours per week.

Local 25 of the International Ladies Garment Workers Union will be recognized and workers' membership therein no longer grounds for dismissal. Few factory owners, however, have agreed to "closed shop" arrangements, where only union members would be hired.

Striking workers will be allowed to return to their former positions.

Union leaders have declared victory and taken to pro-labor journals to celebrate their gains. Other publications—more sympathetic to the owners—have described such improvements to the workers' lot in sarcastic vein. But a fair-minded correspondent must acknowledge the harsh price paid by the striking women and temper any modest gains, the factory owners' complaints notwithstanding. Above all, any victory in this battle, however small, belongs to those women—girls really—of the picket lines.

Should the reader forget, it was union leaders who cautioned moderation at Cooper Union this November last. Were it not for the courage and eloquence of young Clara Lemlich, no strike would have occurred at all. With her face still bruised from the brutal attack suffered at the hands of ruffians (hired for sure, but by whom?) Lemlich stood at the lectern and declared: "I am a working girl, one of those who are on strike against intolerable conditions. I am tired of listening to speakers who talk in general terms. What we are here to decide is whether we shall or shall not strike. I offer a resolution that a general strike be declared—now."

It was the women of the picket lines who bore the violence of detective agents hired by the owners, and who were hauled before a judge should they have raised a finger in self-defense. It was the women of the picket line suffering the indignity of known prostitutes in their midst—paid by the owners—to give policemen pretext for arresting the strikers under the very charge of prostitution.

And so, the slowest season for shirtwaist factories is drawing to an end and the busiest about to begin. Factory owners have calculated that paying detective agents and picket-breaking workers will be too expensive and it is therefore in their interest to settle with the strikers. With the so-called Shirtwaist Kings—Max Blanck and Isaac Harris—being the last to come to terms, the strike has ended.

The women of the picket line have suffered—many months without pay, with little charity relief, and with continual harassment. The gains may seem modest but are nonetheless real.

H.P. MARTIN & CO.

Gowns and Suits
Tailored Linen Suits
$20.00
Embroidered Dresses
$32.00
Custom Design Dresses
$32.00
FIFTH AVE., 48th St.

STOCK REDUCTION SALE
20% Discount

WHITEHALL BROTHERS
LADIES SHOES
Latest Fashions
Full Selection of Boots
Broadway & 26th St.

TO-DAY

Born on February 10th

Richard Storrs Willis
1819

Walter Parratt
1841

Historical Events

The Treaty of Paris ended the French and Indian War, February 10, 1763.

After nearly three decades away, Voltaire returned to Paris, February 10, 1778.

Part Two

13

1911

Esther sat in the front row. Clara had saved her a seat up front so she might answer a few questions about factory conditions. Rachel was in attendance as well but sat in the back, and Esther quickly lost sight of her. Local 25's union hall was not very large; the leadership had been looking for a bigger location since the strike, when membership increased a hundred-fold. There were about two-hundred members crammed in the hall, however—maybe half were seated in chairs while the rest stood in the back and around the sides. A makeshift dais had been constructed, with a long table and a half-dozen chairs. One man stood and tried to get the room's attention. Esther didn't know him, nor anyone else up there.

"Everyone, please..." he began with his hands raised to quiet the crowd. "Good evening, ladies and gentlemen. For those who don't know me, I am Irving Stein, general secretary for the I.L.G.W.U." He paused, perhaps waiting for an applause that did not come. "I'd like to thank you all for being here for this important discourse. I'd also like to thank our esteemed assemblyman—Mr. Al Smith—for bringing so many distinguished men together." Now there was a small round of applause. Esther's attention went to the one woman seated on the dais.

"Assemblyman Smith—thank you sir," Stein reiterated, and Al Smith stood and waved to the clapping crowd.

"From the National Consumers League, we have Frances Perkins."

The sole woman on stage rose and raised her hand. She was well-dressed, with a silk blouse, beaded pearl necklace, and a narrow-rimmed bonnet. The men all wore suits, of course, but Esther was used to that. Men in suits walked through the factory floor all the time. Besides those she passed on the sidewalk though, Esther was not accustomed to such finely-dressed women. A handful of members clapped for the woman from the National Consumers League.

"And next... We have Chief Edward Croker from the fire department."

This man had gold buttons on his dark-blue jacket. He held a blue, rounded uniform cap in his hand. Esther noticed gold braiding on the cap. He stood halfway and gave a quick wave before sitting again.

"Next, we have Mr. Martin Simpson from the Board of Fire Underwriters."

The next man stood and raised a hand. He wore a finely pinstriped suit and bow tie. His round eyeglasses were folded and sticking out from his breast pocket.

"And lastly, we have Mr. Samuel Bernstein—manager of the Triangle Waist Company."

Esther felt a jolt of fear shoot through her body. She hadn't noticed him at first. He was wearing a suit for one thing, instead of his usual apron over shirtsleeves. And his hair—it was slicked and combed back. But there he was all right. Esther's hands shook. She thought of getting up to leave, but that would only draw attention to herself. Had he noticed her yet? If she hadn't walked the factory translating for him recently, he probably would not have known her. *But now? Who knows?* she thought. Mr. Bernstein stood and waved at the crowd.

Esther saw Clara go from her standing position on the side of the room and march straight up to the dais. Looking angry, she pulled Mr. Stein aside and the two discussed something privately. Stein stepped back onto the dais and Clara waited on the side until he started talking again. When the audience was looking up at him, she came over and knelt in front of Esther.

"I'm sorry," she whispered. "I had no idea he'd be here. Stein says he was a last-minute add-in, insisted upon by Charlie Murphy. He said it was the only way he'd allow the assemblyman to be here."

Esther looked up at Mr. Bernstein, whose attention was focused on Stein. "Clara, I can't say anything bad about Triangle—not with him watching."

"The union can protect you. We won that right in the strike."

Esther sat on her hands and rocked back and forth. What would happen If she were fired? Rachel was just a trainee, and that smug Mr. Craven wouldn't hesitate to fire her as well. Their mother barely made enough money to cover the rent. How would they eat? "Clara—I can't."

Clara stared at her for a moment, then said: "All right. It'll be all right. Mr. Stein is the only one who knows I was bringing anyone from Triangle. I'll make sure he doesn't ask you anything."

CHARLIE SAT IN THE front row, his cousin, Silent Charlie Murphy, to his left. He fidgeted in his seat and felt guilty about lying to Foreman Jennings. He said it was his mother's birthday and asked to be relieved for a meal break that evening. Married men went home for dinner, after all, so Charlie hoped the foreman would allow it. Jennings, ever stern, but fair, agreed and told Charlie to sign out in the journal. The company journal was a thick ledger kept on the housewatch desk. All firehouse activity—fire runs, equipment deliveries, personnel assignments and excusals—were recorded in it. Charlie ran his finger down the page:

9:30am Telegraph Signal Box 312. H&L 20 responded.

10:05am H&L 20 available from quarters.

12:00pm Fr. Ott relieves Fr. Smith on housewatch duty. Dept. property and quarters in good order.

1:30pm Fr. Mance leaving quarters for haircut.

2:05pm Telegraph Signal Box 334. H&L 20 responded.

2:15pm Fr. Mance returns to quarters.

3:35pm Asst. Foreman Woll records fire activity Box 334—125 Wooster St. B-3 resp. No injury to members reported.

3:35pm H&L 20 available from quarters.

3:35pm Fr. Ott resumes housewatch duties. Dept. property and quarters in good order.

6:00pm Fr. Schley relieves Fr. Ott on housewatch duty. Dept. property and quarters in good order.

The handwriting was perfect script and Charlie was worried he would be too sloppy. He had assisted on housewatch duty, but hadn't recorded anything in the journal yet. He took the pen in hand and added:

7:45pm Fr. Pendergrass going home for dinner.

He rested the pen in the fold of the journal and went to leave. "Leaving quarters," Fred Schley said. Charlie turned. Fred was pointing to Charlie's journal entry. "Fireman Pendergrass is leaving quarters for meal—we don't say going home for dinner, Johnny."

Johnny? Charlie wondered again, but let it pass. He simply nodded and went out the door. He now sat in his front row seat at the union hall and worried about his journal entry. He had lied. He wasn't home for dinner, or meal, or whatever. He didn't want to attend the meeting and had already told his cousin that he had to leave at 9:00 to get back to work. Charlie reached over and took a chained pocket watch out of Silent Charlie's pocket. 8:05. He slid the watch back in the pocket and looked up at his cousin's face.

The big man was listening to the speaker and paying Charlie no mind. Charlie hadn't listened to a word anyone said until a young woman came from the direction of the dais and kneeled directly in front of the young woman to his right. He remained looking forward, but it was easy to hear their whispered conversation. "I'm so sorry, I had no idea he'd be here..." the kneeling woman began.

The speaker on the dais had finished the introductions and now called on Chief Edward Croker to speak. Charlie had his badged uniform cap with him, Silent Charlie had asked him to wear it. But Charlie held the cap under his arm and did his best to keep it out of Chief Croker's view. His blue button-up shirt and canvas pants were not the obvious garb of a fireman, and he was trying not to attract the chief's attention. Surely his cousin must have known Croker would be there. Did the Tammany Hall boss really think Charlie's presence could counterweight the opinion of a man like Croker? The chief's stature among newspapermen, politicians, and ordinary citizens had grown to the point where he was considered the absolute authority on fire safety and an unimpeachable leader of the city's firemen. Charlie joined the fire department knowing very little about it, but he knew about Chief Croker, often pictured in the newspaper in his white helmet staring up at an inferno or speeding to an alarm in his automobile that the papers had nicknamed the *Red Devil*. Charlie watched the chief stand, but for the moment he was still listening to the hushed conversation of the two young women beside him.

"Mr. Stein is the only one who knows I was bringing anyone from Triangle," the kneeling one said. "I'll make sure he doesn't ask you anything."

The gist of the conversation, as far as Charlie could tell, was that the seated young woman was afraid of being called upon to speak. It seemed one of the men on stage frightened her. Charlie knew exactly how she felt. Croker addressed the room:

"Thank you, Mr. Stein and the members of Local 25, and the members of the press here in attendance. And Assemblyman

Smith and the other speakers tonight. I need not remind all in this room of the importance of fire safety, particularly in factories and lofts. As we saw all too starkly this past November in Newark, the potential for tragedy is high. This city may have a fire as deadly at any time. There are buildings in New York where the danger is every bit as great as in the building destroyed in Newark. A fire in the daytime would be accompanied by a terrible loss of life.

"Strangely enough the owners of many such buildings or their lessees are too short-sighted to perceive the immense advantage which a little study and application of the rules of fire protection would be to them. Such men insure, they comply with the law—perhaps—in the matter of construction, and they sit back contentedly, feeling that all is well and they have only to attend to the strictly commercial side of their business."

Charlie thought back to the conversation in Silent Charlie's office. *Short of shutting the factories down and going out of business, what do the politicians want factory owners to do?* Murphy had asked rhetorically, to that factory owner's delight.

"This is sheer folly," Croker continued. "Insurance is an excellent thing, but insurance never makes up for the loss of a thriving business by fire. The value of the physical property may be returned, it is true…" here Croker nodded to the men at the table, "but what about the damages for the loss or injuries of employees in case the responsibility can be fixed upon the employer? These things are never *covered* by insurance."

There was a round of applause from the crowd. Charlie was captivated by Croker. The chief spoke not only with authority, but with measured fairness. It was smart, Charlie thought, to open with an appeal to the financial interest of the owners. There may not have been any owners there, Charlie thought, but there were newspapermen. Croker continued:

"It is the equation in terms of money. There is, of course, another side, that of the obligation, the moral responsibility, which the owner of a building, or the employer of labor has toward his fellow property holders or his workmen. He is neglecting his obvious duty to society as well as his selfish interest if he does not see to it that he is living in a fool's paradise, and that measures proposed to the legislature are really to protect his property and his employees.

"As a matter of fact, unless it was built in very recent times, and probably not even in that case, a factory is very far from fireproof—but that does not mean the fire hazard in it cannot be reduced."

Croker enumerated the various danger spots of factory buildings: boiler rooms, electrical wiring, gas supply and so on. Charlie looked to his right. The kneeling woman had gone and the one seated was listening intently to the chief. She wore a long skirt and simple white shirtwaist blouse. Her hair was chestnut brown and wavy. She had it tied in a bun and Charlie stared for a moment at the smooth, soft skin of her neck. He was suddenly aware that she was beautiful and wanted to keep looking, but she fidgeted in her seat so he turned his head back toward the chief before she noticed.

"...the disposal of waste scraps and ashes and last, but not least, the smoking habits of the employees."

There was another round of applause before the chief continued: "Owners have resisted holding fire drills, citing loss of productivity for the duration of said drill and the time immediately after. Once again, a short-sighted position, for reasons I have put forth earlier. I am willing to assert that ninety-nine out of every hundred lives that have been lost through fire in the last ten years, not counting members of the fire department, could have been saved, if proper methods of drill and of training and proper precautions in matters of building and means of escape had been the rule instead of the rare exception. A well-rehearsed plan of escape as well as clear, unobstructed exit stairs and doors require little investment on the owners' part. That is the tragedy of it to one who has seen so many go to a fearful death."

A very loud round of applause rose up as Croker was taking his seat. "Thank you, Chief Croker," Stein announced. "Assemblyman Smith, Chief Croker has proposed several fire safety measures to the legislature. Can you speak to the assembly's efforts to protect our union members?"

Al Smith stood up. Charlie had heard him speak before, at a Fourth of July parade that ended in the Gas House District. He was a short-statured man with a big voice—not a deep voice. It was high-pitched, almost nasal, but steady and could carry over and command a crowd. "Thank you, Mr. Stein," he began. "And I'd like to thank Chief Croker for his tireless efforts to improve the safety of our city." There was a small round of applause again for the chief. "It was two years ago, I believe..." Smith looked over to the sole woman on the panel. She smiled and nodded. "That a lady knocked on my office door carrying a small suitcase. I thought she might have lost her way from the train station." Smith laughed, though no one else did. "She proceeded to open the case and cover my desk with file after file of factory safety reports. When I asked her why she brought them to me, she said it was a matter of life and death. Do you remember what you told me, Frances?"

The woman smiled and nodded.

Smith continued: "She told me the story of young Abigail Matthews, age nine, who lost her arm when it became crushed by a press while working in a coat factory in Rochester."

Charlie looked around the room. Smith had all eyes on him, and the assemblyman's powerful voice began to tremble as his emotions crept in. "She was not killed by the machine—no in fact the other workers were ordered to move the girl aside and keep working. The girls' mother, who worked in the same factory, was allowed to take the girl. Clutching her child, with her mangled arm, the desperate mother pleaded with passing carriages for a ride to the nearest hospital—where the poor child died ten days later."

Charlie looked up in shock at the sickening end to the story and the crowd behind him collectively gasped.

"That day was the first time I met Miss Frances Perkins," he motioned to the woman. "She works tirelessly to improve conditions in the factories, and largely thanks to her efforts there is a growing consensus in the legislature that more must be done. It is true, we depend on factories for the manufacturing of all manner of goods, and the owners of such establishments have the right to profit from their ventures. But when those profits come at the expense of human lives, it is up to us, as lawmakers in a civilized society, to step in and take measures."

A raucous applause broke out. Charlie noticed the young woman to his right clapping, and he clapped too until he turned his head and saw Silent Charlie's hands folded on his lap. Stein held his hands up and the applause dwindled. "Mr. Bernstein," he said to the man on the end. "It is my understanding you are here to speak about the safety measures currently in place at the Triangle factory." Sporadic boos and a collective hiss went across the room.

"Shame on them," a women yelled from the back of the room. "Arresting girls on the picket line!" There was clapping, and a handful of others yelled: "Shame! Shame!"

"Now, ladies," Stein pleaded—though Charlie had heard men yelling *shame* also. "Let's hear the man out. We can't fight for change if we don't talk about what needs changin'."

❧

ESTHER SQUIRMED IN HER chair as Mr. Bernstein rose to his feet. She leaned forward and put her hand to the side of her face. The owners of Triangle, Mr. Blanck and Mr. Harris, had held out longer than any of the other owners during the strike. They never agreed to union recognition, let alone a closed shop. As far as Esther knew, the only concessions they made in the end were a slight wage increase, the fifty-two-hour work week, and the allowed return of striking workers. Despite not recognizing the union, the owners promised to not use union membership alone as grounds for dismissal. Esther was not at all comforted by this promise. During the strike, she had seen union meetings get very heated. If tonight got out of hand, and Mr. Bernstein remembered her, she would be labeled an agitator. They would easily come up with a reason to fire her. She needed to get out of there. But getting out of her seat now would draw attention.

She looked over to Clara, who had so fearlessly inspired all the strikers. Esther wished she could be as brave, but at that moment the only thing she could think about was what would happen if she and Rachel lost their jobs. Clara was staring back at her. She could vaguely hear Mr. Bernstein talking about water buckets placed every fifteen feet. Clara gave a slight nod, then called out loudly while waving her hand: "Mr. Bernstein... Mr. Bernstein..."

"Please hold your question till he's finished, Miss Lemlich," said Stein from his chair.

"But will he talk about the handbag inspectors?" Clara answered undeterred.

The whole room, Bernstein and Stein included, were looking to the other side of the room where Clara was standing. Esther seized the opportunity and got out of her seat, making her way quickly to the side and squeezing through the throng of standing attendees.

***

CHARLIE WATCHED THE YOUNG woman run out and was drawn to follow. He was no longer interested in the meeting or his cousin's pressuring. He needed to find out more about her. He too got up and strode to the edge of the hall. He burst out the door and put his uniform cap on his head. The air was crisp, and he had no coat, so he blew on his hands and looked around. The union hall was the ground floor of the last building on the block and Charlie walked to the corner. She was standing on the sidewalk up the side street a bit—waiting apparently, not leaving. He walked toward her.

"Hello," he said simply. "I'm Charlie."

She did not say anything for a moment, just looked back at him blankly. "Are you a railroad conductor?" she finally asked.

"Fireman, actually."

"Your hat looks like a conductor's hat."

Charlie shrugged. "I guess we both wanted to get out of there."

"Pardon me?"

"I heard you tallkin' to that girl—you wanted to get away from that man. I felt the same about Chief Croker."

"Well, Charlie—you sure are quite nosy."

"No… it's just that, I…"

"I'm Esther, Charlie."

He abandoned his previous attempt at speech and answered simply: "Pleased to meet you, Esther."

"Why don't you want the fire chief to see you?"

"Well, it's just that I'm a new fireman and wouldn't want to be seen presenting myself as some sort of expert. And I definitely wouldn't want to contradict a man like Croker."

"So why did you come?" she asked and smiled. Her amused eyes looked right into his.

"I was going to ask you the same thing."

She looked down. "I owed a favor."

"Well, there you go. That's my reason as well. I owed a favor." He gave a small laugh and hoped she would return the gesture. Her smile was addictive. She looked up again and they locked eyes. She smiled. His heart beat faster. "I like your accent," he said. "Where are you from?"

She was thoughtful for a moment. "I'm from Poland—the Russian part."

"I didn't know Poland had a Russian part."

Esther shrugged. "You like my accent? I've tried so hard to get rid of it."

Charlie smiled. "I do. Are you waiting for someone?"

"My sister—she's still inside."

"I have a few minutes before I have to go back to work. May I wait with you?"

She again shrugged her shoulders.

"So you work in a garment factory?"

She nodded. "Yes—the Triangle factory."

"Is it really that bad?—the factory, I mean. I'd never heard about that little girl with her arm. Is that really what it's like?"

"Sometimes. It was worse in the sweatshops. My uncle had children as young as eight feeding thread and sewing buttons. My sister worked there starting at eleven. The machines at Triangle are electric, with automatic thread feed. There are some young boys who grease the parts that power the machines, but otherwise you need to be able to work a sewing machine, so most of the girls are at least fourteen or so."

"But what about what Chief Croker said? The fire dangers. Are you worried?"

"I don't like waiting in line for the inspector in order to get to the stairs. When we had a fire last year, they made us wait to be inspected before we could leave. I work on the ninth floor. They made us wait all the way up there before we could leave. I don't like that. Otherwise, it's fine I guess."

Charlie was pensively silent. "So, what do you do, Esther?" he finally asked. "When you're not in the factory."

Again she shrugged. "We went to a dance last week at Manhattan Lyceum."

Charlie had heard of the dances down on the Bowery, and other venues throughout the Lower East Side, but had never attended any. "Was it fun?"

Esther smiled and nodded. "The old man on piano isn't half-bad. He even played *Temptation Rag*."

"Ha! They play that on the Victor machine at the saloon. Do you dance to it?"

Esther gave a wide smile. "Of course."

Charlie thought of dancing with her and again his heart started racing.

"Do you like dancing?" she asked.

"I've never done it—but it sure looks fun."

"So, what do you do for fun?"

He shrugged his shoulders and thought frantically for an answer. The last thing he wanted to come off as was boring. "I went to Coney Island last summer."

Esther clutched her hands to her chest, leaned back against the wall and closed her eyes. "Oh, how I'd love to go to Coney Island. Francine at the factory goes in summer—she talks about it all the time."

Emboldened by her enthusiasm, Charlie blurted: "Well I'll take you—this summer I mean."

She stood up straight and opened her eyes. She was quiet for a second and Charlie thought he'd gone too far. Then, she smiled and nodded. "Sound like great fun," she added.

The warm rush through Charlie's body made him forget about the cold air. There was a door facing the side street and it swung out. Charlie turned and his heart sunk. He was face to face with Chief Croker. Far too late to remove his cap and hide it, he had nothing to do but offer a weak salute.

"Who are you?" barked Croker.

"Charles Pendergrass, sir." Out the corner of his eye, Charlie saw Esther. She looked on, as surprised as he was, but not nearly as frightened, he was sure.

"What are you doing here? Talking to this girl? To what company are you assigned?"

"Hook and Ladder Tw…"

"This is my cousin, Chief," Charlie Murphy said while coming out the door. "I asked him to accompany me this evening." Also coming out the door was Al Smith.

"What on earth for?" said Croker. "And who gave him leave from duty?"

"Will you relax for just once in your life, Edward?" said Murphy. He took a silver cigar case out of his inner breast pocket and opened the lid. He offered a short and thin brown cigar to Croker and then to Smith. Both refused with a hand wave. He put one in his mouth and closed the case without offering one to Charlie. He struck a match and lit the cigar.

"I will keep discipline in my department in the manner I see fit," said Croker. Charlie wished he could shrink down and slither into a crack in the sidewalk.

"The boy works in the heart of the loft-factory district," Murphy took along draw, held it a second, then blew a thick cloud of blue smoke into the cool crisp air. "It was my intention to reassure the union that your department has matters well in hand. I need the workers and the owners to support the bill I want passed. That is why I let the Triangle fellas send their man here. But you didn't help matters, Edward, with your sanctimonious soliloquy."

"I should have known Tammany was up to something," Croker replied. "I won't stand by and see you pass a toothless law just to shut the Progressive leaders up."

Charlie desperately wanted to slip away now. He looked into Esther's eyes and raised his eyebrows. She looked like she might say something, but it was Al Smith who stepped in.

"Gentlemen, please. We all want to make things better. Isn't that right?"

Charlie was sure the chief wanted to improve fire safety. He wasn't sure what Silent Charlie wanted. "Since the strike, the factory owners and businessmen across the state have banded together on this," Smith continued. "We're to have an uphill fight in the legislature if we're to get anything done—you're right about that Charlie. But the law need not be toothless, Mr. Croker. Miss Perkins in there has been spreading the word statewide for over two years now—building consensus, gaining support."

"You really think anyone in Albany cares what one woman is doing?" Murphy retorted wryly between puffs of smoke.

"What about twenty thousand?" said Esther. Charlie was shocked, so were the others apparently. No one answered her. "The Strike of the Twenty Thousand, myself included. Did they listen to us, Mr. Charlie?"

Silent Charlie lived up to his name, and young Charlie couldn't tell if his cousin's expression was bemusement or reproach.

"I'm in Albany, Charlie," said Smith. "I care a great deal what that one woman says."

"And you have the votes to pass a law?" Murphy asked.

"Not at the moment," said Smith. "Probably won't before the session ends. There are too many holdouts. But I'm hoping to by the end of the year. The Democrats will have our own law."

"Without the Progressives?" Murphy asked.

"Without the Progressives."

"This is ridiculous," said Croker. "I don't care whose bill gets passed, as long as it makes the factories safer."

"You will be pleased with the law, Mr. Croker," said Smith.

"Does it require fire drills?"

Smith gave a melancholy grin. "I'm afraid fire drills are out. The owners all agree. It costs them a half-hour or more of productivity. No bill is possible with fire drills. They'll fight it till the end."

"Horse shit!" Croker yelled. "They'll have blood on their hands—mark my words." The chief began walking to the corner.

"Are you not coming back inside?" called Murphy.

"I've got to get back to work," Croker answered and turned again to walk away. "Let's go, Pendergrass," he added without looking back.

Charlie looked at Smith and Murphy, both nodded and Charlie turned to Esther. He pulled her elbow and she stepped toward the corner with him. "It was nice to meet you, Esther."

"Very interesting, Charlie," she said with a chuckle.

"When is the next dance at the Manhattan Lyceum?"

"Third Saturday of the month."

"Will I see you there?" he asked.

Esther gave him one final smile and nodded.

He was about to speak again, but an automobile pulled up at the corner. "Pendergrass—get in," yelled Chief Croker from the driver's seat. Charlie managed to say goodnight to Esther as he ran to the chief's car and got in the passenger seat.

<hr>

EDWARD SHIFTED GEARS AND accelerated with boyish enthusiasm. Though he'd had the so called Red Devil, a 1904 Sampson Model 3A that had replaced his original motor buggy, for several years, it still excited him. He sped down Broome Street toward the Mercer Street firehouse. "Truck Twenty—right?" he asked young Pendergrass. "Murphy said you were in the heart of the loft factory district."

"Yes, sir," Pendergrass answered timidly. He was gripping the door handle and dashboard tightly.

"How long have you been assigned there?"

"A couple of weeks, sir."

"Ah—the new probationary men. And right to Truck Twenty. I suppose your uncle saw to that." He stared at Pendergrass waiting for an answer. The car continued speeding forward.

"He's my cousin, actually, sir. But yes, I suppose so."

"You suppose?"

"I didn't ask him to. I didn't know nothing about the fire department, or what to ask for."

Edward thought for a moment, then pulled the car over at the corner of Broome Street and Mulberry. "What is it you want from this job, Pendergrass?" he said brusquely, looking the young man dead in the eye.

Charlie Pendergrass looked down at his hands, thoughtful for a moment, and then he looked up and answered. "I didn't know what I wanted at first. Cousin Charlie came to me and told me to apply. Like I said—I didn't know nothin' about it. But sir, we had this fire last week, in a tenement. Mr. Woll—he pulled this lifeless man out of the smoke, and we passed him out to Nine Truck. The man lived, sir. When I saw Mr. Woll do that, sir—that's when I knew."

"And what did you know, Pendergrass?"

"I knew I wanted to be a fireman."

Edward put the car in gear and let off the clutch. They jerked forward and as they rolled through the intersection, he said: "Good answer!"

He drove to the corner of Prince Street and Mercer. "It's best you get out here, Pendergrass," Edward said once they'd stopped. Pendergrass got out and said, "Thank you, sir."

"Don't let your uncle's ideas get in the way of what you've said," Edward told the young man. "Go *be* a fireman!"

"Yes, sir, I will." The young man smiled and ran quickly up the street toward the firehouse.

Edward pulled away and swerved around a horse-drawn carriage heading west down Prince Street. As he spun the steering wheel and worked the gearshift, Edward made eye contact with a man walking on the sidewalk. He wore canvas pants, a blue button-up shirt, and a badged cap. He was clutching a short length of rope tied to the collar of a Dalmatian.

14

1902

EDWARD SAT AT A table inside Lyons's Restaurant—dining alone. Oswald had made plans to eat at home, and even though—in light of the bad news—he'd offered to stay, Edward had refused. He ate a thick pork chop, a baked potato with butter, and washed it down with soda water and whiskey. Unfolded on the table was the bulletin that had arrived that afternoon:

HEADQUARTERS FIRE DEPARTMENT (Form No. 4)

New York, Aug. 19th, 1902.

Special Orders, No. 121 (Extract.)

I. Chief of Department Edward F. Croker is hereby relieved of command of the uniformed force beginning the date of 19th inst. The Chief of Department will appear at headquarters for the purpose of answering the charges that have been preferred against him.

II. During the hearing of the charges and pending the Commissioner's decision thereupon, Deputy Chief of Department Charles Krueger shall be Acting Chief of Department.

By orders of

Thomas Sturgis Fire Commissioner

Edward looked down at the page while chewing his pork chop. Mayor Seth Low had been sworn in that past January, vowing to free the city of Tammany Hall's grip once and for all. A Republican, Low rode the wave of Teddy Roosevelt's popularity and the rise of the Progressive movement to city hall. With reform in mind, he appointed Thomas Sturgis, a Civil War veteran and member of the Civil Service Commission, to be fire commissioner. New York's police and fire departments were to be purged of corruption and machine-picked leaders, including the Squire's nephew, Chief Croker.

His thoughts were interrupted by a visitor to his table. "Excuse me, Chief Croker—I figured I'd find you here."

Edward looked up. "William Gunn Shepherd! You know, If I were you, I'd insist the papers print my middle name. I often see a simple G in your byline."

"Some do, some don't," Shepherd answered with a chuckle. "Guess it depends on how bloated my submission is."

"Hah! Sit down—I'll have the waiter bring you something." Edward folded the sheet and put it in his pocket. He need not have bothered. Shepherd knew what it said.

"I heard the news, Chief. They're all talking about it at the Broadway Hotel—sorry to say."

"Well, yes—it's a very sorry affair. I'd expected Sturgis to come after me. Just thought it would take a bit longer." He signaled for the waiter. "What'll you have, Shepherd?"

"Same as you."

"Two more whiskey and sodas," he called out before the waiter had even reached the table.

"So, what does the commissioner have against you anyway? Is it just your uncle?" Shepherd would have normally been scribbling notes while talking to the chief, but now he just sat with his hands on his lap. The waiter arrived with the drinks, and Shepherd picked one up. "To good health," he said, raising the glass to Croker and then sipping.

"It's that simple, I'm afraid. And it goes much deeper than the old charge of nepotism..."

Shepherd interrupted: "I think you've laid that charge to rest." He laughed and sipped again.

"Well, thank you—but this is much more personal. He was in business with my uncle. He and Richard were both shareholders in an ice company together. He blames my uncle for losing a small fortune."

"That would explain the animus—but does he really think your uncle's sins extend to your leadership?"

Edward downed his remaining whiskey soda and melted ice, and picked up the next glass. "It's the only explanation—the charges against me are ludicrous. If he'd had anything substantive, he'd have used it."

"What exactly are the charges?"

"Firstly, that I showed an incompetence of leadership at the Seventy-first Regiment Armory fire, when the Park Avenue Hotel across the street caught fire."

"I remember the fire," said Shepherd. "What does he think you ought to have done?"

"That's just it, Shepherd. I'd do the same thing all over again. It was a big fire—the armory—for sure. And the wind was carrying embers blocks away. What you won't read in the charges is that there was also a third alarm fire going on, not very far away. I was short on resources. I had to decide which buildings to protect with the few companies I had on hand. The roof of the hotel was covered in snow. And besides, the hotel had *their* men checking the building, so I dispatched the two remaining truck companies I had to protect apartment buildings nearby. And do you know what, Shepherd?"

"What, Chief?"

"The fucking hotel caught fire!"

Shepherd stared back at Croker, seemingly nervous about how to respond, until Edward laughed. The reporter laughed as well, then said: "'When ill luck begins, it does not come in sprinkles, but in showers,' Mark Twain says."

"Indeed," said Edward as he took another sip. "And also, they've thrown theft of public property into the charges as well."

"What's that, sir?"

"Ten lengths of two-and-a-half-inch cotton jacket hose, delivered to the Polo Grounds, on loan to the New York Giants."

"Baseball enthusiast are you, Chief?"

"Well yes, of course. But I didn't steal any hose. The goddamned commissioner himself asked me to have the hose delivered. I have the request in my desk drawer."

"So, what will you do about these charges, Chief?"

"Fight them—by the gods—every one."

EDWARD WALKED OUT OF Lyons's Restaurant and headed up the Bowery toward Great Jones Street. The bay doors to the firehouse were open and Edward could see both his motor car and Engine Company 33's horse-drawn rigs in their perpetually ready position. He went past the housewatchman and climbed the stairs. The door to his office was open. He was sure he'd left it closed. The foreman from Engine 33 came up the stairs and turned to go to his own office.

"Mr. Dunn," Edward said. "Has anybody been in my office today?"

Dunn thought for a moment. "Not that I know of. We were out on a run—gone for over an hour. I haven't seen anyone up here since we got back."

"Thank you."

Edward went inside. He switched on a lamp and looked around. A half-smoked cigar teetered off the edge of the desk, right where he'd left it. His favorite fountain pen was atop a stack of papers.

There was a tall filing drawer under the desk and Edward noticed it was open a half inch or so. He sat, pulled the drawer out, and knew right away what was missing: the hand-written request from Commissioner Sturgis requesting Edward have ten lengths of hose delivered to the Polo Grounds.

WHEN EDWARD ARRIVED AT Fire Headquarters on 67th Street the next morning, a handful of reporters were waiting on the sidewalk, including William Gunn Shepherd.

"Chief Croker," a *Tribune* reporter called out. "Any comment on your suspension?"

Edward looked up. They all were waiting, notepads in hand. "It's preposterous," Edward replied. "I intend to fight these charges—no administrative judge in his right mind would agree there's any merit to them."

"Are the charges politically motivated?" asked Shepherd.

"Well, William, I'm going to leave it to the powers that be to explain their motives." With that, Edward entered the six-story firehouse which housed the commissioner's office. He stopped at the base of the stairs and looked at the harnesses hanging from the ceiling—at the ready, one set attached to a steam pumper and the other set to a ladder truck. How many times had he hitched horses, donned his leather helmet and slicker, and charged out the bay doors? Every fireman knew that any run you went on could be your last. Edward had proudly served fully aware of that fact. But now he wondered if his last run was behind him and felt a wave of nostalgia for every one of those runs. He sighed and climbed the stairs.

A secretary seemingly expected him and walked Edward straight into Commissioner Sturgis's office. "Here he is now!" Sturgis exclaimed. He was a stern looking man, tall and lean with graying hair and a bushy mustache. Edward knew that Sturgis had been an officer in the Union army during the Civil War and had a reputation for stubbornness. Sturgis was standing behind his desk. Seated in a leather sofa along the far wall was Alderman John Callaghan, whose beady eyes were trained directly on Edward's.

"Come in Mr. Croker," Sturgis added. Edward noted the *Mr.* In prior meetings, the commissioner had addressed him as *Chief*. Edward was not offered a chair and did not ask to sit. He stood silently and waited for Sturgis to begin. He did not have to wonder why the hell Callaghan was there. It all made sense now. For all of Mayor Low's promises of reform and Sturgis's platitudes, Tammany Hall was still Tammany Hall and like rain seeping through a leaky roof, no matter how many holes you plugged, the water would find another way to drip in. Sturgis may have hated Richard Croker for personal reasons, but he still knew how the game was played.

"You will have read the charges carefully, I assume, Mr. Croker?" Sturgis began.

"I have, sir," said Edward. "And I look forward to a trial where I shall clear my name."

Sturgis looked over to Callaghan, whose slender lips managed to grin beneath his waxed mustache. "Well, there will be no trial," the commissioner said. "The city charter grants commissioners the right of summary action in cases where gross incompetence is involved."

"Gross inc…" Edward realized how futile it would be to argue and simply asked. "What is it then?"

"You are hereby terminated from this department, sir," Sturgis announced triumphantly. "Effective immediately."

Edward's hands were at his side, and he balled his fists. He gritted his teeth and fought the urge to wring Callaghan's neck, and Sturgis's for that matter. Any outburst now would harm his ability to fight this injustice. He nodded, turned, and left.

15

1911

Esther sat at her station working the delicate cloth under the firing needle. The sleek, cast-iron Singer was fast, and didn't give her foot cramps like the foot-pedal powered machines did. The downside was noise. The electric motors hummed while the needle driving mechanism pounded continuous rapid-fire thuds. Multiplied by the noise of over 270 machines on the ninth floor, the sound gave Esther an ever-present ringing in her ears. She sat as upright as possible on her wooden stool. The seamstresses at her father's factory in Bialystok had taught her that. If you lean forward too far, halfway through the day your back will start to ache. She also liked to keep her face as far clear of the needle as possible. A broken needle shot up once and cut her cheek. Esther considered herself lucky that her eyesight was good, and she could watch what her fingers were doing without having to lean in too close.

She pushed the last stich through and held the blouse's torso in her lap, worked her fingers along the seams checking for imperfections, then lay the piece in the bin and grabbed another unfinished piece from the pile. She nimbly squeezed the two cut ends together and fed the fold under the needle. She was always surprised by how much she could think about while also concentrating on her work. Some of the girls held full-out conversations, whispered of course, with their neighbors, but Esther found that distracting. Thinking, on the other hand, came naturally. It actually took great effort on her part to keep her thoughts from drifting away while stitching piece after piece after piece. She thought of Charlie. He was handsome enough—but truth be told his looks were far from stunning. Joe the elevator operator was far more handsome. *How funny would that be?* Esther wondered. *If Rachel and I each fell for the two elevator operators here in the building.* Charlie's looks were more rugged, more down-to-earth. Still, she was attracted to him. There was a kindness in his eyes. He seemed genuinely moved by that story about the little girl's arm being mangled. That was endearing.

THAT EVENING, CLARA LEMLICH was waiting again in front of Esther's building. She was not alone. A horse drawn carriage stood parked out front and once Esther and Rachel arrived Clara called Esther over.

"You remember Assemblyman Smith and Miss Perkins, from the meeting?" Clara said.

Esther saw Al Smith and Frances Perkins seated across from her friend and nodded. "Of course, good evening."

"Clara tells us you were one of the strikers, from Triangle," said Smith.

"Yes, that's true."

"We understand completely..." Frances Perkins added, "why you didn't want to speak at the union meeting. I don't understand why that Bernstein fellow was allowed to be there."

"Will you come have dinner with us?" Smith asked.

"I uh—my mother will have cooked already," Esther said nervously, glancing up at her apartment window.

"Est—go ahead," said Rachel. "I'll let *Mame* know, and maybe you can bring what she cooked in for lunch tomorrow."

"See that," said Smith as he opened the door of the carriage. "It all works out."

Esther nodded again and smiled. She tried not to show too much excitement. She was pretty sure they would take her to a restaurant, and she would eat better than she had in some time. They rode to a small place on Allen Street, just south of Houston Street. There was no sign or even lettering on the window, but the restaurant was busy. A man in an apron met them at the door and walked them to the back room where a table set for four was waiting. If anything was said between Smith, Perkins, or the man in the apron, Esther didn't hear it. They each took a seat and the man left a handwritten menu on the table.

"I asked Clara if you only ate kosher, but she didn't think so," said Smith.

"In Bialystok we were more observant—but became much less picky about our meals here."

Smith smiled. "The tenement I grew up in had two German families on the ground floor. Day in and day out, we smelled boiled sauerkraut coming in the air shaft window. Before my father died, when we had supper every day, I hated that sauerkraut smell—used to make me sick."

Esther smiled, feeling completely at ease. She wasn't sure where this story was going, but Smith's kind manner was completely disarming.

"Then after my father died—when food became much scarcer in our household, the smell would make my stomach growl with hunger. I'd have given anything for a bowl of sauerkraut." He laughed, and the others joined in. "I know it's not the same thing as following kosher rules, you see. But I do know how hunger, real hunger, can change your mind about food."

"Alfred, will you please put that sauerkraut story to rest," said Perkins. She then looked right at Esther. "I've now heard it three times!"

"Only three," he quipped while reaching for a piece of sliced bread. "Wait till you know me a few more years." He looked up at Esther and winked.

"Esther, dear," said Perkins. "Alfred and I have been nudging the legislature for two years now."

"Don't let those fancy clothes or New England accent fool you," said Smith while buttering his bread. "Tough as nails, she is." He pointed to Perkins with the butter knife.

"I thought the strike would light the spark of reform," Perkins continued. "But, in truth, the modest reforms you strikers gained seemed to have let the air out of the balloon in the legislature. It's as if they feel the problem has been solved."

"This is where you come in," said Clara.

"Me?" Esther tensed up. She sensed another request for testimony. "Look—I want to help. I really do. But the strike nearly ruined us. The relief money ran out after the first month. I got roughed up on the picket line by a policeman who was arresting another picketer." She paused and looked at Lemlich. "And Clara here was nearly killed by those brutes."

"I won't lie to you, Esther," said Perkins. "There are risks you must consider. But Mr. Smith is working hard to get a committee in the Assembly. If he succeeds, we'll need to move fast—before the factory owners can launch their counterattack. We'll have Clara to speak, of course. But she has become so well known, such a symbol of the union's fight, that I fear her ability to persuade indifferent assemblymen is weakened. It's as if she's yesterday's news."

Esther looked over to Clara, who seemed not bothered in the least by Perkins's assessment.

"You, dear," said Smith. "You work for the mighty Shirtwaist Kings—the very men who held firm against the strikers. If we can demonstrate to the legislature that safety measures are still lacking, even in the biggest factories, I think we have a chance at moving a proper bill forward."

"And if I am fired?" Esther asked the table.

"Then I shall give you a job myself," answered Perkins without hesitation. "So help me God."

16

CHARLIE PULLED THE RUBBER hose from stall to stall, rinsing the cement floor and letting the horse-piss-laden run-off drain down the gully and into the drain hole. Fred Schley had taken Snowball and Apollo out to be reshod. Ott took Jack for a walk around the block for exercise, so Charlie was using the opportunity to clean out the stalls and put down some fresh hay. He put the hose away and dragged the two tin pails full of horse shit and dirty hay to the bay door. The three horses belonging to the second section and the one that pulled the battalion chief's carriage were tied up outside. He was unsure if he should walk them back inside or wait till the stalls were dry. Remembering that he couldn't throw down fresh hay until the floor was dry, he decided to wait. He retrieved a can of brass polish from the work bench along with a rag and went to the long brass pole near the housewatch. He started about a foot above his head and rubbed the polish on with small, circular patterns and worked his way down. He would have to get a ladder to reach the higher part of the pole, but figured he'd get the lower section out of the way while the stalls dried.

While he was wiping off polish and buffing the pole to a bright shine, a mounted policeman strode in on his horse through the bay door and rode between the two ladder trucks directly to the stalls. He dismounted, put his horse in a stall, and looped the reins around a rail. Charlie watched in silence as the man walked toward the kitchen door and unbuckled the thick leather gun belt he wore over his pea coat. The policeman hung the belt—holstered pistol and all—on a coatrack outside the kitchen door and went in. The swing door squeaked open and shut and Charlie looked back at the stall where the policeman's horse now stood. He heard a toilet flush and out of the small bathroom beside the kitchen came Floyd Mance with a folded newspaper under his arm. He walked to the housewatch, sat back in the chair with his feet on the desk and opened the paper. Charlie said nothing about the policeman and went back to polishing the pole.

When he thought enough time had passed for the floors to be dry, Charlie wondered how to proceed. Should he take the policeman's horse out so he could put down fresh hay? Just then, Ott returned with Jack. He walked beside the horse, holding the rein, and stopped beside Charlie at the pole.

"Why are the horses outside?" he asked.

"I was going to bring them in now—but I have to put down fresh hay."

"So…" Ott stared impatiently.

Charlie motioned his head to the stalls and Ott saw the police horse.

"Oh—for fuck's sake," he said and walked Jack to the stall. Charlie followed.

Not only was the policeman's horse standing in the stall, but there was also a huge pile of fresh shit underneath the hind legs.

"Lousy scurf!" Ott cried. He unwrapped the horse's reins and walked him out of the stall. He handed both those reins and Jack's to Charlie and grabbed a shovel. In one quick motion he scooped up the steaming pile of manure and turned toward the police horse. "Open the saddlebag," he said the Charlie.

Charlie had no qualms. He was still smarting from his brief stint in jail. He folded back the leather flap and Ott dumped the horse shit right in. Charlie closed the flap, laughing.

"Tie him up to the workbench and put down fresh hay," said Ott. "I'll start walking the horses in."

Later, Charlie was assigned his first housewatch. It was after lunchtime, and because they had spent most of the previous night at a fire in an abandoned warehouse on Hudson Street, the foremen and senior firemen all went up for a nap. Only Ott remained on the apparatus floor with Charlie. The company journal was open to the current page and Charlie grabbed the pen:

3:00pm Fr. Pendergrass relieves Fr. Ott on housewatch duty. Dept. Apparatus and Property in good order.

He straightened up the desk and threw a two-day-old edition of the *World* in the waste basket. Ott came from the kitchen holding a wedge of Limburger cheese wrapped in a thin, greasy cheesecloth. He sliced off a piece with a small knife and offered it to Charlie.

"Ugh—that stuff stinks."

"Yeah, but it tastes good," Ott said, still chewing.

"No, thank you."

"Your loss." He put the new piece in his mouth while still chewing the last.

"And Ott," Charlie added. "Thanks for helping with the horses. That policeman just strode right in like he owned the place."

"Yeah," Ott answered—mouth full. "We get along with most of the coppers in the Sixteenth Precinct here on Mercer Street. They're usually pretty good to us. That guy today is just a bit of a blunderbuss. I think the horse is smarter than him."

Charlie laughed. "That was a great idea with the saddlebag."

"Old navy trick. I had this petty officer once. What a horse's ass! He made us shovel twenty yards of coal into the two bunkers near the boilers. I tried to tell him that all the coal in that pile was bad coal—and we usually filled one of the bunkers with good coal. He told me to shut up and shovel. Then when we was just about finished—the master chief came down and started yelling at us for not filling the second bunker with good coal. We had to shovel out the bad coal and re-shovel in the good."

Charlie had no idea what Ott was talking about. Ott must have read his face. "You know about bad coal and good coal?" he asked.

Charlie shook his head.

"There's hard coal, or good coal. Burns hotter and holds heat longer. Then there's soft coal, or brown coal—bad coal. Burns at a lower temperature. We used bad coal for easy floats—harbor to harbor and so on. But when we needed that extra kick, we used good coal. You see?"

"Yeah—I get it. Makes sense."

"The Spanish—they had a hard time getting good coal. Our ships were always faster."

"So what does that have to do with horse shit?" Charlie asked.

"Oh yeah—that." Ott started laughing before even finishing the story. "So later on, when the shit-headed petty officer went up to the bridge, we brought a load of bad coal and filled his bunk with it."

Now Charlie was laughing. "Did you get in trouble?"

"Nah—not really. He knew who did it, but couldn't prove it. He was too embarrassed to go tell the officers. But he did cancel my next leave when we docked in Havana, said it was because I was out of uniform while changing an oil filter. Ah! It was worth it."

Charlie smiled.

"That's where I got the idea for the saddlebag trick. When an ass gives you shit, shovel it right back at 'em!"

Charlie and Ott both cracked up laughing. "I like that," Charlie said. I'm going to use it some time."

"I hated that goddamned coal," Ott added.

"I unloaded steam freighters on the docks," said Charlie. "Sometimes the crates were covered in black dust."

Ott nodded. "The worst was the coalings—all-hands on deck. The coal passers had the worst job, poor bastards. But during a coaling we all shoveled. They tied up a barge right alongside the ship and the coal passers shoveled it into canvas bags then hoisted them up on deck. Then we dumped the bags into a chute that went down to the fire room. Then we had to shovel the coal into different bunkers."

"Sounds rough," said Charlie.

Ott swallowed the last morsel of Limburger. "Um-hum," he said while chewing. He then took the greasy cheese cloth and bunched it up into a ball and stuck it in his mouth.

Charlie watched in a combination of shock and disgust. But Ott kept chewing, and talking: "I was just a kid—thirteen when I joined. I was just happy to be away from home—didn't care that they made me shovel that filthy crap. Boy was it filthy—it took longer to clean the deck after a coaling than it did the coaling. And the coal passers, they were black. If we didn't have to shove off right away, they were allowed to jump in the sea. Otherwise, they just stayed filthy—washed their face off in buckets of water."

"Thirteen?"

"Yeah," Ott giggled and then swallowed whatever was left in his mouth—cheese or cheesecloth. "Ran away from home so my old man wouldn't kill me."

"Why would he kill you?"

"We had a farm out in Jersey—and we'd go out there in summertime. One day I took this horse out of the stable by myself and was going to try to ride her out in the field. I didn't know how to saddle a horse, just figured I'd jump on. So, I lead her toward the gate, but she doesn't want to go. So, I pull on her mane—and it spooks her somethin' good. Next thing you know she neighs loud and bucks up on her hind legs."

Charlie hung on every word. Despite the fact that he'd grown up sweeping a saloon, he'd never met anyone who told such lively stories. Ott was holding his hands up mimicking a rearing horse.

"She steps back and falls into the well. Don't know how the hell she fit in that goddamned well, but she shot straight down to the bottom and died."

"Oh—shit," Charlie couldn't help but laugh.

"Well—there was no getting that fucker out."

"Oh—shit," Charlie repeated.

Ott's big face was fully animated. When he spoke, every muscle in his body participated in the story. His grin was pure joy. Charlie suspected he had told this story over and over and loved doing so each and every time. He was visibly excited to have found a fresh listener.

"So, I thought it was best to get the hell away for a while. Ran straight to the recruiter. I was tall even then, and when I lied about my age the recruiter didn't ask too many questions."

"What happened to the horse?"

"Just rotted away in the well—contaminated the water and everything."

"I see why you ran away," Charlie added with a chuckle.

"Damn sure," said Ott with a wide grin.

EDWARD SAT AT HIS desk puffing his cigar. There was a foreman standing at the other desk in the office. He was gathering up toiletries from the drawer and packing them in a small case.

"Are you sure I can't change your mind, John?" Croker asked.

The foreman stopped packing and sat. "Chief, I'm highly grateful for your faith in me these past years. But you and I both know it's not a foreman's place to be a chief's aide. I should be leading men, not driving one man."

"One time I let you drive," Croker quipped. "And now you're a driver?"

The foreman laughed. "It was more than once. But you know I'm right."

Edward *did* know he was right. He himself would have never accepted a clerical role when he was a foreman. He always wanted to be the first man into a burning building. He still did. He stood and held out his hand. "I want to thank you, John. When Oswald retired, and I was uhh.. Well you know... Having a rough go of it at home. You offered to step in—not just as an aide, but a friend. That meant the world to me at the time. Still does."

John stood, shook his hand and smiled warmly.

"Good luck out there," said Croker. "If you're ever in need, I'm only a call away."

"Thank you, Chief. I'll have one of the men downstairs come up and show you how to answer it." He laughed and pointed to the telephone sitting on the aide's desk."

Edward sat, leaned back, and took a long draw from his cigar. "Yes—and perhaps I'll call headquarters and cancel your reassignment!" He winked.

"Touché," said John, and he took hold of the case and went out.

Edward looked over at the empty aide's chair. *Now what?* he thought.

There was a knock, and a young fireman peeked his head in. "Chief, there's a police captain here to see you."

"Send him in."

Dominic Henry was captain of the 16th Precinct on Mercer Street. Average height, average build, with a thick brown mustache, he marched in with his cap under his arm and went straight to Croker's desk to offer a handshake.

Edward leaned forward and raised his ass out of the seat only slightly as he shook the captain's hand. The cigar was still clenched in his teeth. "Grab a chair, Mr. Henry. How are things over on Mercer Street?"

"Same as ever, Chief. Same as ever."

"What can I do for you today?"

"Well, an issue has arisen with your firehouse down the street from us—Hook and Ladder Number Twenty, I believe."

"Yes."

"Right. So, it seems one of my patrolmen went inside to use the toilet and when he came out, one of your firemen had filled his saddlebag with horse manure."

Edward laughed, then controlled himself when he saw the captain's stern expression. "Sorry. Go on."

"That is all, sir. I would like to know what you will do about it."

Edward puffed his cigar and answered. "I could have an engine company open a hydrant if he'd like to wash out the saddlebag."

"Is this but a joke to you, sir?"

"No, Captain. Not a joke. But I *am* wondering why you came here instead of going first to Battalion Chief Worth at the Third Battalion. He's in that very firehouse. This hardly seems like a matter for the chief of department."

"This, sir, is a matter of discipline. Is it not?" Henry's anger was making his voice tremble.

"I suppose it is," Croker replied calmly.

"Is that not your field of expertise? Was it not you who went on a crusade to rid the police ranks of loafers?"

Now the reason for Henry's visit was clear to Edward. The captain had come to gloat. He wanted to embarrass the chief for his firemen's behavior. Croker's tone changed. "I specifically denounced the patrolmen assigned to walk the factory district overnight. If they weren't off sleeping or getting drunk, some of the worst fires we've seen in this city could have been detected, *and* extinguished, much earlier."

"A message better suited for the ears of the police commissioner, sir, instead of the newspapers."

Edward exhaled a mouthful of smoke and looked across the desk at Henry. "Dominic, is it?"

"Yes, sir."

"Well, Dominic. For as much as I detest politics, I've been at this post long enough to know that, sometimes, the only way to win is to play along. I asked the legislature to require sprinklers in factories. They refused. I asked the mayor to hire a dozen more fire marshals to stand overnight as fire guards. He refused. To neutralize my constant pestering, he had the police commissioner announce increased foot patrols overnight in the Second, Fourth, and Fifth precincts. The men were supposed to walk the factory district and look out for smoke. Instead, they disappeared to God knows where."

"Well, sir, I think..." Henry began, before Edward cut him off.

"You're goddamned right I went to the press. It's the only way to get anything out of these good-for-nothing politicians—embarrass them."

"And the poor patrolmen you embarrassed? What of them?"

"To hell with them. It's their duty to protect this city—not sneak off and hide."

Henry stood and put his cap on. "Well, perhaps you are right, sir. The only way to get something done is to embarrass someone." He stepped toward the door, then stopped and took a folded piece of paper out of his pocket and laid it on the desk. "The patrolman says he knows the fireman guilty of this insult. Says he's had words with the man in the past."

Captain Henry walked out, and Edward picked up the fold of paper and read the name. He put the cigar in his mouth again and leaned back.

17

THICK SMOKE PUMPED OUT the front door and large showcase window that Fred Schley had just smashed with a six-foot hook. Engine Company 13 had arrived first and stretched a two-and-a-half inch hoseline into the ground floor. The fire appeared to be in the back of a carpet store. Charlie looked up at the front of the five-story loft building. The block of Broadway was all lofts from corner to corner. The iron shutters on the upper floors were all closed, except for one window on the top floor and smoke was seeping out, but the worst of it was coming from the ground floor. Foreman Jennings and Andrew Ott got down on their bellies and crawled in along Engine 13's line. Charlie got down and followed them in. The smoke was thick as soup, and he held his breath for a minute but then breathed in and his nose and throat burned. There was no visibility at all, but Charlie felt tears flowing out of his eyes. It was difficult to keep them open, so he just shut his eyes tight. There was nothing to see anyhow. He crawled on his elbows and knees, holding a six-foot hook in one hand and the hoseline in the other. As they moved in further, he could hear the water flowing out from the hose nozzle and crashing across ceilings and walls.

"Shut it down," Charlie heard someone yell out in the smoke, and the water flow ceased.

"Twenty Truck," the voice called out again. "You guys in?"

"Over here," Jennings answered.

"Main body of fire is knocked down, if you wanna try to clear some smoke."

"See if there's any rear windows or door to open up, Ott," Jennings said. "Pendergrass—give' em a hand."

Charlie crawled forward with Ott and they smashed two large windows. The smoke began to clear. Charlie stood to reach the upper pane and hanging shards with his hook and felt the sharp heat stinging his ears. "It's hot as hell," Charlie said. "Why'd they shut the nozzle?"

"Gotta clear the smoke," Ott answered. "Once the main body is knocked down—it's better to let the smoke clear so the engine men can see what their hittin'. You see those cast-iron columns, holdin' up the whole building above us?"

Charlie turned but couldn't see more than a few feet back. He knew the columns Ott was talking about. Often quite tall in lofts—twelve or fifteen feet depending on the ceiling height. The columns were decorative, but functional, prefabricated cast iron that supported tremendous loads.

"They get brittle when heated and then suddenly cooled. Water from the hose can cause them to crack. Two years ago, two firemen from Engine Twenty-seven were killed when they hit a hot column with the hose stream. The whole floor above collapsed down on 'em." Ott was standing and clearing glass with his claw tool. He stopped speaking to let out a short coughing fit, then continued: "One almost came down on top of me one time—would've broken my thick skull if I hadn't got pushed outta the way."

Charlie coughed and kept clearing away glass shards. He wondered if he'd ever be able to remember all the things that could get you killed at a fire.

Charlie was scrubbing the truck's wheels with a wet brush when Foreman Jennings slid down the fire pole with a sheet of paper in his mouth. His hair was wet and neatly combed from a shower. Once his feet were on the ground, he took the paper out of his mouth and asked Charlie: "Ott down here?"

"I think he's still up showering," Charlie answered.

"Who's on the housewatch?"

"Mance asked me to listen up while he showers. Sorry, sir—I just figured I'd scrub the wheels while I was down here—I'll go sit at the desk."

"No—it's fine. The wheels should be scrubbed as soon as possible or the mud and horse shit will cake on." Jennings walked to the back and checked the kitchen, then went up the spiral stairs. Charlie finished scrubbing the wheels, then rinsed the floor down with the hose. His pants and uniform shirt were still wet and he had soot on his hands and face. He figured he'd just wash up in the sink once someone came down to take the housewatch. Showering felt strange. His apartment had a basin tub in the kitchen and he usually bathed once a week. The first shower stall Charlie had ever seen was in the firehouse.

At last, Stafford, Schley, and Mance came down. Stafford and Mance by stairs, Schley slid down the pole. A few minutes later, Ott winded his way down the stairs. He was holding a piece of paper and his face lacked the usual jovial glow. "I've been transferred," he announced, holding up the paper."

"What the hell are you talking about, Johnny?" said Mance. "Didn't you just get here yesterday?"

Charlie stared on in silence.

"What d'ya mean transferred?" asked Schley. "Transferred where?"

"The chief of department's office," Ott answered solemnly.

18

1907

ANDREW OTT HAD SETTLED into the Little Germany section of the Lower East Side once his enlistment in the navy was up. He worked for a while in his father's French-German bakery before starting an apprenticeship with an elevator company. With his size and strength, he was well suited for the role of elevator mechanic and the dawn of the skyscraper era kept the company busy day and night. After a few months, Andrew was offered a permanent position. He and his wife, Elizabeth, were expecting their first child and moved into a two-bedroom apartment, not far from the Ott Bakery.

A new skyscraper was going up in the Financial District, with steel and concrete work during the day and elevator installations at night. Though early fall, it was a warm night and the men were sweating running rails up the open shafts and installing the cables, counterweights, and cars once the rails topped out. Andrew worked in a white, cotton short-sleeve shirt—the kind the navy had started issuing to sailors as undershirts. His biceps and forearms bulged, and sweat poured down his face and neck as he held a massive cast-iron wheel in place over the open shaft. If he lost grip, the wheel would plummet twelve stories and crash through the roof of the car his coworkers were assembling at the base. His white shirt was translucent with sweat and stuck to his chest. "Will you hurry the fuck up, Hal," he said through gritted teeth.

"Hold your horses," Hal answered as he slid a steel rod through the wheel and rested the ends in twin cradles on either side of the shaft opening. The machinery room, perched on the new building's roof directly over the elevator shaft was jammed with tools and equipment. Right behind Andrew was a massive spool of coiled steel cable. Once the two had secured the wheel, they would begin feeding in the cable. "Just hold her another minute," the man said. "Let me tighten down these bolts so she doesn't walk."

It was after 11:00 pm by the time the crew had fed in all the cables and attached the ends to the top of the car and also to the counterweights which lined the sides of the shaft. Hal and Andrew walked the stairs down to the base of the elevator shaft in the basement, where the other four men were putting the finishing touches on the car. Unlike older, manually-operated elevator cars, this would be automatically controlled by buttons the passengers themselves could push. These were rare, as most people distrusted operator-free elevators. Ott had never installed such a system before. The control panel inside the car had a hinged cover and it was swung open. His foreman, Mr. White, was kneeling before the panel fiddling with a screwdriver. "Ott," he called out without looking away from his work.

"Yes, skipper."

"Take the pail down to the corner and fill 'er up, will you?"

Andrew smiled. "Yes, skipper!"

∞

Andrew walked into the saloon and placed the tin pail up on the bar and sat on a stool. The bartender came over knowing what to do. He flipped the handle over, grabbed the pail by the rim, and held it under a spout. He was about to start pumping the tap handle, but Andrew stopped him.

"That'll take a while—I'm sure. Why don't you start by filling a glass first—give me something to do while I watch you fill that thing."

The bartender laughed and filled a glass for Andrew.

"*Prost!*" Ott uttered as he held up the glass before downing a third of it.

"When will you boys be finishin' up over there?" the bartender asked as he pushed the pump up and down. Foamy beer spurted into the bucket sporadically. "Just laid the first car tonight," said Andrew as he took another sip. "Still got the second car and the service elevator to put up—but can't do that until the last section of roof is in. I'd say a couple months."

"Sailor man, aye?" asked the bartender, looking at the tattoo on Andrew's bicep—an anchor with U.S.N. underneath.

Andrew twisted his arm and admired the ink work as well. "Yes, sir—sure am." He held out his arms, palms up, to show off his forearms as well. There was a panther on the left forearm and a hula girl on the right.

"You a married man?"

"I am."

"What does the misses think of that little sweetheart there?" He stopped pumping for a second to point to the hula girl.

"That little beauty is good luck. Every sailor who visits Hawaii gets one. It means that sailor will never run adrift and always get home safely."

"Well, my wife would chop my arm off," the bartender answered dryly.

"Ha!" Andrew spout as he tilted his head back and drained the glass.

When the pail was nearly full, the bartender lay a clean white towel over the top and placed it down gently. Andrew left a few coins on the bar and took hold of the handle. "Thank you, sir," he said as he gingerly walked toward the door.

As he slowly made his way down the block, he noticed a small crowd of people gathered in front of the new skyscraper. The sidewalk had been empty when he went out just a short time ago, now there were a half-dozen policemen. There was a horse-drawn police wagon parked along the curb. As he neared the entrance, Andrew stashed the beer bucket atop the short stoop of a neighboring building's doorway. He walked down to the skyscraper.

"Where do you think you're going?" a policeman called out before Andrew could get inside.

Andrew stopped and turned, pointing to himself.

"Yeah—big man. You!" the policeman added.

"I work here."

"Is that so," he stepped to Andrew and grabbed him by the arm, walking him inside. "Sergeant—this fella says he works here," he announced in the vestibule.

Andrew looked over to the elevator lobby. The hoistway doors lay on the pavement and there were bricks and angled pieces of iron bars lying in a tangled mess before the open shaftway.

The sergeant came over. He was taller than the policeman holding Andrew's arm, but not as tall as Andrew. He'd taken off his cap and his wavy brown hair and mustache were drenched in sweat. "You with the elevator crew?"

"Yeah."

"Where were you a few minutes ago?"

"Went on break—I was only gone a little while. What happened?"

The sergeant looked back to the elevator. "Patrolman Cooper, there, was on his post and heard a loud crash come from this here building. He ran over to investigate. When he came in, he found this." The sergeant now took hold of Andrew's elbow and led him to the open shaftway.

Andrew could now see inside—the top of the elevator car was visible. It was twisted, the whole car was off track.

"When he went down to the basement to see, he found them," added the sergeant.

"Found who?" Andrew asked dumbly.

"The men inside—all dead."

"Dead?" Andrew felt a cold shock jolt his senses.

"All five."

"All Five?"

"Do you know how this could have happened?" The sergeant asked, not without a hint of empathy.

Shock was now replaced with panic. *The wheel!* Andrew thought. *Did I install the fucking wheel wrong?* He stuck his head into the shaft and looked up. It was dark, but, luckily, enough moonlight shone into the machinery room for Andrew to see that the wheel was still in place. The cable must have failed somewhere else. But where? They had fastened the U-bolts and saddles tightly. The counterweights were securely on their guide rails. He looked in the shaft again. The intervening floors were too dark.

"I don't know," he said at last.

"Well, they must have plummeted from high up. I won't tell you what the inside looks like," the sergeant said.

Andrew walked outside into the night air. It was cooler outside than in the building and his shirt was still wet, giving him a slight chill. He'd thought the policemen would make him stay longer. But the sergeant only asked if the elevator company had a telephone number and then let him go. They never even asked him his name. He walked down to the stoop where he'd left the pail of beer and retrieved it. Then he went back to the saloon, sat a table, drank the entire bucket himself, and then ordered another, drank half of that, and passed out with his head on the table.

He woke up with a startle and sat up quickly with the sun shining brightly through the plate-glass window. The saloon was deserted. His head hurt and he had to piss something fierce. After finding the toilet and a glass of water. He let himself out the locked door and walked home.

He opened the apartment door and heard his wife scream. The apartment was full of people. His mother and father, a priest, and a man he didn't recognize wearing a black suit sat at the table. His wife ran to him with tears streaming down her cheeks.

"Lizzy, dear. What's wrong?"

"You're dead!" she cried.

"I'm what?"

"You're dead—they said you were dead."

"Who said?"

"A Mr. Bateman—said he was your manager. Came here last night with a policeman. It was after midnight, and they were banging on the door. They said there was a terrible accident and your whole crew was dead."

Andrew began to laugh—then thought clearly enough to hold it in. "Well now you see me, Lizzy. I'm safe. The other men all died. I wasn't in the elevator with them at the time." He looked over at the table. His mother had tears in her eyes. "It was a horrible accident. I don't know what went wrong."

"But…" Lizzy started between sobs. "Andy—where have you been? We were planning your funeral. Where have you been?"

Andrew's head was pounding and his mouth was dry. He felt nauseous and wasn't sure if it was because of his brush with death or the bucket and a half of beer. He was about to speak when he felt it building. First in the pit of his stomach. Then, up his throat. A metallic taste overtook his mouth and it rose quickly to spew out. He ran to the kitchen sink and vomited.

19

1911

Andrew walked in through the open bay doors. The housewatchman recognized him and gave a cursory nod before returning attention to his newspaper. Andrew lay his helmet and slicker coat over the fender of the chief's automobile and went up the stairs holding his transfer order. He raised his hand to knock on the chief's office door but a voice called out from within and beat him to it.

"Ott?" the voice called out.

"Yes, sir—it's me."

"Come in—come in."

Andrew entered and saw Chief Croker standing at the window and looking out. "Saw you walking down Great Jones Street with your things," he said. "Big man as yourself had to be the man I'm expecting from Twenty Truck." He was still looking out the window. "Sunny day—still cold as hell—but sunny."

Andrew didn't know if he was supposed to reciprocate the small talk. He stood quiet, looked down at the transfer order and found his courage. "Can I ask a question, Chief?"

"Why are you here?" the chief responded.

"Yes, sir."

Now Croker turned and gave the hint of a smile. "Have you ever heard the expression 'Kill two birds with one stone'?"

Andrew had no idea what the chief was talking about. "No, sir."

"It means to solve two problems at the same time—with one action."

Andrew looked on, blankly.

"You put horse shit in that copper's saddlebag. Did you not?"

It took all of Andrew's strength not to laugh out loud. He struggled just to keep from grinning. Croker walked toward him. The chief was shorter than Andrew, by a lot. But he raised himself on his toes and put his face right in Andrew's. "Is that funny, Mr. Ott?"

Now Andrew could not keep himself from a snort and quick smile, before straining to make his expression serious.

"Will you be laughing when the mayor calls the fire commissioner and asks for your termination?" Croker raised his voice and Andrew felt any urge to laugh flee instantly.

"Think of this transfer as preventative medicine."

"I'm sorry, sir?"

"Preventative medicine! If such a telephone call were to come my way, when the commissioner asks me what discipline I intend to mete out, I can respond that the guilty member has already been removed from his company. That should satisfy."

"Thank you, sir," was all Andrew could think to say. He hadn't imagined this all to be such a serious infraction.

"Besides," the chief added. "My last aide just left. I could use a good hand around here."

"Yes, sir."

"See, Ott—two birds with one stone."

20

CHARLIE STOOD AT THE sink washing dishes. Though he'd rolled his sleeves up, one kept sliding down and soaking up sudsy water. One by one, the other men walked over and plopped their dirty plates in the water, splashing Charlie. No one spoke to him. Every time he thought he was finished, another dirty plate appeared. Charlie even glanced over at the cupboard shelf to see if they were simply grabbing clean plates and throwing them in the sink to mess with him. He wanted to get the plates out of the way so he could soak the greasy baking pan while he cleared all the chairs out of the kitchen and swept and mopped the floor. As probie, these chores naturally fell mostly on Charlie, but most nights the others made small overtures to help out. Fred Schley usually stacked the chairs out on the apparatus floor, and Floyd would even sweep some nights, so that Charlie just needed to grab the mop after finishing the dishes. This night, however, no one lifted a finger.

Even Foreman Jennings seemed oddly cool. Or was that just his imagination? Jennings was never one for many words, but he'd exchanged pleasantries while handing Charlie his dirty plate. Tonight—nothing.

Once all the kitchen chores were finished, Charlie went to the stalls to check on the horses. Snowball's trough was nearly empty, and he added some hay and oats. All the horses needed water. He then grabbed the shovel and bent under Jack to scoop out the manure—but strangely, there wasn't any. He checked under Apollo, and even the chief's horse, Sunset, as well. Nothing. *Perhaps the others decided to give me a hand after all,* he thought.

Charlie busied himself rubbing an oily rag over the wither straps and reins hanging off the front of the ladder truck. He massaged the thick leather and worked the oil into the seams and inspected for cracks. There was a certain serenity in the thoughtless repetition. It allowed him to daydream without the appearance of idleness. John Stafford sat at the housewatch desk reading a book and paying him no attention and, though just a few feet away from the desk, Charlie felt completely alone in his thoughts.

He thought about Esther—the soft skin of her neck beneath her wavy hair, the depth of her eyes. He wanted to see her again and, as luck would have it, his next day off was the day of the dance at Manhattan Lyceum. He'd made up his mind to go.

He thought about his mother. He'd reluctantly admitted to her that he liked being a fireman. She didn't gloat, never said 'I told you so'. She simply kissed his cheek and told him to wash up for supper. But now he doubted himself. Something had changed since Ott was transferred and he couldn't say what. After Charlie, Ott was the next junior member of the company, and he was the most approachable of his coworkers. Without that buffer, the others all seemed more distant. What's more, Ott's jovial nature and love of storytelling had made Charlie's first few weeks in the firehouse enjoyable.

Charlie's thoughts were cut off by the muffled clanking of the telegraph bell hammer's motor. Then, the bell rang out:

Ding... Ding... Ding...
[Pause]
Ding...
[Pause]
Ding... Ding... Ding...

Charlie stuffed the oily rag in his pocket and ran around to his boots.

"Box Three-One-Three," Stafford yelled out while scribbling on the chalkboard. "Broome Street and Broadway."

Charlie kicked off his right shoe and grabbed the two loops of his right pull-up boot. As he started to slide his foot in, he was smacked in the face with the stench of manure. He stopped and saw that his boot—both boots actually—were filled with horse shit. He threw the boots aside, slid off the sock that had touched shit and slid his bare foot back into the shoe. He swung his denim coat over his shoulders and fed his arms in the sleeves as he ran to the stalls to take hold of Snowball.

Once he'd hitched the horse, he climbed up on the side step and donned his helmet. Smokey dutifully ran out the bay door first and then the team of horses stepped off. As the long rig turned right onto Mercer Street, Charlie gripped the handrail tightly and seethed with rage.

21

Max Blanck sat in his office on the tenth floor. The door was closed as he spoke with his partner Isaac Harris and factory manager Samuel Bernstein.

"Orders have increased, as expected," said Harris. "Shirtwaist orders are strong—but all for the new French style—with the plain collar. No one wants lace ruffles anymore."

"How are we with inventory, Samuel?" Blanck asked.

"Here we've moved most of last season's stock—but several bolts of lace and six crates of lawn remain," Bernstein answered. "But Mr. Wegener says the Wooster Street loft is still packed to the ceiling with last season's shirtwaists. All ruffled collars."

Max took in the information but held off on commenting. He had other matters he wanted to discuss. "What of this Chief Croker?" he asked. "What will come of his push for fire drills?"

"I thought you said Charles Murphy gave assurances," said Harris.

"Silent Charlie is good at offering agreement without offering promises. That damned fire in Newark set us back, I'm afraid. We were in a good position when the strikers gave in. Now, things are again uncertain."

"Would a fire drill be so terrible?" Bernstein asked. "Not often, but perhaps a couple of times per year."

"Forty minutes!" Blanck shot back.

"Excuse me?" said Bernstein.

"Forty minutes—at the Wooster Street factory. That is how long it took to get every girl lined up outside, a head count taken, and then walked back inside and returned to work with the machines up and running again."

"Thirty minutes," said Harris as he lit a cigarette.

"Same thing," Blanck replied angrily.

"Does that not prove the necessity?" said Bernstein. "Perhaps with practice that time could be halved."

"How much does thirty minutes of lost productivity cost us?" asked Max. "Have we not spent enough on those damned water buckets? Are we not careful here? Did you not fire a man just last month, Isaac? For smoking on the factory floor. And what is next? You know Croker won't be happy until all the factories have sprinklers installed. We're talking about untold thousands of dollars."

Harris took a long draw of his cigarette and nodded.

"How much have we spent, Isaac, these many years to move our operations out of the tenement sweatshops and into lofts? The amount of air and light on the floor downstairs is truly magnificent. Anyone who'd complain about working there surely never worked in the old shops. All other considerations are secondary. Our workers have plenty of fresh air and light."

"So, what do we do about Croker?" asked Harris.

"It's not the chief I'm worried about. It's not even the mayor—I think Murphy can keep him in check. I want to know who Croker is leaning on in Albany. We'll need our detective friend again."

"Fine and well, Max, I'll have Schlansky come in" said Harris. "But what about the inventory. What do you want to do with the old waists?"

Max was quiet for a moment and then looked at Bernstein. "That will be all, Samuel. Now if you'll excuse Isaac and me."

Max's mansion stood on West End Avenue, overlooking the Hudson River on the Upper West Side. Harris's own spacious house was just around the corner. The two had come a long way from the Lower East Side tenements of their youth. Max's household included his wife, six children, and five servants. He was a very busy man—always putting in long hours at the factory. But Max made sure to take time for his children every evening after dinner. His neck was thick and his face frozen in a scowl from sunup to sundown, but he was not too dour to get down on the floor and play with the young children. It was Max's favorite time of the day—the half hour or so each night, laughing and reveling in the little ones' joy. So, when the butler entered the parlor room and announced visitors, Mr. Harris and another gentleman, Max was none too pleased.

"Show them to the study, Hanley. I'll be right with them," said Max begrudgingly. He was kneeling still, and fixed the tail of his shirt which had come untucked. Mimi, four, laughed and took the opportunity of Max's hands both being busy to jump onto his shoulder and nearly knocked him to the ground. Max forgot about the shirt tail and his annoyance, and spun the girl to the carpet to tickle her. Henrietta, twelve, tried to rescue her sister by tickling her father under the arms. Max squealed with laughter as he clamped his arms down and squirmed.

The butler left, shutting the pocket doors behind him as Max continued the match with great enthusiasm.

Isaac Harris sat on a leather sofa in Max's study sipping a glass of brandy. Max sat at his desk, and in a caddy-cornered armchair sat Max Schlansky, owner of a private detective agency.

"It's this Perkins lady, mostly, leading the push," said Schlansky. He sipped brandy from a short, rounded glass. His knuckles were permanently swollen and one of his fingers was so disjointed as to practically stick out sideways. "Smith is her patron. The two of them have been quietly building support for a committee hearing."

"Bernstein said as much after that union meeting," said Max.

"Well—they've also got Johnson, from Rochester. He's very influential. He can bring almost all the Democrats with him."

"And where does Murphy stand in all this?" asked Harris.

"It seems Silent Charlie is leaning toward backing the reformers. Doesn't want to get pushed aside by the Progressive wave." Schlansky took another sip of Brandy and looked at Harris and Max, apparently thinking he'd said enough. But the Shirtwaist Kings expected more. "But there's a hook," he then added.

"Go on," said Max.

"I hear old Charlie is looking to undercut this Perkins lady and push a Tammany-sponsored bill—call it the Factory Fire Safety Law or somethin'. He figures he can make the Progressives happy and keep the factory owners happy at the same time."

"What does he get out of that?" asked Max.

Schlansky laughed. "You don't pay me enough to figure that out. What ever goes on between the businessmen and the Tammany men is none of *my* business. From where I sit—it just seems like Murphy wants to control everything."

"This is an opening," said Harris. "We can exploit this."

"How so?" said Max.

"If Murphy wants a bill, one more suited to our wishes, but one that keeps the Progressives at bay—we should help Murphy get his bill."

Max laughed. "You really think it will end there? Next thing you know we'll be the ones taking orders from our workers."

"Speaking of your workers," said Schlansky. "One of them is working for Smith."

"What *ever* do you mean?" Max asked.

"A sewing machine operator—from the Triangle floor. My man tells me Perkins met with her twice already and she's going to talk to the committee about Triangle."

"Simple solution," Harris sneered. "A sacked employee makes a much weaker witness."

"That won't do," said Max. "We need to make an example of her. If these girls think the picket line was tough, let them see what happens when they try to cross us up in Albany."

"What did'ya have in mind?" Schlansky asked.

"Your usual. Don't get carried away—remember what we talked about. Just send a message."

Schlansky nodded.

Max stood, hoping to usher the two men out. But Harris had another matter on his mind. "I also mentioned the excess inventory."

Max sat back down. "Ah, yes—that. Which do you prefer, Schlansky? One location or two?"

"One is best—raises fewer eyebrows. Whichever spot has more insurance—move it all there."

Max looked at Harris and then answered for both of them. "Triangle, for sure. We'll let you know when it's ready."

22

1901

Samuel Bernstein hated laziness. He had worked hard from an early age and couldn't abide men less than capable of a full day's work. When the teamster yelled out from atop his loaded truck to wait, he scarcely gave it a thought. The man pulled his dray onto Wooster Street from Houston and stopped right in front of the loft building Bernstein had been locking up for the night. The sun had already set, and all the machines were quiet. Samuel and another man, Thompson, were closing up the shop. The loading dock had a heavy wooden door on rollers that slid across. Thompson pushed it over and Samuel held the padlock waiting for the clasp hooks to line up. Then came the truck load of cloth—several hours after expected delivery time. Samuel heard the man calling and watched him steer his horses toward him.

"Damn Betsy here threw a shoe on the Brooklyn Bridge," said the teamster.

Without a word, Samuel hung the open padlock on one hasp and started pushing the door back open.

"But it's closing time, Mr. Bernstein," said Thompson. "We're gonna unload that thing now?"

"Work is work, Thompson. Do you want to work or not?"

"I want to go home—it's late."

"Go home."

Thompson stood quiet for a moment. Apparently deciding to accept Samuel's directive at face value, he turned to walk away.

"Don't come back tomorrow," Samuel added.

Thompson turned with a shocked expression, but Samuel hardly noticed. He went to the bed of the dray—loaded high with a canvas tarp cover. He and the teamster untied the tarp and Samuel slid two heavy bolts of cloth down, resting one on each shoulder, and carried them inside the loading dock.

WHEN THE DRAY WAS unloaded, Samuel pulled the sliding door shut and bolted the padlock. It was fully dark save for the weak, flickering streetlamp on the corner. Wooster Street was deserted. Moonlight reflected off the cobblestones still damp from the afternoon's passing shower. He started to walk home when another carriage turned down the block from Houston Street. This was a smaller passenger buggy. The corner lamp was bright enough to see the faces of his brother-in-law, and his cousin.

"I told you we'd find him here," Max Blanck said.

"We went by your place," said Isaac Harris. "Get in."

Samuel hopped aboard and Blanck jiggled the reins to get the horse moving. "Where we going?"

"To see the new factory," said Harris.

"Wait'll you see it, Sam," said Blanck. "Ten stories high!"

"Ten stories?" Samuel was incredulous. "What on earth will we do with all that space? Are we shutting down Wooster Street?"

"We're just renting the eighth floor," answered Harris.

"For now!" added Blanck.

The carriage rocked and bounced along the cobble-stoned roads north to Washington Place. From Broadway straight across to Washington Square Park, Washington Place was brightly lit by streetlamps to accommodate the students and faculty of nearby

New York University. They arrived at the corner of Greene Street and were met at the side entrance by a stocky man with a cane.

Samuel climbed down from the carriage and looked up. The moon shone bright above and he clearly saw all ten stories in its stone majesty. The top floor windows were rounded arches with a molded cornice jetting out above and stone coping below.

"Joseph," said Blanck. "This is Sam Bernstein—my wife's brother as it turns out. He runs our loading dock on Wooster Street."

"Pleasure to meet you, Sam," said the man as he limped over and offered his hand. "Joseph Asch."

"The pleasure is mine, Mr. Asch."

"Please—Joseph. Don't mind me, Sam. The knee's been acting up again." Asch used the tip of the cane to point to his right knee."

"Sorry to hear that, Joseph," Samuel added.

"Well, gentlemen," said Asch. "Shall we head up?"

"Indeed," said Harris, walking to the Greene Street door.

"Sam, I asked Joseph to meet us here this evening to discuss something with you," said Blanck.

Samuel found this last statement odd. Ever since his sister, Bertha, had married Max Blanck, Samuel felt like Max's kid brother. Blanck never asked his opinion on anything, really. He just expected Samuel to go along.

They stepped into the service elevator and Asch pulled the iron gate shut and hung his cane on a hinge of the criss-cross steel gate. He pulled the brass control handle forward and the car jerked upward.

"So, you're related to this whippersnapper?" Asch said to Samuel while nodding his head to Blanck.

"Actually," said Harris. "He's related to both of us."

Samuel smiled silently and watched the floors float by through the gate until they reached the eighth floor. Asch pulled the control handle back, grabbed his cane, and then pushed the gate open. The spacious loft was well-lit by electric lamps. Samuel stepped out and was struck by the height of the ceilings and how open the floor space was.

"Joseph thinks we could fit as many as two hundred sewing machines and still have room for the cutter's table," said Blanck. "All together on one floor."

"It will be quite the operation," Samuel answered. "We can barely keep up with orders now."

"That's right, Sam" Harris responded. "We've reached the peak of our capabilities with just the one factory. It's time to grow—but it will be difficult to manage two factories at the same time."

"What he's trying to say, Sam," Blanck interrupted. "Is that we're naming you manager of this factory. You won't just be running the loading dock—you'll be running the whole shebang."

Samuel was shocked. He had honestly believed he'd risen as high as he would ever go working for Max and Isaac. Managing a factory had never occurred to him. "Thank you," was all he managed to say.

"What the hell is a shebang?" asked Asch.

"Oh, Joseph, take your head out of your ass once in a while," said Blanck.

Asch let out a loud guffaw and tapped his cane on the wooden floor planks. "Good one, Max—you're quite the shebang yourself."

"That's not what that..." Blanck shot back, then paused. "Why don't we show the manager here his new factory? Aye?"

Samuel watched in amusement and followed the three to the elevator doors in the far corner.

"You'll see the passenger elevators here, gentlemen," said Asch. "And that corner there, Isaac, didn't you say you wanted it built out with a coatroom?"

"Yes, that's right," said Harris. "We'll still have plenty of floor space."

"Jolly-Oh," said Asch. "And here's another staircase," he added, indicating a thick door beside the elevator. "With the one back there by the service elevator, that makes two stairwells."

"Two stairs!" said Blanck. "See that, Sam. How many factories have two stairs?"

"The city inspector said I needed three," said Asch.

"Three! What on earth for?" Blanck asked in astonishment.

"The floor space. Said I need three stairs with this much floor space. So I had them add a fire escape outside this here window." Asch went over to the set of tall windows and slid the lower panel of one up.

In the shadows beyond, Samuel could see a narrow strip of wrought iron forming a tight walkway and steps. He stuck his head out, looked side to side, and down. "What's with these iron shutters?" he asked.

"Fire code for manufacturing buildings with other buildings nearby," said Asch. "If you close 'em, keeps fire from spreading building to building."

"Yes, Joseph, of course," Samuel said. He was well aware of the functionality of iron shutters. "I mean what's with how awkward they are on the fire escape, they don't fully open, and if they do, they block the stairs."

"It's all just a formality," answered Asch. He knocked on the stone coping around the wood window trim. "This building is fireproof."

"Let's get a move on, you two," Blanck called out from across the floor. "I'm hungry."

23

1911

Samuel stood before the service elevator unsure what to do. Frank, the service elevator operator, kept one hand on the gate and the other on the top of the stack of lace bolts to keep it from tipping over. This was the third day in a row the teamsters had brought excess inventory from Wooster Street. Samuel wasn't sure where he'd put this last batch. The crates of ruffled-collar shirtwaists from yesterday were piled between cutters tables on the eighth floor. And long rolls of lace and lawn were stacked up higher than some of the cutters' heads.

"Bring these up to the ninth floor," he told Frank, who pulled the gate shut.

None of this made sense to Samuel. Why the hell would they bring all the excess from Wooster Street here to Washington Place? If no one wanted the ruffled collars anymore, why hold on to the stock? Max and Isaac could probably sell off the excess at a loss to some midwestern department stores, then at least they'd be rid of it. Now, he was going to have to deal with all these bolts and crates cluttering up the floors. He decided to see, at least, if he could stop any more arriving tomorrow.

He went up to the tenth floor, past the secretary's station and knocked on Harris's door. Harris pulled the door open. "What is it, Sam?"

"The overstock keeps coming over from Wooster Street—I've nowhere to put any more. It's cluttering up the cutters' station and I just had to send a bunch up to ninth floor."

"Oh, no," Harris said. "It all must be kept together. Find a corner on either floor and pile it all together in one location."

"What in God's name for?"

"It's just the way we prefer it," said Harris as he turned his eyes down to a sheet of paper he was holding and shut the door. Samuel turned to head back down to the eighth floor. He remembered something—an overnight fire they'd had two years prior in the Wooster Street factory. That's why the excess fabric was being consolidated. A flash of anger rushed up to his head. One of the shipping clerks stepped in his path and Samuel pushed the poor fellow aside and kicked the stairwell door before stomping down the stairs.

24

The evening air was getting cooler and Charlie pushed his hands in his pockets to keep the chill from his fingers. He headed down Third Avenue until it became Bowery and every so often, a train would rattle on the elevated tracks overhead. He was still angry about the manure. Perhaps he had been too hasty believing the fire department could be a permanent career. He didn't fit in. Ott had been friendly, but now he was gone. He would be back at the firehouse in the morning, and he was not looking forward to it. Instead, he tried to focus on his evening. He hoped to see Esther at the dance but wasn't at all sure what he would do or say if he did.

There was a small crowd in front of the Manhattan Lyceum and Charlie stepped up behind them. He flipped a quarter-dollar coin in his fingers, alternating between the head of Lady Liberty and the eagle. He *did* like the steady pay. On the docks, he didn't work every day. He had to show up every morning and 'shape'—mill around with other hopefuls until the foreman figured out how many men he needed that day. If he didn't get picked, he didn't get paid. And if he did get picked, he couldn't be sure what job he'd get. With any luck, the riggers needed a hand. Charlie liked rigging—the ancient craft of knotting ropes around cargo just right so it holds during the hoisting but can also be easily untied. The perfect knot would never slip but could be quickly backed out once the load was let down. He was fascinated by the mechanics of a block and tackle pulley system—how such an ingenious use of ropes and wheels can cut the weight of objects in half, or more. If the riggers didn't need help, sometimes he'd catch a spot loading pallets or he would just be sent away. At the firehouse, at least, he didn't have to wonder if he'd be picked. He still didn't want to go back in the morning, however.

He made his way into the Lyceum's lobby and handed his quarter to a young woman seated at a table. He could hear piano music in the theatre. This was his first dance and he wasn't sure what to do next, but went through the open double-doors and looked around. There was an old man on stage playing piano, and two main groups of people. One huddled around a set of tables and chairs in the back of the room and the other centered in what he could see was the dance floor. He scanned the hall for Esther but could not find her.

"Well, I'll be damned—Charlie Pendergrass!"

Charlie turned to see a young man, his age, walking toward him with a hand held out. His other hand was clasped tightly around the pretty hand of a young woman with wavy blonde hair.

"Hey, Jack, good to see ya," Charlie said genuinely.

"This is Anna."

"Nice to meet you, Anna."

"Ain't she beautiful?" said Jack and Anna let out a thin smile. "I didn't know you came to these things."

"My first."

"Hey," Jack's face lit up with the excitement of a brilliant idea. "You should meet Anna's cousin—Madeline. She's lookin' for a dance partner. Isn't that right, Anna?"

Anna again smiled and nodded enthusiastically.

"Thanks—maybe in a bit," Charlie answered. "I'm looking for a friend."

"One of your new fireman friends? Hey, how is the new job? Do you get to slide down that pole?"

"The job is good." Charlie didn't really want to talk about it.

"Too bad," said Jack.

"Why's that?"

"Seamus Flaherty had a pallet crush his foot—poor bastard's gonna be lame for life. They're lookin' for a new rigger. Word is it'll be a union man. Cranky old Jenkins is lettin' the shapers fill in for now till he decides which one he'll pick."

Charlie felt a pang of remorse. That could have been him trying for the spot of union rigger. Old Jenkins had always liked him—picked him over other men when he was shaping. "When will Jenkins decide?"

Jack shrugged. "He'll probably drag it out until the union puts up a stink and makes him pick one."

Charlie was silent and Jack added: "We're gonna hit the dance floor. Come find us when you find your friend."

"I will."

Charlie looked around the room again for Esther. No luck. He went to the back of the room and bought a bottle of Coca-Cola. The young woman selling the soda popped the top and handed him a foaming bottle. Charlie quickly swigged the suds and the first third of the bottle in one gulp. He then sat on an empty chair and took a tin flask out of his pocket and topped off the Coca-Cola with cheap whiskey. He swirled the bottle and took a sip. He looked around the room, everybody seemed to be having a grand old time. He made up his mind to finish his drink and go home.

Jack, Anna, and another attractive young woman came running over to the soda table, laughing. Jack was out of breath. "There he is!" he said when he noticed Charlie sitting nearby. "Charlie, this is Madeline."

Madeline was almost as tall as Charlie, with a slender body and curly brown hair which sat magically atop her head in the *bouffant* style. She wore a long gray skirt under a white shirtwaist that puffed out slightly at the shoulders. *She could be a Gibson girl,* Charlie thought. Famed illustrator Charles Dana Gibson's sketches of young women were considered the ideal of modern feminine beauty and graced the covers of many magazines. Charlie had seen many a ripped-out Gibson girl sketch pinned up in outhouses on the docks.

"It's nice to meet you, Madeline," Charlie said as he stood and offered her his hand.

"Jack told me all about you," she answered. "Says you're a fireman now." Her eyes were deep and serious even though she was smiling.

"The girls here want a Coca-Cola," said Jack. "Then we're gonna dance some more."

Esther walked into the Lyceum with Rachel, who immediately ran off to search for Gaspar. She wondered if Charlie would show up. It was just a passing query, after all: *If I come to the next one, will I see you there?* That was weeks ago. God knows what could have come up in his life in the meantime. She looked around the dance floor. No sign. Not knowing what else to do, she decided to go get a Coca-Cola.

As she approached the table she was captivated by the sight of a tall and beautiful woman. Her hair was up in the *bouffant* style so popular in all the fashion magazines. She was speaking to someone with his back to Esther and as she got closer, Esther could make out the pleasingly soft tone of her perfectly pronounced words. Esther was suddenly self-conscious of her Polish accent. While still speaking, she made eye contact with Esther and the young man turned around. Esther froze when she saw it was Charlie.

"Hey, there... Esther," he said with a nervous smile.

Esther's smile was equally nervous, and Charlie added: "This is Madeline."

"Pleased to meet you."

"Nice to meet you, Esther," the woman said kindly.

"I just came for a Coca-Cola," Esther said, looking at Charlie. "Excuse me one moment."

She stepped over to the table and paid for a bottle. When she turned and saw Charlie still talking to Madeline, she took her soda and went the other direction. She wanted to find Rachel, but saw Ida first.

"Holla," Ida said.

"Hi, Ida—will you do something for me?"

"Sure I will."

"Will you find Rachel? Tell her I wasn't feeling well and went back home. Then will you walk her home later?"

"Of course. Are you ill? What's wrong?"

"Just an upset stomach is all. I'll be fine. And Ida... Thank you."

"Of course. Hey, Coca-Cola is good for an upset stomach. My mother gives it to me and my brother."

Esther held up the bottle and sipped. Ida patted her shoulder and went toward the dance floor. Esther headed for the door.

The crisp air outside felt nice and Esther was enjoying her Coca-Cola as she walked down Bowery toward Houston Street. She wasn't upset about Charlie with that other girl, but was no longer in the mood to be at the dance.

∞

CHARLIE NODDED POLITELY AS Madeline finished her story about bicycles. Glancing over her shoulder, he noticed that Esther was no longer at the soda table. He couldn't see her anywhere.

"So, who's ready to dance?" Jack asked and Anna bounced on her heels and clapped her hands.

"Will you excuse me?" said Charlie. "I need to find my friend."

"You ain't gonna dance with us?" Jack responded incredulously.

"Sorry, maybe in a bit." He smiled at Madeline and walked in the direction of the dance floor, scanning the room for Esther. Wading through the throng of people who had just entered, he made his way to the vestibule and out the door. He ran out to the middle of the street. A train rattled the elevated tracks on the Bowery. He ran to the corner and looked north but could only see a couple of blocks as the streetlamps faded under the shadows of the great El-train pillars. Turning south he strained his eyes to see down to Houston Street and for just a quick second, he caught sight of Esther before she turned left.

HOUSTON STREET WAS QUIET and Esther crossed mid-block to the south side, hopping over several piles of manure along the way. On each corner stood a streetlamp but the light only stretched so far and by the time she was mid-block the sidewalk was dark. Some of the windows in the tenements above had dim candlelight flickering, but still Esther walked faster toward each corner where the lamplight offered a sense of safety. From the direction of Allen Street, she heard the clopping of a horse and soon a carriage appeared. An old man sat atop working the reins and went by without noticing Esther. She was happy to reach Essex Street and hoped to see her neighbors sitting out on the stoop, but the chilly evening air would probably prevent it.

She could see the stairs of her tenement down by the corner of Stanton Street and also a man on the sidewalk heading toward her. As he got closer, Esther saw his Bowler hat was pulled down low almost over his eyes and his hands were buried in the pockets of his long coat. He was just a few feet away when he looked her dead in the eye. A chill went down her spine, but Esther kept walking and passed the man. She was staring at her building when she felt a crashing pain across the back of her left leg. It was as if someone pushed her backwards down a flight of stairs. She crumbled to the ground and let out a scream. Towering over her was the man in the Bowler hat. He had a short wooden club and raised his hand high and then crashed it down on Esther's other leg. Three quick hits crashed over Esther's legs. She winced in agony every time one landed. He raised his arm for another and she screamed.

From behind, someone grabbed the man's arm and prevented the blow. The man's Bowler hat slipped off as he was jerked back hard. Esther saw Charlie struggling with the man and she used the opportunity, with great effort, to kick him hard in the shin. He grunted with pain and Charlie grabbed the arm with the club with both hands as the two struggled for control. Esther saw the man quickly ball a fist with his free hand and strike Charlie square in the nose. Charlie fell back and the man ran away.

| ONE CENT | Evening Edition | SPECIAL EDITION |

VOL. 4.   THURSDAY, FEBRUARY 6, 1904   **NO. 37.**

CHIEF CROKER REINSTATED

WILLIAM G. SHEPHERD

New York, NY., Feb. 6—Here are the inside facts about Fire Chief Edward F. Croker's year-and-a-half fight to clear his name. The Appellate Division of the Supreme Court has ruled, in unanimous decision, that Croker be reinstated immediately as Chief of the Fire Department. The Corporation Counsel has stated that the city will not appeal the decision, putting a close to the matter forever.

Fire Commissioner Nicholas Hayes said he would happily comply with the court's order. It was the actions of Hayes's predecessor, Thomas Sturgis, on which the court based its conclusions. In their written decision, the magistrates took issue with Sturgis's acting unilaterally without affording Croker the opportunity to defend himself. Furthermore, the judges stated: "that the evidence presented as to the charges did not prove the relator guilty, but, on the contrary, with respect to some of those upon which he was found guilty, he was entitled to an acquittal, and with respect to the others he was prevented from fairly and fully presenting his defense."

The magistrates also described Sturgis as having "manifested a prejudice and bias which affected his judgement," and this reporter cannot disagree. This ordeal began with a campaign promise. Seth Low pledged that he, as mayor, would finally free the levers of government from the grip of Tammany Hall. And what better target than the nephew of the Squire himself, Richard Croker.

Since the days of Thomas Nast, Tammany men have been publicly scorned as corrupt and wholly self-interested. But a fair-minded observer of public affairs must recognize Chief Croker for the honest and dedicated servant of the citizens that he is. Seth Low served out his two-year term as mayor. The reforms he introduced to the civil service system may well prove to be an honorable legacy. His defeat this November past to Democrat George McClellan, however, is evidence enough that Tammany Hall is alive and well. Perhaps Edward Croker was not the target for which he ought to have aimed.

Women's Coats
$5.00

J. Whitman & Co.

Dresses & Skirts
$3.00

Open Mon.-Sat.   784 N. Atlantic Ave.
10 A.M.- 7 P.M.   Brooklyn, New York

BOOKER & SON
CUSTOM BICYCLES
Men's, Ladies' & Children's
Starting at $9.00
Mon-Fri 10AM-6PM
Sat 10AM-4PM
Corner of 14th ST., & SEVENTH AVE.

FRIEDRICH'S COMMERCIAL FURNITURE
Oak Roll-top Desks $25
Standard Desks. $13
Bookkeeper's Desks. $14
Typewriter Desks $14
Revolving Chairs $4
Stackable Bookease
   $3 per section.
COMMERCE MARKET
Brooklyn, First Floor

TO-DAY

Born on February 6th
Queen Anne of England
1665
Aaron Burr
1756

Historical Events

Julius Caesar defeated Pompey at the Battle of Thapsus, February 6, 46 B.C.

Massachusetts became the sixth state to ratify the U.S. Constitution, February 6, 1788.

Part Three

25

1904

EDWARD SAT AT THE bar inside the Broadway Central Hotel, beside his lawyer, Mr. Abrams. It had been a whirlwind couple of weeks. His wife and young daughter had been thrown from a carriage. Young Edith escaped serious harm, but Mrs. Croker hit her head and was knocked unconscious. She had spent a week in the hospital out in Shinnecock Bay, Long Island. For almost twenty-four hours the doctors couldn't say if she would regain consciousness. Luckily, she pulled through, and was now at home resting. Then, after nearly two years of frustration and waiting, the Appellate court ordered he be reinstated as chief of department.

The bartender put down two glasses of whiskey and soda water. Edward raised a glass and looked Mr. Abrams in the eye. "Thank you again, Walter. I couldn't have succeeded in this without you."

The lawyer clinked glasses and drank. "My pleasure, Edward," he said. He took another sip and went on: "May I offer you further counsel—free of charge."

Edward laughed. "I like the price. Go ahead."

"Set things right at home."

Edward's smile disappeared. "You know, I think that's one fire I'm at a loss for how to put out."

"You have a second chance now. Your case is resolved—you've been reinstated. Mrs. Croker is healing well. She'll look to you. You have this opportunity to get beyond the past."

"If only it were that simple. It hasn't been easy these last months. When I was working, I was at the firehouse most of the time. She had her life in Shinnecock, and I had mine here with the Department. But without my work, I was home more. And you'd think that would have brought us closer, but it's as if she resented me even more. She thinks I'm too demanding when it comes to the boys. Thinks I'm too obsessed with my work."

"Are you?"

Edward sipped his drink and didn't answer.

"Edward, look... In addition to a client, I've come to think of you as a friend."

"Sounds like you're buttering me up for a spanking."

"I know things were strained at home. And I don't fault you for renting the apartment here in the city after you had to vacate the quarters at the firehouse."

"I needed to be in Manhattan—my lectures were my only means of supporting my family."

"I know. And I understand. But I think the notice you published, however well intentioned, hurt your wife deeply."

"It was the responsible thing to do," Edward answered. But he was not sure if he really believed it. While he was out of work and scrambling for money, his wife had resorted to asking the local merchants in Shinnecock Bay for credit. When he found out, Edward was enraged. He took great pride in providing for his family and had never been in debt in his life. Furthermore, when he confronted his wife, she blamed *him* for getting fired from his job. Edward immediately sold the two horses he had stabled in Shinnecock and paid back the merchants. He left the rest of the money at the house for her to use, and then published a notice in the local paper that he, Edward F. Croker, would not be responsible for any further debts incurred in his name by his wife. "I've worked very hard to build my good name. I won't have it sullied by unpaid debts."

"All I'm saying, Edward, is that you have a chance to start over."

Three men approached the bar, all reporters. "I told you boys we'd find him here," said one. It was William Gunn Shepherd.

Edward beamed a wide smile. "Willy Gunn! I was hoping to see you today."

"Why is that Chief?" asked Shepherd.

"For your piece today. Thank you. It's good to know I still have a friend in this town."

"Well, I write it like I see it. I won't print something I don't believe—not even for a friend."

Edward slapped Shepherd on the shoulder. "Good man!" He turned to the other two and held out a hand. "I don't believe I know you gentlemen."

"The first man gave a handshake and said: "John Brinkley, Associated Press." Then the second: "Amos Sheffield, Tribune."

"Pleasure, gentlemen—this here is my attorney, Walter Abrams."

The men all nodded and exchanged pleasantries before Shepherd got straight to business.

"Chief, do you have any comment on the *Brooklyn Eagle*'s report?"

"What would that be, Mr. Shepherd? I haven't read it."

"They say your victory in the Appellate court and reinstatement make you the most powerful man in city government. Even Mayor McClellan is under your shadow. They say you're well positioned to be the next mayor."

Edward reached for his drink and sipped. "Can I get you boys something?"

All three declined. They stood with pad and pencil in hand waiting for the scoop: *Will Croker Run for Mayor?*

"I haven't read that story in the *Eagle*, but I've heard those rumors as well, boys. And I've given the matter much thought."

He paused and looked each in the eye to impart the gravity of his words. "Please take down this statement, gentlemen—I'd like it out there in no uncertain terms."

Shepherd flipped to a clean page. He was ready. Edward spoke to the three reporters and to Abrams. He spoke to convince an entire city. He spoke to reassure himself:

"I've no ambition in this world but one, and that is to be a fireman. The position may, in the eyes of some, appear to be a lowly one; but we who know the work which the fireman has to do believe that his is a noble calling."

He paused briefly to allow the reporters to write.

"There is an adage which says that, 'Nothing can be destroyed except by fire.' We strive to preserve from destruction the wealth of the world which is the product of the industry of men, necessary for the comfort of both the rich and the poor. We are defenders from fires of the art which has beautified the world, the product of genius of men and the means of refinement of mankind."

Another pause.

"But, above all, our proudest endeavor is to save lives of men—the work of God himself. Under the impulse of such thoughts, the nobility of the occupation thrills us and stimulates us to deeds of daring, even at the supreme sacrifice. Such considerations may not strike the average mind, but they are sufficient to fill the limit of our ambition in life and to make us serve the general purpose of human society."

Shepherd and the others were scribbling furiously. "Well, boys," said Shepherd. "We have our answer. Thank you, Chief."

"Thank you, gentlemen." Edward reached for his drink and the reporters all ran off to file their stories.

"I guess I have my answer as well," said Abrams.

"What do you mean?"

"No one who makes a speech like that is ever going to be content looking after his wife out in the country."

Edward sipped again, nodding pensively. He was about to say something, then didn't.

26

1911

Charlie sat on a wobbly wooden chair in the kitchen of Esther's apartment. He held a damp towel under his nose, checking every so often to see if the bleeding had stopped. The tiny kitchen had a basin-type bathtub along the wall and Esther sat on the rim fully clothed except her shoes and stockings. Her skirt was pulled up and her bruised legs were soaking in cold water. Esther's mom was boiling something on the stove and speaking to her daughter in Yiddish. Tears ran down her cheeks. Charlie didn't understand what they were saying.

"Why do you think he hit only my legs?"

It took Charlie a second to realize Esther was talking to him now. "I dunno," he said in a nasally heavy voice. He lowered the towel to check it.

"Oh, you poor thing," said Esther. "Your nose is twice it's normal size—and crooked."

He self-consciously put the towel back to his nose.

The mother said something else in Yiddish, but this time Esther answered in English. "No, *Mameshi,* he didn't take my handbag. How about you, Charlie. Did he take anything from you?"

"No—just punched me in the nose and ran off."

"But why would he attack me, if not to rob me?"

"On the docks, they send leg-breakers after ya when they wanna send a message," Charlie answered absent mindedly while looking at the towel. The bleeding had stopped. He looked up at Esther, who looked like she'd just seen a ghost.

※

ESTHER STOOD ON THE front stoop. Her legs were sore, she had bruises on both thighs and a huge welt on her calf. "Thank you, Charlie. I don't know what would've happened if you hadn't come." She put her palm against his cheek. His nose was bruised and swollen. There were black and blues under each eye.

"I'm sorry about earlier," he said. "At the dance."

"You did nothing wrong."

"Yeah—but the whole reason I even came to the dance was to see you."

"It was?" She blushed slightly and hoped he wouldn't notice.

"Of course. That's why I followed you home. I wanted to explain."

"There's another dance next Saturday," she said and smiled.

His face became dour. "I'll be at the firehouse—my next day off is in ten days."

"That's too bad. You must love your work, to stay there so much. I couldn't imagine sleeping at the factory."

"Well," he paused and looked down at his feet. "I don't know."

"You don't like your work?"

"I thought I did, It's just..." He noticed Esther's legs. "It doesn't matter. Can I see you on my day off? Maybe I can meet you at the Triangle factory in the evening and walk you home."

Esther raised herself on her toes and kissed his cheek. "I would like that, Charlie."

He smiled and stepped down from the stoop and began to walk away, then turned back. "Esther, I don't know your last name."

"Greenberg," she said.

"Esther Greenberg," he said. "I like that. I'm Pendergrass, by the way. Charlie Pendergrass."

Esther gave a big smile. "Good night, Charlie Pendergrass."

27

Edward came down the stairs in a hurry. The housewatchman had rung the bells and called out, the Seventh Battalion had just transmitted a second alarm for a factory fire on 18th Street. From his office above, he'd heard the motor of the Red Devil roar to life. Oswald always started the car for the chief and then scooched over to the passenger side, and John had usually done the same. But Andrew Ott sat behind the wheel wearing a leather cap and goggles. Edward checked the backseat to ensure his slicker coat and helmet were stowed and yelled over the purring engine: "Slide over, Ott."

Ott turned his head to look at the chief and shut off the motor.

"What on earth are you doing, man?" Edward barked.

"You brought me here to be your aide, Chief. I didn't ask for it. The aide drives the chief—that's the way it works."

Edward felt the blood boiling up through the muscles tensing in his neck and jaw, to the top of his head.

"Third alarm!" the housewatchman yelled.

Ott started the motor. "We're gonna miss it, Chief, if you don't get in."

Edward bit his tongue and got in the passenger side. He would deal with Ott later. The second he lifted his leg off the running board and his ass touched the seat, Ott hit the gas. The Red Devil lurched forward and out the bay door in flash. Edward looked back to make sure they hadn't run anyone over on the sidewalk. The car was capable of going fifty miles an hour and Edward thought they may very well have hit that number before even making it to the corner. Ott had the car on two wheels as he turned north on Lafayette Street.

Edward squeezed the armrest with one hand and held the dashboard with the other while Ott weaved through the crowded streets. "Give me some bell, Chief" Ott said as he furiously worked the steering wheel and gear shift handle.

Edward reached up and clanked the bell.

They arrived at the fire in mere minutes. Ott tucked the Red Devil behind a hose wagon a block or so from the burning factory. Edward did not loosen his grip until the motor was off. He turned to say something to his aide, but Ott was pointing ahead and spoke first: "Look at that bastard burn, Chief. Gotta be three floors of fire."

Edward lay his tweed cap on the front seat and donned his slicker coat and helmet. Ott put his leather cap and goggles on the dash, donned his own slicker coat and helmet and ran off down the block.

Edward shook his head, smiled, and headed down after him.

CHARLIE WORKED THE MOP back and forth across the kitchen floor. He took the bucket and used it to prop the door open, then dipped the mop head in the sudsy water and wrung it with his hands. From outside the door, he reached in with the mop to scrub the final few feet without stepping on the wet tiles. Fred Schley and Floyd Mance came back from the housewatch, around the rig, and stepped over the mop handle in Charlie's hands into the kitchen. The were wearing their pull-up boots—caked in soot—as they strolled over to the counter and poured themselves cups of coffee. Black, ashy footprints littered the wet floor. Charlie said nothing. He stood at the doorway, mop in hand, waiting for them to leave so he could mop up the footprints.

Schley came out first. "Mmmm," he offered as he sipped his hot coffee. Mance was behind him. "You know, Fred," he said. "I think Johnny looks better with his nose smashed in."

Schley laughed. Charlie flipped the mop and dropped the wet, dirty head atop Mance's head. "And you look better with long hair," he said.

Mance had brown soapy water running down his face and soaking his shirt. He dropped the coffee cup and threw a punch. Charlie was ready and side stepped the blow, then offered one of his own, connecting with the side of Mance's head, knocking the big man to the ground. Schley, for some reason, chose not to spill his coffee and went quickly to the workbench and placed the cup down. He then came back and grabbed Charlie just as Mance was getting up and readying to charge.

"Enough!" yelled Foreman Jennings from the base of the spiral stairs. The three froze instantly. "What the hell is going on here?"

No one spoke.

"Well?" Jennings was heated. "Pendergrass... What's the meaning of this?"

Charlie said nothing.

"The kid's a rat," said Mance. "Got Ott lifted outta here."

Charlie thought of a loaded pallet on the docks—when the rope snapped, and it crashed down on top of someone. That is how he felt in that moment. *What the hell does he mean? Got Ott lifted?* He was utterly confused. Is that what everyone thought? Ott's transfer was Charlie's fault?

"Enough, Mr. Mance," said Jennings. "Pendergrass, go wait for me in my office."

CHARLIE SAT ALONE IN the office, waiting. At last, Jennings came in.

"The men are pretty worked up, Charlie," he began.

Charlie nodded. "They been givin' me the business since Ott left."

"How did Chief Croker know about the manure prank with the cop?"

Charlie shrugged. He looked Jennings in the eye and then realized the foreman was awaiting further comment. "I really have no idea."

"Do you know Chief Croker?"

"Yes, sir. He's the chief of department."

"Yes, he is. But do *you* know him. Are you friends?"

"No, sir."

"You were seen getting out of his car."

Charlie felt slightly nauseous. "Yes, sir. He gave me a ride."

"From where?"

"From a garment workers' meeting. My cousin asked me to attend. He wanted me to talk about fire safety, but I didn't want to. I went for a little while—then came back." Charlie thought quickly. He was going to have to admit to lying about going home for his mother's birthday. He just hoped Jennings didn't ask who his cousin was.

Jennings had been standing, but now sat at his desk. "And when was this?"

"Couple of weeks ago. The night I asked to go home for my mother's birthday."

"You shouldn't have lied to me, Charlie."

"I know, sir. I'm sorry."

"I may be your foreman, but I'm not your enemy. If there was a meeting about fire safety, perhaps we all could have gone."

"Yes, sir." Charlie was happy to leave it at that regarding the meeting. "But I didn't say anything to the chief about Ott."

"Well, that's not how it looks to the men, and I can't say I blame them. You were dishonest, got caught in the lie, and then one of them gets kicked out of here. You see where I'm going, Charlie?"

At that moment Charlie could only think of one thing—what Jack had told him about the opening for a union rigger. Being a fireman wasn't what he thought it would be. Everyone was in his business all day long. On the dock, guys hardly even spoke to one another. Everybody just worried about themselves. But here in the firehouse, he was expected to live with these guys. And they were *all* watching him—the probie—*all* the time. "Mr. Jennings, sir," he said softly. "I don't think this is the job for me."

Apparently surprised, Jennings asked him to repeat it.

"This, sir, being a fireman. It's not for me."

"Over this Ott business? If what you told me is true, it'll sort itself out. You'll see. Things always get better."

"Thank you, sir. But I've made up my mind."

Jennings was quiet for a moment. He then went to a filing cabinet and found a form. He put it down in front of Charlie and handed him a pen.

28

Esther stepped out into the brisk morning air. She buttoned her coat. Her hands began shivering and she couldn't be sure if it was the cold or her nerves. She stepped down the stoop and her legs creaked. The pain was deep in the muscles of her thighs and calves. Her knees seemed to resist bending. Rachel hooked her arms around Esther's arm and they walked in step. Leaning against a wrought-iron gate, Clara Lemlich was waiting for them.

"Sisters-in-arms!" Clara exclaimed.

Clara had always lifted Esther's spirits. Her indomitable nature was an inspiration during the darkest days of the strike—when policemen arrested picketers, and relief money dried up, and even after thugs assaulted her and other strike leaders. But Clara was the last person she wanted to see this morning.

"Your legs, *ziskayt*," said Clara. "How are your legs?"

"Good morning, Clara," said Esther. "How did you know?"

Rachel squeezed her arms tighter and answered. "I told her—yesterday when *Mame* sent me to fetch onions. I went to the union hall, Clara was there."

"Why would you do that? Rachel—without telling me." Esther pulled away from her sister, but regretted it after her knees went wobbly. Still, she was too proud to grab on again.

"Est—this is serious. We can't let those bastards get away with this." Rachel's young eyes blazed with fury.

"She's right, Esther," Clara agreed. "We can't…"

"*This* is me this happened too—no one else. I will decide what I do next." Esther wanted to get away from them but could only walk so fast.

"Do you know why they hit your legs?" Clara asked.

Esther turned to look at Clara and hear her answer.

"It's so there wouldn't be any bruises on your face. You see they learned their lesson with me. When my picture was in the newspapers, all bruised up, lots of people turned to support us. Even though the bastards denied anything to do with it—people knew they was to blame, and we got a lot of support from that. Now, you see, they learned their lesson. No more bruised faces."

"I don't know how they know, Clara. But they know I was helpin' the assemblymen with the fire safety hearings. They *are* bastards—but I get paid every week. If I quit, or get fired, I'll have to go work for some other bastard—or maybe not get paid at all."

"Don't you want to make it so the bastards can't just do whatever they want?" Rachel asked.

"You've seen what happens to any one of us who stands out. Both of you." Esther's voice was raised and shaky. "I know you have."

"The strike was a tough victory, but it was just the start," said Clara.

"I'm not talking about the strike—or the picketers." Esther had tears running down her cheeks. "I'm talking about *us*. We came to America to get away from the violence. But if we don't keep our mouths shut, it finds us here."

"So you're gonna let them get away with it?" asked Rachel as Esther began walking as fast as she could.

"I'm going to work. And that is all I am doing from now on," she said. Rachel and Clara didn't move. Esther turned her head while she continued toward Houston Street. "Tell Mr. Smith and Miss Perkins to find somebody else."

MAX LIKED TO START his day early. Both he and Isaac lived on the Upper West Side and took chauffeured carriages to the factory, but he usually arrived well before his partner. He drank coffee and examined telegraphed purchase orders from each and every salesman across the country. He was particularly pleased this morning by an order for two thousand shirtwaists from a department store in Chicago. The sun had just made its way up above the tenements and Broadway lofts to the east and light poured in the tall office windows facing Washington Place. Max looked up and took in the first morning rays. He thought about the early days in those dark, stuffy sweatshops and again wondered how anyone could complain about working in such a modern and spacious building. Max had read in the papers what that damned fire chief was saying now: unless the owners shelled out for sprinklers and fire drills immediately, there would be another Newark fire. And worst of all the chief was asking for fire inspectors. Max knew exactly what that would mean—someone else coming around with their hand out.

Max employed hundreds of people—men with families; widows with young mouths to feed, girls bringing home much-needed money. If all those bureaucrats and politicians really cared about those workers, they'd help Max hire more of them. He resented the implication that he didn't care about the workers. He gave them air, light, and money. And those damned newspapers—always sensationalizing everything. They wouldn't be happy until they stirred the girls up into another strike. That would be a disaster. The busy season was just about to start up again. At least Schlansky had done his job. Let that be a lesson to any would-be agitators. And if their go-to private detective could take care of the other issue soon, Max and Isaac would have an infusion of cash to kick off the busy season. They could invest in the newest designs.

"May I get you another, Uncle?" a young woman said.

Max's daze was broken, and he turned from the window toward the doorway. He held up his coffee cup and saw it was empty. "Yes, Mary—that would be nice. Thank you."

"The telautograph is scribbling," Mary said as she stepped over and took the cup.

Max jumped out of his chair like a puppy who just saw a ball bounce. He'd argued with Isaac about spending money on the telautograph, but now wanted to see how it worked. On a narrow table behind the secretary's desk, an oval-shaped machine perhaps a foot high and a foot and a half at its widest was spitting out rolled paper from underneath a pen attached to hinged brackets that moved back and forth, up and down, all on its own. Before the paper had even finished rolling out from under the pen, Max ripped the sheet off. He read the cursive writing aloud:

All excess materials moved to

9th floor. Please don't send any

more.   S.B.

Samuel's at it bright and early, thought Max. The ninth floor was perfect. Schlansky was good at what he did, and Max was confident things would not get out of hand. But just in case, it was better to have a handful of sewing machines damaged than the cutters' workstations.

∞

Samuel was the first to arrive on the eighth floor that Monday morning. He had stayed late on Saturday bringing the last of the overstock up to the ninth. Sunlight poured through the upper panes of the Greene Street windows, but it was still fairly dark by the table outside the dressing room that held the telautograph console. He stared at the stylus hovering over the note he'd scribbled, amazed how a wired signal could teleport his words upstairs. He was happy to have the machine save him a trip and conversation with his brother-in-law, who, he knew, was upstairs sipping coffee, reading sales reports. He didn't even want to use the telephone right beside the telautograph—instead of taking a message, Mary might put the call through to Blanck.

Gradually the cutters and their assistants began arriving. Unlike the sewing machine operators, they used the passenger elevators on the Washington Street side. "Good morning, Mr. Bernstein," they said as they put their coats in the dressing room and donned aprons over their shirtsleeves. Samuel wanted a smoke before the day's work kicked off and went to the passenger elevator bank and rang the bell. A moment later, the door was pulled open by young Joseph, the operator. Two cutters stepped out, and Samuel went in.

"Spent the night up here, did you Mr. Bernstein?" Joseph said with a chuckle.

Samuel returned a small laugh. "No—I *do* actually have a home, ya' know. Just an early start is all, Joe."

Samuel stood outside in the cold March morning air and rolled a pinch of tobacco in thin yellow rolling paper. He struck a match on the side of the building and took in a long drag as he held the lighted match to the cigarette's twisted tip. It tasted good and calmed him. He had slept badly. He couldn't shake his annoyance at Blanck and Harris. Samuel had done well for himself at Triangle; hard as he may have worked, it paid off. He was manager of the factory. His sister's husband was one owner, and his cousin was the other. Come what may, Triangle was his home—his family. Blanck and Harris were both millionaires but they acted as though they'd just stepped foot in America without a penny to their names. They squeezed every dollar out of every turn and despite good heads for business, they always chose the short-term good over the long-term. And now, just as the busy season was about to kick off, the Shirtwaist Kings were resorting to their go-to tactic for quick funds. It didn't matter how hard Samuel had worked to organize the factory so efficiently. They didn't care how much clean-up would be involved. They wanted quick cash—without touching their own accounts.

At the corner of Greene Street, he could see the sewing machine operators, mostly young women and girls, lined up for the service elevator. There was a bit of a commotion and a group of girls seemed to gather around someone lying on the sidewalk. Samuel threw the last of his cigarette into the street and went toward the crowd. He pushed his way through and kneeled to see who it was—a young woman lay on her back, trying to get up and protesting against the attention.

"Please—let me be, I'm fine. Just let me get up," she said with teary eyes.

Samuel stared at her face. He knew her from somewhere. It didn't take long to figure it out. She was the seamstress who translated for him when Harris's cousins came to visit. *And* he had seen her at the I.L.G.W.U. meeting recently. He recognized her there, talking to Clara Lemlich—everyone knew Clara Lemlich—but she left early. "Are you hurt?" he asked her.

"I'm fine, Mr. Bernstein—I just tripped coming up onto the sidewalk here," she answered. Her voice was shaky.

"Her legs gave out," another young woman in the crowd added. "She got black and blues all over her legs. Her skirt slid up—they're all bruised."

The injured young woman quickly tugged the bottom hem of her skirt to ensure full leg coverage, and then shot a nasty look at the other.

"What's your name, dear?" Samuel asked.

"Esther Greenberg."

"Esther, can you stand?"

"Yes, Mr. Bernstein. I'm fine, really I am." She put a hand on the sidewalk and pushed herself up. Samuel could see her wincing.

"Esther!" a young girl shouted as she waded through the crowd. "What happened?"

"Rachel, I'm fine. Just tripped is all."

Samuel noticed the family resemblance. "You're her sister?"

"Yes, Mr. Bernstein—Rachel Greenberg."

"Your sister seems to have injured her legs."

"No—I'm fine, Mr. Bernstein," Esther protested.

"She's not fine, Mr. Bernstein," called another woman's voice sternly. Samuel looked over the shoulders of the crowd and saw it was Clara Lemlich. "This is what your goons do to hard-working girls."

A gasp went out among those gathered around. "I beg your pardon," said Samuel.

"Go ask the Shirtwaist Kings how Esther's legs got bruised," Lemlich was shouting.

Samuel stared at Lemlich, momentarily paralyzed. *What's this all about?* Then, he went with his first instinct, which was to restore order. "You girls—get upstairs. All of you, now. It's nearly starting bell." He was commanding and accustomed to being obeyed. Now was no different. The seamstresses headed for the service entrance on Greene Street, though a few were leering back with nasty looks. Esther limped toward the entrance with her sister at her side. Only Clara Lemlich stood still.

"You're good at what you do, Miss Lemlich," he said, without malice.

"I could say the same for you," she answered.

"And what is it that you think I do?"

"Make money for the Shirtwaist Kings."

He laughed. "I suppose I do." He turned to walk back to the Washington Place entrance. "Good day, Miss Lemlich."

Samuel stepped off the elevator on the eighth floor to find all the cutting stations teeming with activity. Assistants laid perfect stacks of fabric, up to an inch thick. Cutters wielded giant scissors with surgeon's precision. Above each table hung templates of cuts stretched tight over wires.

"The samples of the new design are ready, Mr. Bernstein," said a middle-aged woman holding a shirtwaist.

"Thank you, Dinah." Samuel took hold of the blouse and inspected it. The sleeves were pleated at the shoulder seam, and the collar was thinner than the last season's style, and without ruffles. While turning over the garment, he noticed that a cutter at the far end of the row was seated and crouched forward. He handed the shirtwaist back to Dinah and quickly went to the station.

"Jacob!" Samuel shouted.

The cutter sat back quickly and tossed something in the scrap bin under his table. A faint whiff of smoke wafted up.

"You damned idiot," Samuel added as he pushed Jacob off his chair and slid the scrap bin out from under the table. He furiously pulled out small cuttings, tossing them aside until he found what he'd been looking for: a smoldering cigarette butt. He held it up and stared into the cutter's eyes.

Jacob was shorter than Samuel. He had a graying beard over a leathery face. He made no plea. He just awaited the inevitable.

"You're dismissed," said Samuel simply. He turned to leave, cigarette butt in hand. Other cutters and assistants had stopped briefly to watch the exchange but now hastily resumed work.

Samuel was highly aggravated as he rinsed off the butt in the sink. The commotion on the sidewalk outside had kept him from the factory floor, and the second he wasn't looking, a cutter lit a cigarette. Blanck and Harris were resistant to most fire safety rules because they cut into profits. But even the Shirtwaist Kings drew the line at smoking on the factory floor.

ESTHER WAS BUSY STITCHING. It felt good, for now at least, to be seated. The walk to work had been painful. She was no longer angry at Rachel or Clara for pressuring her, now she was doubting herself. Was she doing the right thing? Al Smith and Frances Perkins were trying to make things better. Shouldn't she try as well? But she did try, and look what happened. The next time, she could end up killed—or in jail, or at the least, without a job. *No,* she thought. *I'm doing the right thing. I'm not getting any more involved in the Assembly's business.*

Down the row between the long sewing machine tables came her foreman, Mr. Craven. Every couple of machines, he stopped to nitpick something about the seamstress's work. A wave of hatred washed over Esther. If she had that club, she'd take it to Craven's smug face. Thankfully, he walked past her without stopping.

From the passenger elevators, Esther saw Mr. Bernstein come onto the floor. He circled around the tables and was now heading down her row. She fed the blouse body under the hopping needle and acted as if she'd not noticed him.

"Miss Greenberg," Bernstein said. Esther stopped sewing and looked up at the foreman, as did all the seamstresses within earshot. She didn't speak.

"I shall inform your foreman, and the elevator operators. Until your legs heal, you may use the passenger elevators to leave at the end of the day, to save you from the stairs."

Esther was dumbstruck. Before she could respond, Mr. Craven returned.

"Is there a problem, Mr. Bernstein?"

Esther's spell was broken. Craven's beady eyes were trained right on her. He was just waiting for an excuse, she thought. He wanted nothing more than for Bernstein to say Esther had messed something up. Suddenly she knew what she had to do.

"Thank you, Mr. Bernstein," she said. Tears formed in her eyes. "You have all been so kind to me here since my terrible accident. Mr. Craven has been like a father to me."

"Craven's eyes bulged, and he opened his mouth: "Why, I ne..."

"That's very commendable, Mr. Craven," said Bernstein.

"He was so attentive," Esther continued. "When they messed up my sister's pay—offering to speak with you. I feel very fortunate."

Now it was Craven's turn to be dumbstruck. "I... I..."

"What does she mean, Craven?" Bernstein asked sharply.

"Yes, Mr. Bernstein. The younger Miss Greenberg was started at a trainee pay scale."

"Yes?"

"Well—she does have the experience to warrant a full salary," Craven admitted. "I was going to inform you."

"Very well—I'll inform Miss Lipshitz," Bernstein answered and turned to Esther. "And I'll let the elevator boys know."

"Oh, thank you, Mr. Bernstein,' Esther said. "But going down stairs is not so bad at all. I will be fine walking down with Rachel."

"Fine," Bernstein replied plainly. "Tell Mr. Craven if you change your mind." With that, the manger turned and left.

Esther shot a quick glance at Rachel, who was doing her best not to smile. She then turned back to Mr. Craven, who was staring at her. His beady eyes narrowed and Esther braced herself. But instead of her foreman's voice, she heard a loud yell from across the room.

"Damn you—I say damn you," Bernstein's voice boomed across the ninth floor. All two hundred and seventy-odd seamstresses looked up. "What the hell happened here!" he shouted.

Craven ran down the aisle toward the back windows.

"Why are these crates against the window?" Bernstein continued his tirade. "Miss Burrows, Mr. Craven... Who moved these? These windows with fire escapes mustn't be blocked!"

As intimidating as Mr. Bernstein could be, Esther had never heard him yell before. All the seamstresses, including Esther, went back to their sewing and pretended nothing was happening. Thankfully, the growing pile of bolts and crates in the back of the room had nothing to do with her.

29

The legislative chamber of city hall was stifling hot. Cast iron radiators stood along the walls, one under each tall window, and pumped steam heat into the room. The onset of March and impending spring had no effect on the boilermen's schedule and somewhere down in the century-old building's bowels the furnace blazed. Andrew had sweat running down from his temples over the collar that choked his thick neck. He wanted to unbutton his dress-uniform shirt and take off the tie, but Chief Croker had insisted he look as spiffy as possible for the hearing. He sat beside the chief at a long oak table. Members of the Board of Aldermen manned the dais while a representative of the Protective League of Property Owners read a written statement.

"Estimates run as high as twenty-five cents per square foot," the man stated. He too was seated at an oak table facing the dais. He had a stack of papers laid out and switched from sheet to sheet as he read. His glasses were positioned on the tip of his nose, so he could look up bare-eyed at the aldermen between sentences. "Imagine a loft building, sirs, with eight floors of manufacturing space—each consisting of twenty-five hundred square feet. That would make the cost of installing sprinklers five thousand dollars—for just one building, sirs. How will the owners bear such an expense?"

"Chief Croker," called an alderman. "What say you, sir?"

"I say hogwash, sir."

"I beg your pardon," the owners' representative objected.

"I could sprinkler a building myself for a fraction of that figure," Croker added.

The man held up a sheet and reiterated: "Twenty-five cents per square foot!"

Croker looked over at Andrew, then said: "Your Honors—even should I concede the accuracy of such wild estimates, there is one figure that is undisputed. Since the advent of automatic sprinklers in factories, not one single life has been lost to fire in an outfitted building."

Andrew took his cue and stood, walked over to the representative, and grabbed the sheet of paper from his hand. The seated man looked up at Andrew's light-colored eyes staring down intently at him and made no objection. Andrew looked down at the paper, lingering close to the man and letting the physical bulk of his presence loom over. He noticed the silver bullet and was sure Croker would too. He returned to his seat, slid the paper across to the chief and pointed to the key passage.

Croker was still talking but glanced down and then cut himself off mid-sentence. "Gentlemen, it would appear the cost estimate in question was given for a grouping of factories in Pennsylvania, outside of the nearest town, and includes the cost of running a water main. I need not remind this body that all the streets in this city's factory district are already connected to water mains."

"The factories in Pennsylvania were three-stories high," shouted the representative. "Lofts in this city are three times as tall. If anything, that estimate is low!"

An alderman banged a gavel down on his table. "Let the chief speak, Mr. Samson. He did not interrupt *you*."

"Your Honors," Croker continued. "As I've written about for some time now, I believe three steps taken either by this body here, or state-wide in the legislature, could save countless lives in the years to come. First and foremost would be the requiring of automatic sprinklers in factories. Second would be mandatory fire drills in manufacturing plants where twenty or more employees are assembled. And third would be the creation of a new bureau in the fire department, consisting of inspectors to visit these factories on a regular basis and ensure compliance with these and other existing laws."

"Mr. Samson," said the gavel-wielding alderman.

"Yes, sir."

"I suggest you advise the Protective League to commission a new study. I propose another hearing in ninety days' time. That ought to suffice your clients' needs, sir. I would like to see *real* cost estimates for outfitting factory lofts—in *New York City,* mind you—with automatic sprinklers."

Croker leaned into Andrew's ear. "He's letting the fox decide how high to put the chicken wire."

The alderman continued: "And I want you to invite Chief Croker to a factory—during business hours—and have him demonstrate a proper fire drill. You may make your case against such drills in ninety days, but I will not sit through more blubbery about costs in other states." The alderman slammed the gavel and stood.

"And the bureau of fire inspectors? Your Honor, what about that?" Croker called out.

"You'll have to take that up with the mayor, Chief Croker," said the alderman as he turned and stepped off the dais.

EDWARD SAT AT HIS desk sorting through the bag of intra-department mail that arrived while he was at the hearing. Ott came in with two cups of tea, placing one on Edward's desk before sitting at his own and sipping.

"Thank you, Mr. Ott."

Edward flipped through requests, special orders and directives—some pages coming from chiefs in the various divisions going up to headquarters, and some from headquarters going down to the divisions. He made two piles: one of forms requiring his signature, and the other simple information he needed to read. He got to the last sheet and read it thoroughly.

"What on earth is this, Mr. Ott?" He flipped it over to show his aide. Ott stood and leaned closer.

"Resignation!" Ott read aloud. "Charles Pendergrass, Hook and Ladder 20. I don't believe it. Not Charlie."

Edward reread the form. As battalion chief, deputy chief, and now chief of department, he'd fixed his signature to this form a handful of times over the years. Most young men had an idea of what they were getting themselves into by joining the fire department; and if they didn't, they soon learned and for the most part got along just fine. But every so often, a probie got a taste of a fireman's life and decided it wasn't for him. For the first time, Edward had a face to go along with the name on the form. He'd only met the young man that one time, but somehow seeing the name handwritten in the blank line of the preprinted form made Edward sad. Still, it was not his job to question this. The young man had a foreman, and a damn fine foreman at that. Edward had always been impressed by Jennings and the tight ship he ran. If Foreman Jennings signed the form, Edward was confident the matter was handled well. He picked up a fountain pen to sign his name, angled the wide and thin tip along the sheet and swirled a beautifully calligraphed *E* before raising the pen mid-signature. No. This wouldn't do. He folded the form and stood.

He drained his cup of tea in one long swig and reached for his peacoat and fedora from the coatrack. "Let's go, Mr. Ott," he said on his way out the door.

※

ANDREW STEERED THE RED Devil around two carriages and turned south on Mercer Street. The chief no longer argued with him about who would drive and Andrew had become quite the automobile enthusiast. The Mack *Manhattan* model truck he'd learned to drive at the elevator company had been much bulkier—the Red Devil, on the other hand, was built for speed. He stepped on the clutch and pulled back the stick as they rolled to a stop in front of the open bay door of the firehouse. Battalion Chief Worth and Foreman Jennings stood on the sidewalk with Smokey laying on his paws between them.

"Just the two men I'm looking for," Croker announced as he hopped out of the car.

Andrew turned off the motor, put the stick back in gear, and climbed down. He knelt down on the sidewalk and held out his arms. Smokey jumped up and ran over to lick Andrew's face.

"What can we do for you, Chief?" asked Jennings.

Andrew was petting the dog eagerly but listening in on the conversation.

"What happened with this Pendergrass fellow?" asked Croker.

"Not really sure, Chief," said Jennings. "Just not a good fit, I suppose. I tried to get him to hold off. Seems some of the men were ridin' him a bit, but those things always blow over."

"And you knew about this?" Croker asked Worth.

"Not until Mr. Jennings here brought the resignation form over to my office for signature. Bit of a mystery, anyhow," said Worth. "How the boy got here."

"What's that now?" asked Croker.

"Well, I mean, Chief Kenlon has been good to his word, only sending Twenty Truck men over six-foot-two. This kid comes out of nowhere and Chief Kenlon says he has no idea how he got here."

"Well, division commanders make requests and I sign off on them," Croker responded. "But the commissioner's office has final say about staffing."

Andrew switched from petting Smokey behind the ears to rubbing his belly. The animal happily obliged by rolling over. Andrew was a little surprised to hear Croker admit to any small detail of the fire department he did not personally control.

"What's this have to do with anything?" Croker asked.

Andrew looked up to see Worth and Jennings exchange glances. "Let's have it!" Croker chided.

"I think the men gave the kid a hard time after you lifted Ott," Jennings said bluntly. "They assumed you were the one who put him here, and they figured he was the one who told you about the horse shit incident."

"That's preposterous." Croker raised his voice.

Part of Andrew wanted to melt away, he didn't think he should be hearing this conversation among officers, but couldn't resist the chance to get all the details. So, he continued petting the dog.

"I've met the boy one time," Croker continued. "And it was that idiot patrolman's captain who told me about the horse shit. Why would you, as foreman, allow such nonsense to continue?"

Jennings was silent and Worth spoke up. "Chief, Foreman Jennings here came down hard on the two main instigators—has them doing extra overnight housewatches and extra stall sweepings. He keeps the men in line."

"I did try to convince the kid to stay, Chief," said Jennings. "But perhaps I didn't try hard enough. Truth be told, I didn't believe him when he said he didn't squeal on Ott here. He'd already gotten caught up in an other lie."

"What was that?" Croker asked sharply.

"Said he was taking meal break at home for his mother's birthday. Turns out he went to some garment workers meeting."

Andrew felt guilty that Charlie had been treated badly because of him. But why was Chief Croker getting so involved? He'd assumed a probie quitting would hardly be given a second thought by the chief of department.

Croker stepped back and pulled a cigar out of the inner pocket of his peacoat. He struck a match on the Red Devil's running board and puffed the cigar to life. "Do me a favor, Mr. Jennings—will you?"

"Sure thing, Chief."

"Fill out a request for special leave without pay for Pendergrass, backdate it two days ago, and sign it."

"Right away, Chief." Jennings went straight to the spiral stairs and disappeared.

Croker climbed into the Red Devil and sat in the passenger seat pensively stoking his cigar. "Did you have the second alarm on Broadway the other day, Mr. Worth?" he asked.

Worth stepped forward and rested his hands on the car's hood. "Yes, Chief. The companies all did well. We had the upper hand quite quickly."

Andrew stood and Smokey took the opportunity to head back inside the firehouse. Andrew walked around the car and climbed into the driver's seat. His leather cap and goggles lay on the dashboard. He only donned them for fire runs. A moment later Jennings came back out holding a sheet of paper and handed it to Croker. The chief examined it and handed the form to Andrew. He then reached in his pocket and pulled out another sheet. Andrew could see that it was Charlie's resignation. Croker tore the page in two and handed it to Jennings.

"To Lyons's, Mr. Ott," said the chief. "Straight away, I'm hungry."

30

CHARLIE STOOD OUTSIDE THE gatehouse at the entrance to the pier. For the second day in a row, the foreman hadn't picked him. Perhaps he was still sore at Charlie for having quit to join the fire department. And there Charlie was thinking he could be offered the union rigging position. That didn't seem likely now. He waited a while—to be sure no one else was needed—and then set off towards home.

"You look like the cat that missed the canary, Johnny," a gruff voice called out.

Charlie looked up. Waiting up at the street corner was Andrew Ott. Surprised, Charlie stared up. "What is this *Johnny* business about?"

Ott laughed heartily. "I thought that was your name?"

Charlie smiled. Ott hadn't been around when the other guys decided to ride him, and besides, Charlie liked Ott too much to hold any kind of grudge. He walked toward the big man and patted his shoulder as he went by.

"Where're ya' goin'?" Ott asked.

Charlie shrugged. "Home, I guess.

"Come with me."

CHARLIE SAT AT THE kitchen table in Andrew Ott's apartment. He held a steaming cup of coffee, with fresh cream and sugar. He sipped it slowly and let its earthy warmth settle over his whole body. It had been a windy morning on the pier, waiting for nothing.

"Wait'll you taste Lizzy's fried eggs," Ott said from his seat across the table. He leaned out of his chair and pinched his wife at the point where the buttock met the back of the thigh. As if she'd been expecting Ott's attempt, Lizzy swung a spatula around and whacked his hand. "Hoo-hoo," he squeaked, shaking his hand and then picking up his coffee. "She can work a spatula all right!" Ott made himself laugh, and Charlie couldn't resist chuckling himself.

"Andy—you didn't forget about our appointment today, did you?" Lizzy asked without turning from her cooking.

Ott had a mouthful of coffee and spat it back in the mug. His eyes bulged and—as he was clearly trying not to laugh—Charlie laughed harder.

"Andy!" Lizzy had now turned and was menacing her husband with the greasy end of the spatula. "We're meeting the agent at one o'clock. I told you last week."

"I know. I know," said Andrew. "I didn't forget." Lizzy turned back toward the stove and Ott made a funny face at Charlie. "I get one day off and I gotta go gallivantin' across Brooklyn."

Charlie was about to speak, but Lizzy beat him to it. "We're looking at a place in East New York, Charlie," she said with the same enthusiasm as if Charlie had asked her their plans for the day. "Have you ever been to East New York?"

"Can't say that I have. Been to Coney Island, though."

"Ha!" said Ott. "We love it there. Took the kids last year."

No sooner had he said kids than a baby began crying from the other room. Lizzy hovered the frying pan over the table and slid two fried eggs onto Charlie's plate and two onto Andrew's. "Charlie's hungry," she said.

Charlie *was* starving, but hadn't thought he'd exhibited any particular signs.

"Not you," said Ott. Charlie looked up and Andrew was pointing his fork toward the living room. "She means lil' Charlie, back there in his crib. Lil' Helen is around here somewhere too."

"Oh," Charlie smiled. "You named your boy after me?"

"No," answered Ott with an uncharacteristic serious look on his face. "Then we woulda had to call him Johnny!" He held strong for a minute, then began laughing.

"Will you please tell me where the hell Johnny comes from?"

Ott had no interest in answering—he was too busy cramming fried eggs in his mouth. It seemed to Charlie that he scooped them all in and swallowed in a single motion. Before he was done chewing, Ott got up and went to the hutch and brought a glass-covered cake plate to the table. He removed the domed top to reveal a tall, powdered-sugar coated cake baked into a ring.

"What on earth is that?" Charlie asked with a mouth full of eggs.

"Kugelhopf!" said Ott proudly. "From my pop's bakery. Wait'll you get a mouthful of this." He cut out a large wedge and slid it onto Charlie's egg-greased plate.

A scent of orange hit Charlie's nose and he could see bits of almonds and raisins dotting the golden spongey middle. "Thanks," Charlie mumbled as he swallowed the last of his eggs. "This is some breakfast."

"Where do you think *this* comes from?" said Ott as he gripped the sides of his belly with each hand and squeezed.

Charlie had been thinking the same thing. *No wonder he's such a big man!* Ott was indeed big, but not fat—just a jolly mass of muscle. Charlie glanced down at his own wiry frame, then cut off a piece of cake and forked it into his mouth. His taste buds flared with the touch of powdered sugar and then coalesced into a sweet, citrusy heaven. He'd never tasted anything like it before. He couldn't help but smile as he chewed.

"Listen, Charlie," Ott began, almost solemnly. "You're probably wonderin' why I brought ya here. I wanted to butter ya up a bit—in case you was still sore at me."

"Sore at you for what?"

"I feel like it's my fault the guys gave ya the business. The whole horse shit thing was my idea—and when the chief transferred me, the men thought you'd squealed on me or sumthin'."

"Look, Andrew..." Charlie put his fork down and looked straight into Ott's eyes. "I didn't say nothing. Not to the chief. Not anyone."

"I know. I know. That pain-in-the ass copper went crying to his captain. It was the captain who told the chief."

Charlie shrugged and took a sip of coffee. "Well, it's no difference now. I'm not a fireman anymore."

"Yes, you are." Solemnity having run its course, a friendly smile returned to Ott's face as he bit into the huge slice of cake he held in his hand.

"No—it's too late. I resigned."

"No," Ott insisted with a mouthful. "You didn't. Chief Croker ripped up your resignation. He got Jennings to put you on seven-days' unpaid leave. You're due back next week."

"But, I... I don't..." Charlie couldn't organize his thoughts.

"How are things going down on the docks?" asked Ott.

Charlie's face dropped. He shrugged.

"That's what I thought. See you at the firehouse."

Charlie was silent and Ott stood. "Gotta piss," he said and went out into the public hall, where the toilet cabinet was located.

Charlie walked into the living room where little Helen was playing with a set of wooden blocks on the oval rug. He could hear baby Charlie still fussing from the bedroom. Opposite the sofa, there was a fireplace built into the plastered wall with a thin molded lip for a mantel. Two framed pictures stood atop. One was a photograph of Ott with Lizzy on what appeared to be their wedding day. The other was a cut-out newspaper photo. It featured a team of pallbearers—all in military uniforms—carrying a coffin up a set of stairs. There was a horse-drawn hearse and scores of well-dressed women and men, dignitaries apparently, gathered up the steps. Charlie stepped closer to look at the pallbearers: soldiers, Marines, and sailors. Holding the back corner of the casket, wearing the distinct navy dress blues, blue neckerchief, and white cup hat, was Andrew Ott.

"Guess who's in the box?"

Charlie was startled by Ott's voice behind him. "Who?" he said, still staring at the photograph.

"President McKinley!"

"You're kidding me!"

"Honest to God—secretary of the navy wanted the tallest sailors and Marines he could find."

Charlie turned to see Ott standing in the middle of the room, holding another wedge of Kugelhopf. He bit into it and dropped crumbs on the carpet. "Oh—shit!" he exclaimed and then crouched down, still chewing and hurriedly scooped up the crumbs while sneaking peaks toward the bedroom door. Charlie watched the gentle giant, so tough at a fire, afraid of his wife's scorn. Charlie smiled. He thought about how interesting Ott's life was and how boring, until then, his own life had been. Charlie smiled and remembered what he had liked so much about being a fireman.

31

EDWARD SAT BACK IN his chair, feet up on the desk and blew out blue cigar smoke. It was a bright and sunny day, though still cold. He had the windows swung open and let the crisp March air circulate through the smokey office. There was a knock on the door.

"Enter," he called out.

The door creaked open and a young fireman in uniform cap poked his head in. "Chief, you have a visitor."

"Thank you, Mr. Stephens. Send him up."

A moment later the door swung fully in, and Edward was shocked. Filling out the entire door frame was none other than the Squire, Richard Croker. "He is not here! He has risen!" the Squire bellowed. "Remember how he told you, while he was still with you in Galilee!"

Edward sat up and lay his cigar on the edge of the desk. "Comparing yourself to Christ now, aye Uncle?"

Richard laughed. "I was talking about you, ya wily lil' bastard-ya. They sack ya, but here ya are—risen from the dead."

Edward stood and shook his uncle's hand. "Just a little parting gift from you I guess—delivered by one Thomas Sturgis."

"That sour prick," answered Richard.

"When did you get back?"

"Couple of days ago. I missed the smell of America," he said with a grin.

"I'll bet," Edward replied skeptically. "I'd heard you were into horse racing."

"Indeed, I am. A man of many interests."

"And what interests you now? Here in New York?"

Feigning insult, Richard stepped back with his hand on his heart. "Can't a man pay a simple visit to his dear nephew?"

"I'll bet," Edward said again as he reached for his cigar.

"A mighty fine office ya got here, Nephew. This firehouse is a work of art. I secured twice the usual funds for this design—sat with the architect myself. Every brass knob in this firehouse is of my own creation. Yet that horse's ass Scannell gets his name on the plaque out front."

"What brings you here? Really?"

Richard spun the aide's chair around and crashed his portly frame down hard. He was rounder at the gut, and grayer on top than the last time Edward had seen him, but still spoke with a youthful clarity. "I needed to settle some affairs here with the banks and so on—and I'm selling off the remaining property I hold. All boring stuff to a man of action such as yourself." Richard reached into his pocket and produced his own cigar. Edward took a match from the box on his desk, struck it, and held the dancing flame out for his uncle.

"Where will you stay?" Edward asked as he took his seat.

"Took a room at the Claremont. So, how is the family?"

"Good—Richard has finished his studies and took his commission, and Edward is doing well. Edith is sixteen, now. Lovely little lady she is."

Richard blew out smoke and frowned. "I hear things you know."

"What sort of things?"

"You spend all of your time in the city here. You are estranged from your wife—she's raised the children on her own."

Edward balled his left hand into a fist. He took a long draw from his cigar and held it in for a while. When at last he exhaled, he simply nodded.

"Sad business—really," said Richard. "Through all my ups and downs, Elizabeth has been by my side. The children are another story all together. Richard and Howard hardly ever write. Only my dear Florence shows any respect for her parents."

Edward was silent, and after a few moments Richard revealed the true reason for his visit. "The aldermen are getting antsy," he began. "The Tammany men are split on your sprinkler proposal. Murphy is against it. He wants the state legislature to pass a watered-down law without sprinklers—thinks he can have his cake and eat it too, if you ask me."

"How so?" Edward asked.

"Well, he's no fool. The Progressives have a strong showing at the ballot box and can't be ignored. But since the civil service was reformed and patronage has all but gone away, the only way for Tammany Hall to hold power is to keep the wealthy of this city happy."

"What's any of this got to do with me?"

"You can have your sprinklers."

Edward knew better than to get too excited. He casually puffed his cigar. "What's the catch?"

"Catch?"

"The catch—you're not here out of charity. If there's a deal to be had for the sprinklers, I'm sure it's to your benefit."

The Squire was unfazed by the assumption. "McKay is the key. He can secure enough votes to pass a city ordinance for sprinklers in the five boroughs. Word is the mayor will sign off. Far cry from my day, if you ask me. It would have been unimaginable for a Tammany alderman to even consider voting against my wishes."

"Until they were done with you and ran for cover."

"Ha!" Richard coughed out smoke. "True enough."

"So how do you fit into all this, Uncle? Tell me the truth."

"You'll remember my compressed air-pipe company..."

"From the Elevated Railroad debacle?"

"Goddamned Goulds! Father and son, both crooks."

Rather rich, Edward thought, the Squire complaining of crooks.

"They promised me the contract for compressed pipes on the elevated lines and reneged."

"It's been ten years, Uncle. I think the time has come to let bygones be bygones."

"Couldn't agree more. Anyhow, the company is still doing well enough."

Edward was starting to put the pieces together. "And you still own your shares, I take it."

"Indeed, I do. They made me sell my interests in the ice company, but not the air-pipes."

"And let me guess—McKay is giving you the inside track for sprinkler installations."

Richard pulled his cigar from his lips and raised his eyebrows: "It's a very natural progression. We'll be the first company certified to install fire sprinklers. The others will have to wait months."

Edward was not in the least surprised. He was, however, unsure how any of this pertained to him. "Uncle, I've made my thoughts on the necessity of automatic fire sprinklers quite clear. It would seem to me that any service I'd be to you or the alderman has already been rendered."

"Not so fast, my boy. The aldermen are still stuck on the whole fire drill question. Drop the whole fire drill business—and the inspectors. Be vocal in your support of a stand-alone sprinkler ordinance and it will pass the Board."

"It is the Board's prerogative to pass whichever ordinance it sees fit," Edward insisted. "But it's my job to make honest recommendations. The fire drills and inspectors will save lives."

Richard sat back, casually making his way through the cigar. "I'm afraid it's sprinklers only or no law at all. Or worse—the state legislature's bill." He waited a moment and then added. "You may ensure the quality of the sprinklers yourself, of course. My partners are willing to offer you a stake in the company."

Edward quickly protested: "My position and my conscience would never allow such an arrangement!"

"The stock need not be in your name, if that's what worries you."

"Uncle—my answer is no."

Richard took another draw. "Suit yourself, lad"

32

It was already dark, and many workers from the Asch Building had already come out. The Triangle factory, however, was still working. Charlie stood across the street on Washington Place, waiting. He'd bought an evening edition from the newsboy on the corner and now leaned against a brick wall and read the folded paper. Esther had said she worked at the Triangle Waist Company. He'd read about it during the strike and knew where it was, he thought. But now he doubted himself. *What if there's more than one factory?* He decided to wait fifteen more minutes.

At last, scores of young women poured out of the building's Greene Street entrance. It was a steady stream and Charlie put the rolled-up newspaper in his pocket and crossed the street to get a better look at the faces. It was quite some time before he found Esther. She was gripping the arm of a younger girl and limping. Through the sea of exiting seamstresses, she saw Charlie and smiled.

"Are you well?" he asked. "Your legs—still sore I see."

"They're fine," she answered.

"Are not!" the other girl objected.

"Charlie, this is my sister, Rachel—Rachel this is Charlie."

"Pleased to meet you, Rachel," he said and held out a hand.

Rachel lay her hand in his and let him shake. She giggled a bit when she said: "Hello, Charlie." Then, apparently remembering her objection she added: "I think her legs are broken."

Charlie looked uselessly at Esther's skirt. "Probably not broken. She wouldn't be able to walk. But it wouldn't surprise me if there was a fracture."

"They're just bruised," said Esther.

"She fell this morning," said Rachel.

"You should be resting," he said.

"I can't miss work," Esther answered quickly.

"Can I walk you home?"

Esther smiled and Charlie held out his arm. She grabbed hold and they walked while Charlie told her about his resignation and conversation with Ott. The walk was slow, but Charlie wanted it to last forever. He liked her leaning on his arm.

"Will you help her up the stairs?" Rachel asked when they reached their stoop. Charlie happily agreed and Rachel went up.

"Are you going back, then?" Esther asked as she eased herself down to sit on the step.

"Yeah—I think I'll go tomorrow morning and talk to Foreman Jennings."

"Smart boy, Charlie," Esther said with a smile. The temperature had dropped, and her hands were shaking. Charlie sat and took her hands in his and rubbed for a moment to warm them, then he just held them and looked into her eyes.

"Is it all right that I came to your work to meet you?"

She smiled. "I'm glad you did."

"I'd like to see you again. I have to see about work now, when I go to the firehouse tomorrow. But my next day off, I'd like to see you."

"I'd like that too."

He put his palm on her cheek, then gave a quick glance up and down the street to check for onlookers. Confident they were alone; he leaned in and kissed her lips—softly and only briefly. She quietly allowed the kiss and then stood, slowly while holding the handrail for balance. Once she was upright, she looked down at him, still seated. She reached down and grabbed his chin, then leaned down and met her lips to his again.

She turned to go inside, and Charlie stood and followed her awkwardly, not knowing how best to assist. He was behind her on the steps and decided to put a hand on her shoulder. She made no objection, and continued her slow ascent with both hands on the railing. Each time Charlie stepped up to follow, his face neared the back of her head and he caught the scent of her hair.

Esther lay awake in her bed well into the night. Every time she thought her sister was asleep, Rachel turned over and asked for more details. How did it feel? Were his lips soft? Did he hug you in his arms? Esther didn't mind. She was still reveling and playing the kisses over and over in her mind anyway.

"I wish Gaspar would kiss me," Rachel said, hugging her blanket close to her chest.

Esther smiled and remembered when she was Rachel's age. It was young to be working fifty-two hours a week in a factory. Others her age went to school. At the dances, Esther could always tell the students from the workers. The girls wore full dresses instead of shirtwaists and skirts; the boys wore blazers. And they acted differently, seemed to have a language all their own. Esther had only ever socialized with other factory workers at the dances. Still, she wished Rachel could have been in school, instead of working as a seamstress. Not that Rachel seemed to mind. She was a happy girl, and—truth be told—Triangle would be worse for Esther if she didn't have her sister with her all day. Esther closed her eyes and drifted toward sleep—for the first time since Saturday thinking about something other than the attack.

Sometime later, Esther awoke with a startle. Rachel's deep breathing was peaceful, and the apartment was otherwise quiet, but Esther's heart was racing as if there'd been a loud, sudden noise. She stared at Rachel's back and felt a pang of guilt.

Clara and Rachel *had* seemed to understand why she didn't want to help the legislature anymore. But it was more than just her physical safety she worried about. She had a deep uneasiness. The life she'd been working so hard to build—the job, the apartment, the language lessons, the dances—could be gone in an instant. It was like Bialystok just before the pogrom. They had the factory, their home, their friends. She'd had her father. And in the blink of an eye, they were all gone. Being a public witness for the legislature would bring attention. The Jewish factory owners and textile workers in Bialystok had gotten attention. Esther wanted to avoid it.

33

Charlie was up before sunrise. The coffee pot had just begun boiling and he paced across the dark kitchen, fully dressed, waiting. He was trying to be quiet, but must have awakened his mother nonetheless. She came into the kitchen in an old nightgown and grabbed two cups from the shelf, set them in tandem on the table, and sat without speaking.

Charlie poured two cups. He set out the sugar and remembered how proud he'd been to be able to afford it. He slid open the window that faced the tenement's airshaft. Outside on the windowsill there was a glass bottle with a rag stuffed in the top. He brought it in, set it on the table and closed the window. His mother removed the rag stopper and poured the cold milk into her coffee and reached for the sugar. He added milk and waited for the sugar. After she'd taken a proper sip, his mother spoke: "Gettin' out extra early today. Think that'll make'm pick ya?"

"I'm not going to the docks."

"So, then. Where are you off to?"

"The firehouse."

"What on earth for? I thought you quit."

"Well, I'm going to talk to the foreman. Maybe I can go back."

"What will be different this time?"

He swirled the coffee around in his cup and sipped. "With the other firemen—maybe nothing. But I'm different."

There was a long silence and Charlie wondered if she'd drifted back to sleep. It was too dark to see her eyes. But at last, she spoke: "Why did you quit? Really?"

"I told you."

"You told me the other fellas didn't like you. So what? Surely some of the scoundrels at that saloon were mean to ya. And how about the docks? Don't tell me every man down there is a saint. So, some of the fellas was mean to ya. You're tougher than that—been through worse. Didn't you tell me how much you was likin' being a fireman?"

"That was before."

"Before what?"

Frustration was building, Charlie didn't like where his mother was taking the conversation. He'd made up his mind already to go back to the firehouse. What difference did it make why he'd quit? "I just... You don't understand."

"I'm a smart old broad—try me."

"It was starting to feel like the saloon all over again. I hated working there—working for *him*. Everyone saw me as Big Charlie's nephew, even though he ain't my uncle. It's *his* fault Pa is gone, and he gets to act so smug like he's takin' care of me. When the men thought I squealed to the chief and got one of them in trouble, they looked at me like the men in the saloon used to."

"So, what now?" She stood and refilled her cup. Faint light was creeping in from the living room windows and the kitchen now had a soft, almost candle-lit aura. "You're different you say. How so?"

"I see the life I want and I'm taking it. Don't care what the other men think—and I don't care what *he* thinks. I ain't letting him parade me around anymore at no meetings or anything. That's what started all this trouble. I don't owe him nothing."

CHARLIE KNOCKED ON THE firehouse door wearing his rubber slicker and leather helmet, and carrying his denim coat, boots, and a duffle bag. He'd left the door key that Foreman Jennings had given him in his locker when he resigned. He waited a minute and then knocked again. He could hear Smokey barking and then the door swung in. Floyd Mance stood at the door in his uniform cap. Charlie had hoped one of the younger men would be on housewatch.

"Look who's back!" Mance said dryly. He stepped back and held the door open so Charlie could enter.

Smokey jumped up and put his paws on Charlie's chest. He set his things on the floor and began petting the dog behind his ears. "Smokey Boy!—Did you miss me?"

"Yeah—we all went to pieces without ya," said Mance as he let the door swing closed and went back to the housewatch desk.

Charlie moved his gear to the work bench with Smokey following. He looked up into the pole hole. It was dark upstairs. He decided to go make coffee in the kitchen while he waited for Foreman Jennings to wake up.

"You're officially on a seven-day leave of absence—without pay," Jennings said after he had come downstairs and poured himself coffee. Charlie stood awkwardly with his back against the counter as other waking firemen came in for coffee, filled cups and left.

"Thank you, sir," Charlie answered. "I appreciate you giving me another chance."

"Well—it was Chief Croker's idea. He seems to have taken an interest in you."

Charlie gave no response.

"Not that I mind at all," the foreman continued. "I thought you were acting a bit rashly anyhow."

"Yes, sir."

"Good, then. I'll see you first thing Monday morning."

"Monday, sir? I'm ready to start now."

Jennings took another sip of coffee and shook his head. "The leave of absence already went through. I'll not ruffle up any more feathers trying to undo it. You can wait till Monday."

"Yes, sir."

Charlie knelt by the front door and gave Smokey a goodbye petting. He glanced up at Floyd Mance, still at the housewatch desk, with his feet up reading a newspaper. "See you Monday, Floyd," he called over optimistically. Mance kept reading but held two fingers to his forehead quickly in a mock salute.

Charlie walked up Mercer Street and crossed Houston. Vendors pushed their hand carts along the wide street, laden with fruits, vegetables, or baked goods en route to their usual corners and alleys. He continued north a few blocks and then turned right, crossed Broadway and walked east along Great Jones Street. A row of stables on the south side of the street had all its horses out while the stablers swept out and hosed down the stalls. The majestic Engine 33 firehouse had both bay doors open. Chief Croker's Red Devil was pulled up, half in, half outside. Andrew Ott was washing the car with a big sudsy sponge.

"Hay—make sure you get all the shit off the wheels," Charlie said loudly from twenty feet away or so.

Ott kept working the sponge around the shiny red fender. When Charlie was within ten feet or so, Ott swung his other hand up and pointed in his direction. He was holding the end of a black rubber hose and he flicked the valve open with his thumb and sprayed a wide stream of cold water at Charlie. Ott's huge frame heaved with deep laughter as he chased Charlie up the sidewalk.

"Goddamnit!" Charlie yelled as he ran—but he too could not help laughing. In the end, Ott was content to dampen Charlie's hair and coat a little and he ceased the chase. He dragged the long hose back toward the car and rinsed off the suds.

"Did ya go and talk to the skipper?"

"Yeah," answered Charlie. "Just came from the firehouse."

"How'd it go?"

"Good—Mr. Jennings said I was still on leave but that I'd start again on Monday."

Ott tossed the sponge into a bucket and wiped his hands on his pants. He patted Charlie on the shoulder. "See—all good."

"Thanks for coming to find me at the docks. And for lookin' out for me."

"That's what we do in the firehouse. We look out for each other." Ott wrung the sponge and began wiping the other fender.

"Well—we'll see if the others feel I'm worth lookin' out for."

"Who was there this morning?"

"Mance was on the housewatch—he didn't seem too happy to see me."

Ott stood up straight and squeezed the sponge to let brownish, sudsy water run down to the sidewalk. "Let me tell ya somethin' about Floyd," he began. "When I first came to Twenty Truck, he was the hardest on me of all of 'em."

Charlie had no trouble believing it.

"He rode me like an unbroken mule—never let up. Maybe because I'm bigger than him and tend to talk a bit..."

Charlie was about to feign disbelief. *No... not you!* But decided against.

"...probably figured he needed to put me in my place. And he drilled me day and night. Every time we got back from a run, he had me grab the thirty-footer and throw it up on the front of the building—by myself."

Charlie thought about how heavy the thirty-foot straight ladder was. It was really a two-man operation to lift it in place. One time, in the Fire College, he had attempted to raise it by himself. He'd pushed the butts against the building and started at the far end, hands on the rails above his head, walking under the ladder and pushing it up. He got about two thirds of the way before the heavy wooden rails came back down on top of him.

"Well one day—it's freezin' outside, with wind whippin' so hard my hands are numb. Mance has got me out front throwin' up ladders. I thought my hands was gonna fall off. Finally, I had enough and I told Mance I was gonna stick the ladder right up his ass."

"You really said that?"

"I did. And Mance, I'll tell ya, Charlie. He's a tough ol' bastard. He come runnin' at me like he wants to kill me. Allen Smith was on the housewatch and heard the yellin'. He come runnin' out and got between us. He got Mance to go inside and have a cup of coffee. Then he helped me put the ladder away."

"That was good of him," Charlie offered, a little bitter at the fact that no one stood up to Mance on *his* behalf.

"Ya know what Smith told me about Mance?"

Charlie shook his head.

"Said that Mance used to work in Nine Truck. Transferred to Hook and Ladder Twenty a few years before I got there. Said there was a fifth alarmer at the corner of Grand Street and Allen and Mance's foreman was killed."

"I didn't know that," said Charlie.

"Yeah—well, Mance doesn't talk about it, ever. Smith says the foreman was climbing a ladder and the butts slipped out. The foreman fell straight to the ground and died. That's why Mance is such a maniac when it comes to raising ladders. He was at that fire where his skipper died. I don't know if he was the one who raised that ladder or not—but I was the first probie in Twenty for a while and he took it on himself to make damn sure I could raise a ladder."

"But it sounds like he was even more awful to you than he is to me."

Ott smiled. "Yeah—and boy did I hate 'em. Then one day, right before my probation was over, Mance and I was overhaulin' a second alarm in a factory. The engine opened the nozzle on a hot cast-iron column and the son-of-a-bitch cracked. The beam above started comin' down right on top of me. Mance pushed me outta the way and jammed the ten-foot hook he was usin' under the beam."

"That was quick thinking."

"Yeah—it was. He wasn't under the beam when the column cracked. He stepped under it to save me. I didn't hate 'em after that."

Charlie was thoughtful and quiet.

"And don't worry about the men," Ott added. "I'm going over there later on today. I'm gonna tell them you wasn't the one who squealed to the chief."

"Thank you, but don't bother yourself with that. I'm going to come back Monday and work hard. They can judge me on how I work."

"It's no bother—it's the right thing to do."

"It's fine, really."

"Well, we're headin' there anyway. Chief Croker said he needs to talk to Chief Worth."

"Change of plans, Mr. Ott," a loud stern voice called out from inside the firehouse.

Charlie looked in to see Chief Croker coming down the stairs. "Chief Worth is coming here this morning instead," the chief added.

"Aye-aye, skipper," said Ott while rinsing the remaining soap from the automobile.

"Mr. Pendergrass! Enjoying your leave of absence, are you?"

"Yes, Chief," Charlie replied. "And I wanted to thank you."

"For what? My signature? Nonsense. Just remember what I told you after the garment union meeting. Do you remember?"

Charlie thought, afraid to give the wrong answer.

"Be a *fireman,* Mr. Pendergrass," Croker bellowed as he stowed a leather satchel under the seat of the Red Devil. "There's nothing better—right Mr. Ott?"

"Right you are, skipper," Ott shot back enthusiastically.

"Oh," the chief continued. "Don't worry at all, Mr. Ott. We'll have time later this evening to drive to Twenty Truck."

"What for, Chief?" Ott asked.

"You'll need to get all your gear, and the clothes in your locker—not to mention that god-awful smelling cheese you keep in my office—back down to Mercer Street."

Charlie shrugged as Ott looked to him with a confused look on his face.

"You're going back to Hook and Ladder Twenty," Croker said. "I've found a permanent aide."

A big smile came over Ott's face. "What about that police captain?"

"To hell with him! If he were going to do anything, he'd have done it already." Croker gave Ott a smile and winked at Charlie before heading back in toward the stairs.

Ott clapped his hands. Every tooth in his head showed as his smile went from ear to ear. "I'm back, Charlie!"

Charlie slapped Ott's shoulder and for the first time in a while, felt truly happy.

34

Max sat in his study, still working long after supper and after the children had gone to bed. Even the butler had retired for the evening. His wife, Bertha, knocked and slid the study door open. "Max, dear—Samuel is here."

"By God—does he not know the time?"

"Shall I send him away?"

"Ugh. No—you can send him in."

"And Max, dear," Bertha added as she took a step into the room. "Don't forget, you promised Henrietta and Mimi you'd bring them downtown tomorrow."

This brought a smile to Max's face. "Ah, yes of course. They can come to the factory with me for a while. We'll make a day of it. Then we'll ride over to Siegel and Cooper's. It'll be great fun!"

Bertha went out and a moment later, Bernstein came in. "Sorry to call so late, Max."

"Have a seat, Samuel. Would you like a drink?"

Bernstein nodded and stepped toward the side table topped with carafes and glasses. "Top me off, as well," said Max, holding up an emptied glass that had been sitting on his desk.

When Bernstein brought him the refilled glass, Max noticed his hand was shaking. He watched his factory manager walk over to the sofa and was quite sure his steps were unsteady. He spun awkwardly and fell heavily into the seat, nearly spilling his drink. Bernstein was drunk.

"What's on your mind?" Max cut right to the point.

"I don't think... we should use Schlansky anymore."

Max grinned. "Isaac and I are more than capable of making such decisions. Will that be all, Samuel?"

"I didn't mind so much when he was breaking up the picket lines. The picketers were preventing people who *wanted* to work from working. But this is different."

"What on earth are you talking about?"

"That girl. You set him on that girl. And for what? Talking to Smith and that woman he's got with him?"

Max rose and went to the door. He slid it open and motioned for Bernstein to leave. "Goodnight, Samuel," he said sharply.

Bernstein did not get up. "Don't do it," he mumbled.

"I beg your pardon," said Max—his patience gone.

"I know what you're planning to do. The overstock—you had me stack it all together on the ninth floor. I know what you've got planned. It's that Schlansky, I'm sure." Bernstein's speech was slightly slurred. "Is this what we came to America for? To beat young girls and steal money? That's what it is, you know, stealing!"

"So, you are my conscience now. Is that it?"

Bernstein shook his head. "I believe in hard work—I'll be tough with anyone who stands in the way of hard work." He raised his glass to down the remains. "But I..." Trying to speak and drink at the same time, he spilled brandy all over his lap and part of the sofa.

"Oh, dear God," Max bellowed. He grabbed Bernstein by the arm and yanked him up. He took the glass from his hand and shoved him toward the door. "Go home, Samuel. Now."

Bernstein said nothing as he moved unevenly through the hall and let himself out the front door. Max took a handkerchief from his pocket and dabbed the leather sofa pad.

Bernstein was his brother-in-law and a damn fine factory manager. But this was unacceptable. No one would tell him how he and Isaac should run their business. Bernstein knew how to organize production, but he didn't know how to run a business. No one but the emperor knew what went into building an empire. If Max had let the employees dictate factory floor conditions, Triangle would be little more than a well-furnished boutique with three women sipping tea and sewing at their leisure. These young women walked picket lines and shouted that he was a greedy monster. They were too young to remember the tenement sweatshops. They didn't know how good they had it at Triangle—open floor space, windows, light, and air! And most of all a steady job. He kept them all employed. And how did he do that? With sound business decisions. He bought fabric cheap, in great bulk. He sold what he could and then found ways to profit from the overstock. Was he wrong to take advantage of the rules the insurance companies played by? The insurance brokers were certainly happy to collect commission on the high premiums he paid. They weren't asking too many questions.

PART FOUR

35

Saturday, March 25, 1911

Esther was having a hard time concentrating on the stitch she was laying. She kept glancing across the table at Rachel, who seemed equally distracted. The sisters smiled at each other, and Esther fed the fabric under the pounding needle. She couldn't wait to hear the closing bell. Charlie had promised to meet her downstairs and take her out to dinner. There was another dance that Saturday evening, Rachel was going with Ida and Francine. But Esther's legs were still too achy and stiff for dancing, so Charlie suggested dinner at a restaurant instead.

Samuel was eager for the closing bell to ring. He had a headache and his stomach had been off—the lingering effects of over drinking the night before. The morning had been terrible. He struggled out of bed feeling like death itself but was not late for work. Through a foggy memory he thought of his late-night visit to Max's home and fully expected Blanck to come find him that Saturday. But he never came, and Samuel did his best to avoid the tenth floor.

"Mr. Bernstein, Mr. Bernstein," called Dinah, the eighth-floor accountant.

Samuel went from the cutter's table he'd been leaning against over to Dinah's table near the coatroom. There was another young woman by the table as well.

"Yes, Dinah—what is it?"

"I'm sorting out the pay for the new girl here and I can't find her rate in my notes. Do you know by chance what it is?"

Samuel looked at the new seamstress. She was Italian, he could tell. Her olive skin and dark hair were giveaways. She was avoiding eye contact. He closed his eyes and tried to think. The headache was still pounding away. "Fourteen dollars," he said at last.

The seamstress looked up at him, seemingly shocked. Then, in broken English, asked Dinah for confirmation: "He say a Four-teen?"

Dinah looked at Samuel, who said nothing. She nodded, and the seamstress gave a big smile. Dinah made an entry in her ledger and then put some bills and coins in a small envelope and handed it to the seamstress.

"Misters Harris and Blanck take on a new partner, did they?" said Dinah once the seamstress was gone.

"Come again?" said Samuel.

"Fourteen dollars a week is a tad generous. Is it not?"

"I, uhh..." Samuel closed his eyes and put his hand on his forehead. Searching for an acceptable response, he offered weakly: "She comes from H. Simmons and Sons—highly experienced."

Dinah gave an incredulous grin and returned to her ledger.

"Fire!" a woman shouted from across the floor. Her high-pitched scream pierced his throbbing skull.

He turned toward the Greene Street entrance and noticed the smoke. A woman was running toward him. She yelled again:

"There's a fire, Mr. Bernstein!"

Charlie walked slowly down Broadway. The cold of early March had broken, and it was a pleasant spring day. He was a bit early to meet Esther, so he stopped at the barber shop at the corner of Broadway and Astor Place for a shave. Although he was not getting paid for this week, he still had some money left over from the last—enough to take Esther out to a restaurant and to pay for a fancy shave. He was happy to not have to shape anymore. He'd have a steady paycheck.

He lay back in the padded chair as the barber rubbed hot cream over his cheeks and neck and thought of his cousin, Charles Murphy. Silent Charlie went to the barber almost every morning. After his father's death, and while he worked at the saloon, Charlie had always felt the shadow of his powerful cousin looming over him. That shadow still loomed through Charlie's entrance into the fire department. He'd hated the way everyone treated him at the saloon—Big Charlie's little cousin. And he'd hated the other firemen seeing him as under Chief Croker's thumb.

The barber gracefully whisked the razor across his cheek, taking off cream and stubble alike, and leaving smooth, pink flesh in its wake. Charlie felt refreshed by each stroke of the barber's hand, like the old Charlie was being wiped away. Whatever Charles Murphy had done for him had been as much to his own benefit as it had been to Charlie's. He now owed the man nothing and would make his own way accordingly. He had a new start at the firehouse. He had a date that night with Esther.

A block south of the barber was a push-cart apothecary. An old man sold small bottles of powders and potions, but it was the bushel of flowers that caught Charlie's attention. Bright yellow petals adorned long green stems. Charlie had no idea what type of flower it was, but the small paper card pinned on the bushel said *1 cent each*. He handed a penny to the old man and chose his favorite from the bunch. He continued down Broadway with a flutter in his belly. He couldn't wait to see Esther's face when he held out the flower for her. Perhaps he would offer to hold her hand as they walked over to Washington Square Park. They could sit on a bench for a while, before they went to the restaurant.

※

MAX BLANCK AND ISAAC Harris sat in Max's office on the tenth floor, drinking tea. Max's four-year-old-daughter, Mimi, sat on the floor wrapping her doll in the various colors of linen cuts that Max had sent Mary down to the cutters' tables to retrieve. Dressing the doll in wonderful new shades and shapes was Mimi's favorite thing about visiting the Triangle factory, and she had set her doll by the front door of their home the night before so she wouldn't forget it. Twelve-year-old Henrietta, on the other hand, was more excited about the impending shopping her father had promised. She sat on the small sofa and flipped through the catalog from Siegel and Cooper's Department Store. It was her favorite place—selling everything from dresses and hats to books and toys. There was even a hairdresser and restaurant on premises.

"They're conspiring," Harris said while sipping tea. "Bertha and Bella have their minds set on a trip to Europe next year."

"Well, wives have time for fantasies," Max said with a chuckle. "But we have factories to run."

"You wouldn't like to see London—or Paris?" Harris replied.

Max drained his fine demi-tasse and set it on the saucer. "Don't tell me you've gone soft as well, Isaac."

Harris laughed. "How could I? You'd be in the asylum if it wasn't for me."

Max ignored Harris's comment and leaned down to pick up Mimi's doll. "What is Daisy wearing today?" he asked.

Thrilled to talk about her fashion choices, Mimi pointed to the sheer pink cuttings she'd wrapped around the doll and fired off a detailed list of each of the garment's features. "Here are the shoulder straps," she said, indicating the two poorly tied knots she'd fastened. "And here are the peets."

"*Pleats*, darling," said Max, admiring the little folds Mimi had made at the bottom.

"Do you like it, Papa?" Mimi asked softly, looking right into Max's eyes, waiting for his approval.

"I don't recall ever seeing a prettier dress," said Max. Mimi beamed a big smile. "Wouldn't you agree, Isaac?" added Max.

"Yes. Of course. I think Mimi will be head designer here at the factory," Harris answered. "When she's finished school, of course."

"Henrietta..." Mimi called across the room. "I'mma be heddesigner!"

Henrietta was far less excited than her sister and continued flipping catalog pages.

SAMUEL HAD DEALT WITH small fires over the years. The important thing was to apply water quickly, before embers could grow into flames. For this reason, he'd been adamant about keeping water buckets full and readily available. The smoke he saw now, however, was more than just smoldering embers. The cutters and assistants in the area knocked over stools in their scramble to flee. Smoke was already pushing along the ceiling and banking down. He could hardly see the row of windows along Greene Street.

"Dinah," he called back without turning. "Alert the operator." Samuel went to the wall outside the coatroom and retrieved a pail of water. Dinah leaned over her table and picked up the stylus of the telautograph machine. She was frantically scratching out the word *Fire* with one hand while pressing a small red button with the other.

With the water pail in one hand, Samuel went quickly along the back wall toward the fire, picking up a second pail along the way.

"Jonathan," he said to a cutter's assistant. "Bring me the hose from the stairwell—hurry."

The smoke was thick, but Samuel saw it was emanating from the bin under the last cutter's table. The table's worktop was piled high with dozens of layers of lawn and two piles of tissue paper. Samuel put one bucket on the floor so he could upend the other with two hands. In quick succession he threw the contents of each pail into the bin. But this only seemed to anger the flames. Orange licks shot up from the sides and back of the table. The tissue was now engulfed and flames danced up and caught the several cloth templates hanging from wires above. Jonathan handed Samuel the nozzle of the stairwell hose and went back to the Greene Street stairwell to turn the valve. Samuel watched him get pushed aside several times by fleeing seamstresses at the bottleneck of people by the wooden partition enclosing the stairwell door. At last, the assistant made it through, but no water was coming.

<hr />

MAX WENT TO THE switchboard to ask Mary to place a telephone call to his wife. He'd decided to treat the girls to dinner at Siegel and Cooper's and wanted to let her know to dine without them. "Mary, would you..." He was interrupted by a small bell ringing in two-second intervals over and over.

Mary spun in her seat and reached for the telautograph machine. She held her hand under the feeder and waited. Max watched in silence as she stood and leaned over the unit. The bell was still ringing, but the long pen fastened in place by hinged brackets made no move.

"What's going on with that thing?" Max asked impatiently.

"Oh, nothing, Uncle. Someone's just havin' a little fun with the bells is all. There's no message." Mary turned and sat. "They like to fool around at closing time," she added with a wistful smile.

"So glad we paid for that damned contraption. Will you call in a message for Bertha, please?"

SAMUEL WAITED FOR WHAT seemed an eternity. But still, the hose was limp. He turned and looked across the floor. Dinah was still at the table pressing the button on the telautograph. "Dinah," he shouted. "Get all the girls out of here!"

"No one is writing back," Dinah yelled.

"Dinah—get the girls out!"

He watched Dinah abandon the telautograph and reach for the telephone.

Jonathan came back from the stairwell. "I turned the valve all the way, Mr. Bernstein. There's no water."

The suspended templates above the three surrounding cutters' tables were now burning.

"Get the hose from the other stairwell, Jonathan," Samuel shouted and then grabbed two more water buckets and doused the piles of lawn and tissue on neighboring cutters' tables, hoping to stop the spread. He turned and saw Jonathan at the Washington Place stairwell door. He was tugging fruitlessly at the doorknob. The door wasn't moving.

MAX WAS ALMOST BACK in his office when he again heard a bell ringing at Mary's desk. His anger swelled and he was about to discuss getting rid of the telautograph with Isaac, who was still seated in Max's office. Instead, he heard Mary's voice and realized it had been the telephone ringing, not the telautograph. He turned and watched Mary. Her hand held the plug-end of a switchboard wire. Her voice was raised:

"Dinah—I can't hear you. The shouting! I can't hear you," said Mary.

Max watched as panic descended on Mary's face. She let go of the plug and dropped the telephone receiver. "There's a fire on the eighth floor," she yelled.

∞

SAMUEL WENT TO THE passenger elevators beside the Washington Place stairs. He pressed the call bell. Nearby, he heard Dinah yelling into the phone: "Mary—wait... Mary... Mary."

"Dinah," Samuel called across. "Get out."

"Mr. Bernstein," Dinah answered with tears streaming down her cheeks. "Mary didn't hang up the line. I can't call the ninth floor."

At that moment, one of the elevators arrived. Samuel saw the horror in young Joseph's face when he saw the smoke and flames now overtaking the eighth floor. There was a crowd of seamstresses at the rear window, trying to make it onto the fire escape. "Girls, Girls," he shouted. This way. A dozen young women ran for the elevator. Samuel grabbed Dinah's arm and pushed her toward the elevator as well. "I'll go warn the others on Nine," he told her.

It was difficult to see through the smoke. He saw Jonathan still working on the stairwell door. He had a pair of oversized cutters scissors and was trying to pry the door out. Samuel didn't want to waste time. He was determined to make it through the smoke to the Greene Street stairwell to warn those on the ninth floor. He took a few steps deeper into the smoke and his eyes burned. From behind, he heard Jonathan calling out: "Mr. Bernstein, Mr. Bernstein!"

He turned and saw the assistant coming toward him with a dry fire hose. "We got the door open a bit—here's the hose," he said, handing the heavy brass nozzle to Samuel.

Samuel dragged the dry hose toward the Greene Street side, getting ever closer to the flames. He expected a flow of water any second. He waited and waited. He didn't need Jonathan to return and tell him the valve was useless. His anger boiled up. No one had bothered to test the standpipes after their installation. The water tanks on the roof were supposed to feed the standpipes, but something was wrong. He decided to wait another minute, just in case the hose miraculously sprung to life, and for the moment forgot he'd been on his way to warn the ninth floor.

※

Esther's foreman arrived with her pay envelope. Mr. Craven walked along the row of sewing machines distributing the week's wages and Esther took the opportunity created by his back being toward her to reach under the table and pull up her coat and handbag. She'd retrieved them from the coatroom during lunch break. She slipped her arms into the coat and went into her handbag to pull out her time card. She pushed the last blouse she'd been stitching forward—leaving it for Monday morning—and waited with her hands through the bag loops holding the card. She was determined to be the first at the Greene Street stairwell partition once the closing bell rang. She couldn't wait to start her date with Charlie. She had the whole escape planned out. The second the bell rang, she'd run to the exit, punch her time card, and hold her bag open for the inspector. She'd probably be the first one on the stairs, which was good. The stairs were narrow and once they got crowded, the descent could be slow.

She looked across the table. Rachel beamed a big smile and was holding up her envelope. She silently mouthed the words: "Ten dollars." Esther gave a big smile in return.

The bell rang and screeching chairs pushed across the floor. "See you, later," she said quickly to Rachel as she rose and started her sprint. This would be her first attempt, since the attack, down the stairs without Rachel's help. She was determined.

"Have fun, Est," Rachel called after her. Esther's legs ached. Deep in her thigh muscles, sharp jolts of pain shot up, but she ignored them and weaved around the other seamstresses. To her annoyance, there was already a small line of like-minded young women. All around was the sound of laughter and newfound liberty. The line of workers behind Esther was getting long and one of the young women began singing:

Every little movement has a meaning all its own,

Esther knew the tune well. She smiled and mouthed the lyrics softly to herself. Others, however, joined in loudly:

Every thought and feeling by some posture can be shown...

"Look—out there!" someone shouted. The singing stopped. "Look, look," several were saying, pointing at the windows along Greene Street. "Fire!"

Several others screamed just as Esther reached the inspector with her handbag open. She was looking back to the smoke outside the window while the inspector went through her bag. "All good," the inspector said and put a hand on Esther's shoulder nudging her to the stairs.

Esther looked back. *Rachel,* she thought in a panic. *I have to get her.* Esther had to squeeze through the tight partition opening, between the inspector and the women waiting on line. It was slow moving and Esther's anxiety was growing. "Rachel, Rachel," she yelled over the other seamstress' heads.

CHARLIE TURNED OFF BROADWAY and walked along Washington Place. He crossed Mercer Street and felt something was wrong. The street was both noisy and quiet at the same time. All background sound—clopping horses, purring motors, shouting vendors—at once mixed and faded. He could see ahead a handful of people in the middle of the street pointing up. He quickened his pace and followed their gaze. Eight stories in the sky, flames were blowing out the last two windows. For a second, Charlie couldn't believe what he was seeing, and then he looked at the corner of the building to make sure it really was *her* factory. High above the stack of placards stood the bold letters: *Triangle Waist Company*. Sound had not yet returned to his consciousness. There was almost a perverse peace in the crackle of flame he could hear from eight stories below. A gust of wind blew east from Broadway and swirled the column of black smoke rising high above the parapets. Charlie smelled the smoke and snapped alert. *Esther!*

He threw the flower onto the cobble stones and ran to the Greene Street service entrance. A horde of young women poured out. He waded his way through and into the service lobby, but the amount of people filing out of the narrow stairwell door made climbing the stairs impossible. Charlie slid the gate on the service elevator and looked up into the shaft. The top of the shaft was full of smoke and he thought he saw flames. He ran outside and around the building. A thin and gray man stood on the corner with his Bowler in his hands and Charlie nearly ran into him. He put his hand on the man's shoulder and pointed across the street to the fire alarm box.

"Send the fire signal," Charlie shouted. The man looked up one last time and hurried across the roadway.

Edward was in his office explaining his record keeping system to his new aide, William.

"Second alarms or greater generate an entry into this ledger," he said, pulling a thick book down from the shelf. "Don't forget to note the battalion chief's name here. Don't just write the battalion number."

"Yes, Chief," answered William, who, to Edward's annoyance was not looking at the line he was pointing to.

"Enter the name here," he repeated. The telephone on the aide's desk rang.

William looked at it and then at Edward. There was panic in his eyes.

"It won't bite you, William. Go ahead and answer it."

William took the receiver from the cradle and held it under his chin like a microphone. "McGinn here!" he said tentatively.

"To your ear, William," Edward said impatiently. "That part goes to your ear." He then pointed to the horn jetting from the side of the assembly. "You speak into this part."

William did as told and repeated his greeting. "Yes—yes," he added. Then: "He's here." He handed the receiver to Edward.

"This is Chief Croker."

"This is Chief Dispatcher Donohue, Chief."

"Go on."

"We've just transmitted Box Two-Eight-Nine, Washington Place and Greene Street."

"Yes, I heard it. Engine Thirty-three turned out."

"We've also received a phone call from the desk at New York University. They're reporting a fire at the Triangle Factory. It sounds like you got a worker."

"Yes—thank you," Edward said plainly. "I'm on my way."

William ran out of the office and to the stairs. Edward went to the swing gate beside the stairs and pulled it open. He stepped off and grabbed hold of the shiny brass pole. Bringing his feet around he cradled the pole as he slid down to the apparatus floor. He went to the housewatch, picked up a pen and wrote in the company journal:

4:50p.m. C.O.D. Croker responded to telegraph alarm signal box 289.

He turned and saw William sitting behind the wheel of the Red Devil. The aide pressed the starter and the motor revved to life. Edward went to the driver's side. "Move over," he said loudly over the engine noise.

William turned his head to look at the chief. Any notion he may have had to object faded instantly under Edward's stare. He slid across the leather bench seat and Edward climbed in. The car was out the door before his backside settled into the cushion.

※

ESTHER MADE IT PAST the women pushing through the partition. Outside the window to her left, thick black smoke was rising from below. The windows were open and a good deal of smoke was coming in. Esther tasted it as she made her way back to her sewing machine. The tables were long and the aisles were now littered with tipped over chairs and wicker baskets of partially assembled shirtwaists. Rachel was not at her machine. She must have gone to get her coat, Esther thought. Rachel had not retrieved her coat at lunch break. When the closing bell rang, Rachel would have gone to get it. She looked to the end of the aisle, which was clogged with seamstresses trying to get to the stairwell. Esther tried to climb over the table. Her legs ached and it was difficult to raise her knees high enough to get over the top. Her skirt became tangled on the wheel of a sewing machine, and she tore it to get free. She decided climbing over the five remaining rows of tables would not get her to the coat room quicker and went to the end of the aisle instead. At last, she saw Rachel, stuck in a crowd being pushed toward the Greene Street stairs. She called out to her sister.

"Est—Est, I'm here," Rachel answered with tears in her eyes.

Esther pulled her out from the mass and went to the Washington Place stairwell door. There were a handful of women pounding on the door, and pushing.

"It opens inward," Esther shouted over shoulders, not knowing if she was heard.

An older woman, whom Esther recognized as Mrs. Rosen—one of the few forewomen in the factory—took charge. "Stand back," she yelled. The group made a clearing and Mrs. Rosen tried to work the doorknob and pull the door inward. "Damn thing is locked," she hissed. To Esther's left another crowd was forming at the passenger elevator doors. Some were ringing the call bell and others were pounding on the hoistway doors.

BOTH PASSENGER ELEVATOR DOORS opened on the tenth floor at the same time. A number of the shipping clerks and cutters began to board. Max held the hands of each of his daughters firmly and stepped closer to the elevators as the group loaded in.

"Step back—step back right now," Max heard Isaac yelling. He saw Harris push his way to the front of the queue, pulling men back as he went. "Get out—get out right now," Harris shouted at the men who had already gotten into the elevator cars. "We are bringing the girls down first."

Max was relieved Harris was taking charge. His hands were shaking and he was terrified of making the wrong decision. He was thankful Harris was thinking of his two daughters until he realized the girls Harris had been talking about were the women workers on the tenth floor. Harris began shepherding the seamstresses and secretaries to the front of the line.

Max inched forward. He saw the elevator operators, Joseph and Gaspar, helping the women in and moving them around to fit as many as possible. Max wanted to yell—wanted to make everyone get out of his way. But he could not find his voice. He closed his eyes and felt the darkness. The sick feeling that washed over him all those years ago, when that seamstress died at his feet, returned.

The elevators were full when Max got to the front of the crowd. Gaspar had shut his gate and gone down. Joseph was closing his when Harris saw Max and the girls. He put his hand on the gate and pulled it back. He put his hand on Henrietta's shoulder and pushed her into the jam-packed elevator car. He then picked up four-year old Mimi and handed her to Joseph, who cradled the child with one arm and made to close the gate with the other. Mimi began wailing and kicking her feet. She was terrified and her cries woke Max from his stupor. He reached into the elevator, took Mimi from Joseph's arms, and pulled Henrietta out. Joseph shut the gate and the elevator was gone.

"Damn it, Max," shouted Harris. "Now what?"

∞

CHARLIE WENT TO THE Washington Place entrance. A mounted policeman was galloping down the block and pulled up just before the building. The policeman dismounted and looped the reign around a pole. He noticed Charlie entering the lobby.

"You must evacuate," he yelled.

"I'm a fireman," Charlie answered and the policeman made no further attempts to stop him.

The two passenger elevators were in the lobby unloading occupants, mostly young women.

"Are there many more?" asked the policeman.

"Hundreds," answered one of the two elevator operators. He was a handsome young man with slicked dark hair. His face was hard and determined, Charlie thought. There was no panic in his countenance. "We came past the eighth floor—there was a lot of smoke. The call bell on Nine is ringing. We'll head back up," he said coolly as he slid the gate closed.

Charlie pulled open the stairwell door. He found it surprising that no one was coming down these stairs. The Greene Street stairwell was overcrowded. He began climbing the narrow staircase, two steps at a time. The policeman was right behind him.

※

"THERE'S A FIRE ESCAPE, out the back," Esther told Rachel as she pulled her away from the group gathering by the passenger elevators. The smoke that had been creeping along the ceiling from the Greene Street side was no longer a gray haze, but now a black cloud. From the other side of the spacious loft, women screamed. Esther could now see flames near the Greene Street stairwell partition. The windows facing the fire escape were partially blocked by the stacks of cloth bolts and crates of shirtwaists that had appeared over the last week or so. Between that and the group of seamstresses trying to get onto the fire escape, Esther felt hemmed in all around.

There was a loud screech and then a thunderous crash. Shrieks of horror sprang up from the women in front of Esther and Rachel. "It broke away," someone was shouting. "The fire escape fell away!"

Esther pulled Rachel's arm toward the Greene Street Stairwell. Faintly visible through the smoke was a mass of young women huddled on the floor and under tables. The two tables closest to the Greene Street windows were burning, and so was the partition by the stairwell door.

※

SAMUEL DROPPED THE LIMP hose and went back to Dinah's table. She had gone down in an elevator. He looked around carefully, making sure there were no others left behind. He was pretty sure everybody on the eighth-floor made it out, but took nothing for granted. He'd heard the crash outside the window and the screams. He knew the fire escape was gone, so he crawled forward, toward the Greene Street stairs. "Hello! Is anybody here?" he shouted as he went, between coughs. The smoke was choking. The table where he'd first spotted the fire was now a fireball. It was burning his face and ears, but he crawled quickly to the partition at the stairs and made it through where conditions were slightly improved. He was determined to get to the ninth floor. He didn't know if these stairs would be passable, but it was his only choice. He could not get to the ninth floor from the Washington Place stairs. He knew that door was padlocked shut.

The stairwell had some smoke, but no flames yet. He felt his way up with his hand on the banister, and when he found the newel post he reached out for the door to the ninth floor. It was wedged open and behind it was a wall of flames. He could not enter the ninth floor here. His heart sunk. *I waited too long,* he thought. "Damnit," he shouted at no one. "Goddamnit." He pulled the door closed as best he could and went up to the tenth floor.

CHARLIE WAS SPRINTING UP the stairs so fast, he'd lost count of what floor he was on. He reached a landing, paused to gasp for some air, and wondered if it was the sixth or seventh floor. The policeman arrived, huffing, and said: "This is six—two more."

A small group of people came down the stairs. They were all coughing and one middle-aged man was helping a young woman with an injured leg. He paused to talk to Charlie and the policeman. "We finally got the door open—there are still others up there."

"What floor were you on?" Charlie asked.

The man coughed and then said: "Eighth floor."

"Are the people on Nine out?" Charlie asked frantically, thinking of Esther.

The man shrugged and then collapsed on the stairs, holding his hand to his chest. He nearly dragged the injured woman he'd been helping down with him.Charlie pulled the man up and wrapped his arm around his shoulder. "Let's get you down," he said. He looked at the policeman. "I'll come back."

They came out the door and Charlie set the man down on the sidewalk in front of the building next door. After calling over a bystander to assist the man, Charlie heard bells and saw Engine Company 72 speeding along Washington Place from the direction of Washington Square Park. He knew it was 72 even before he could read the gold-leaf lettering on the rig's side. It was the only motorized fire apparatus in the city—the first of its kind. The chauffeur feverishly worked gear sticks and pedals, rolling to a stop at a hydrant just before the Washington Place entrance. The company's foreman jumped down and stared up into the afternoon sky. Charlie followed his gaze. Smoke and flames were now pumping out of the eighth-floor windows on Washington Place.

Six firemen were riding the running boards and back-step. They all dismounted. Stacked atop the standard hose bed were an additional five lengths of rolled-up hose tied in compact bundles. The firemen of 72 Engine each grabbed a roll-up and hurled it over their shoulders. The engineer and another man were hooking the engine up to the high-pressure hydrant at the curb. Charlie knew it was a high-pressure hydrant because it was twice as thick as other hydrants.

"I want two lines into that standpipe siamese," the foreman shouted, and the engineer grunted an affirmative response.

"I'm from Twenty Truck," Charlie told the foreman as he was entering the lobby. "We can get up this stairwell here."

"Show me the way, Twenty Truck," the foreman answered, but just as the firemen were coming through the door with their hose roll-ups, one of the elevator gates pushed open. Women screamed and pushed as they fled. Charlie saw the handsome young elevator operator again. His face was blackened with soot. He still wasn't panicked, but his eyes were somehow distant. As soon as the last woman was off, he slid the gate closed and the elevator went up. Somewhere between fifteen and twenty women had come off the elevator and the firemen had to wait for them the leave the lobby before they could get by with their hoses.

Charlie again charged up the stairs, this time remembering to count floors. He reached the seventh-floor landing and a young woman lay on the floor, coughing profusely. Charlie stepped over her and was halfway up to the eighth floor when he stopped. The door was pushed in about a foot or two and fire was blowing out the opening and up the stairway. Crouched at the standpipe outlet was the policeman he'd seen before. He was fiddling with the valve. There was a hoseline connected to the outlet, but it was dry and tangled on the stairwell floor. "I'm turning the valve, but there's no water," the policeman shouted.

Charlie lay on the landing and reached forward to pull the policeman by his pant-leg. He managed to get him to the landing below. "No one else is coming out that door," said the policeman. He had dark soot smeared on his mouth and nose. "I made it in a few feet—found this woman on a window ledge about to jump."

"Let's get her down," Charlie said. They each grabbed an arm and leg and cradled the now barely conscious woman and started their descent.

They reached the sixth-floor landing and Charlie heard pounding on the door. He looked at the policeman, who was equally surprised. He reached with one hand and tried turning the knob. It turned only slightly. It was not locked so much as stuck. They carefully placed the woman on the floor. He spun his grip on the knob again and put his shoulder into the door. The policeman pushed as well. The door slid in begrudgingly, perhaps a foot.

"Thank goodness," cried a young man. There were several young women with him as well. "The fire escape collapsed," he added. "Several girls fell to the bottom. I had kicked in the window here on six because I saw the fire escape didn't go all the way to the ground."

"I was the last one in," one of the young women said, crying. "I still had one foot on the fire escape balcony when it fell. Two girls—they were screaming—and the sound, oh the sound..." she broke off and heaved heavy sobs.

Charlie looked down and saw she was bleeding quite profusely from her leg. It was soaked through her skirt and pooling on the floor. Charlie wrapped her arm over his shoulder. He told the man to help the policeman carry the other injured woman, and he helped the seamstress with the bleeding leg down the six flights of steps.

It didn't take long, and Charlie again ran up the stairs to meet up with Engine 72. The firemen were screwing hose lengths together and connecting it all to the standpipe outlet on the seventh-floor landing. "Mr. Foley," the foreman called out.

"Here, sir."

"Run down and tell Peters to charge the pipe as soon as he's ready."

"On it, sir," said Foley, who ran down the steps.

"Be ready for water, Mr. McKenny."

"Got it."

A moment later the hoseline jumped to life—first with a few spurts, then with a gush. McKenny crouched and cradled the brass nozzle under his arm. He worked open the valve to let the trapped air escape. The hose thickened quickly and then became solid. There were several sharp bends and Charlie knew that if they didn't straighten out these kinks, there wouldn't be enough water pressure at the nozzle. The foreman went up to the eighth-floor landing and lay on his belly. Charlie could see flames rolling over the dark outline of his leather helmet and the high collar of his slicker coat. The foreman pushed the door inward as far as he could. "Let's move in, Mr. McKenna," he shouted.

McKenna brought the nozzle end up the stairs and knelt at the door opening. The other men, Charlie included, fed the heavy hose up the steps. Charlie saw a kink and bent down to straighten it as the hoseline smoothly went up. He heard the crash of water flowing when McKenna opened the nozzle valve, and the men of Engine 72 pushed their hoseline into the inferno that was now the eighth floor.

The flames that had been pushing out the top of the door were beaten back. Charlie pulled the front of his shirt up over his mouth and nose and charged up the stairs past the eighth-floor landing, around the newel post and up to the ninth floor. The smoke was burning his eyes. The intense heat felt like needles over every inch of his body. Through the blackness he reached out for a doorknob. Running his hand across the wall, he at last found it and spun his grip. The metal knob burned his bare hand and did not spin. He tried once more to push the door open, but it was pointless. He couldn't take any more and retreated down the stairs. All the way down.

HOOK AND LADDER 20's long eighty-five foot ladder truck was moving so fast it nearly tipped over turning off Mercer Street on to Washington Place. Floyd Mance stood as he yanked the reins back hard. The horses neighed as he drew the rig parallel with the building line, closer to the north side of the street. Andrew hopped off the running board and looked up. Flames were shooting out the eighth-floor windows, nearly halfway out across the street in some places. Closer to the corner, a young woman stood on the outside ledge of a ninth-floor window. She was waving a white handkerchief, and Andrew could see flames popping through the thick smoke pouring out the open window behind her.

The street was crowded with bystanders, many of which began yelling: "Raise the ladder!" Andrew began spinning one of the cranks to lower the stabilizers. Mance and Schley were on the turntable cranking up the ladder before the stabilizers were even touching the ground. Once the pad was set, Andrew climbed up to work the wheel that extended the sectioned aerial ladder, while John Stafford rotated the turntable. The four each spun their handles feverishly and the ladder inched painfully slowly toward the unfortunate seamstress.

The ladder was now completely in line with her, and Andrew alone kept cranking to extend. The tip of the ladder reached to just above the sixth-floor windowsills and then stopped. Andrew nearly broke the crank handle as he pushed it around to its final, blunted, end.

"Higher—Higher!" shouted bystanders. Andrew's heart pounded in his chest as he watched the poor young woman wave the handkerchief furiously. His eyes moistened and it seemed as if all the world was moving in the slowed-down, fuzzy haze of a dream. The bottom of her skirt was on fire. She was nine stories up, but surprisingly close to Andrew—he could clearly see her face. She screamed in horror and shook her leg as her skirt burned. Then—in seeming resignation that the ladder would never reach her—she reached out with both hands and jumped. Perhaps she was trying to grab the ladder on the way down. Andrew couldn't tell, but he watched in horror as she plummeted, and the wind fed the flames on her skirt. She dropped like a fireball, straight past the tip of the ladder and in a split-second exploded onto the sidewalk with a sickening thud so loud Andrew though a bomb had exploded.

And then, to Andrew's shock, he saw two more women on the same ledge. He could see them crying. All those stories up, they felt that close.

"Ott—grab the other end," called Schley, and Andrew's stupor was broken. He saw the men of Hook and Ladder 20 unfolding the life net. He jumped down from the turntable and went to help. Engine Company 33 had arrived and some of their men also grabbed hold of the border piping of the large, circular net. No sooner was it open than one of the two women jumped. She flew down fast and when she hit the center, the eight strong men holding the net nearly all toppled in with her. It was all Andrew could do to keep his hands wrapped around the handle. He thought his shoulders might have been yanked out, the force was so great. They tipped the net, and Battalion Chief Worth was there to help the woman off. They immediately raised it and another woman crashed down. The men had not expected it and this time the net was ripped from their hands. The woman hit the cobble stones beneath fairly hard. She was not moving. Andrew and another fireman stepped onto the net to carry her off. He cradled his hands under her arm pits and lifted. Out the corner of his eye, Andrew saw the woman Chief Worth had been escorting collapse down to the ground. The two men carrying the unconscious woman were barely off the grounded net when someone yelled: "Wait, wait!"

Andrew looked up. Two more women—holding hands—had jumped. Before anyone could react, the doomed pair smashed down onto the grounded net. Andrew instantly thought of being on the deck of a battleship during the Spanish-American War. The way the muzzle flashed and the deck shook, and the loud, loud blast—always a fraction of a split second after the flash—that made your ears ring. The women had made the ground shake. It was as loud as those big guns.

Edward was on Greene Street as Engine Company 18 was connecting hoses to the high-pressure hydrant and feeding the standpipe siamese near the service entrance. He jumped when a body crashed down onto the hoseline. He looked up. All the windows on the eighth floor had fire showing, as well as many on the ninth. Any ninth-floor window that didn't have fire had someone standing on the ledge. He watched as a middle-aged man jumped. The sickening, thunderous, thud again made him jump.

The men from Engine 18 left their hose roll ups on the ground and grabbed their life net. There were civilians who ran over and grabbed hold of the piping as well.

Edward saw what was about to happen. "Just one," he shouted. "One at a time." The lost souls on the ledge, nine stories up, could not hear him. Three women jumped at once.

The firemen of Engine 18 and their civilian helpers received the blow of three bodies like a pond takes a falling rock. Several of them did summersaults into the collapsing net. Edward ran over. The women were dead, several of the net holders were badly injured. "Mr. Ruch," Edward said to the engine company foreman. "Put this damned net away—where they can't see it."

"Yes, Chief."

"And get me a hoseline up on that ninth floor!"

Edward walked to Washington Place. Along the way he had to push spectators aside and yell at them to stay clear. Several more victims had jumped. "Keep this damned street clear of people," he roared at a policeman who was also stuck-still staring up at the horror. Around the corner, he found Battalion Chief Worth.

"I had Twenty Truck put the life net aside, Chief," said Worth. The hardened battalion commander seemed on the verge of tears. "It just wasn't effective."

"I told Eighteen to do the same," Edward replied.

"Seventy-two has water on the fire. Water pressure is good," Worth added.

At any other fire, Edward would have relished the pride he knew he'd earned by fighting so hard for the high-pressure water system. The old city water mains would never have been able to deliver water eight stories up. But there was no solace. Any preparations he'd made were inadequate. He was not angry. He knew rage would come later, but at that moment he felt incredibly sad. He pushed it aside. There was still work to do.

"I've transmitted a second alarm," said Worth.

Good, Edward thought. But the people clinging to those windowsills didn't have time to wait for the engine companies to knock down the flames, or for the hook and ladder companies to make their way to those windows to lead them out. There was no time at all.

Two more bodies crashed down. One onto the cobble stones of Washington Place and the other onto the sidewalk. The body had hit a section of sidewalk containing thick, translucent, circular glass panels, called deadlights. Deadlights brought sunlight to the basement area of loft buildings. This body hit the sidewalk so hard, it crashed through the deadlights into the basement.

***

MAX HAD HEARD THE crash coming from the back windows. "The fire escape collapsed," somebody said. Numerous people pressed the call button for the elevators, but they hadn't come back to the tenth floor. "The roof is our best chance," said Isaac, and Max followed him with Henrietta and Mimi each in hand. There was a haze of smoke throughout the floor, but as of yet, no fire. The flames outside the windows meant it was only a matter of time. There was a group of maybe thirty remaining on the tenth floor and they headed for the Greene Street stairwell, the only one of the two that extended above the top floor to the roof level. The door swung in before they arrived, and a sweaty, soot covered, Samuel Bernstein came in and shut the door behind him.

"Samuel," called Harris. "What is going on down there?"

"The eight floor is completely aflame," the factory manager answered. "And I fear the ninth, as well."

"Dear God," Max cried. Henrietta began crying. Mimi seemed to be in shock.

"We need to get to the roof," said Harris. "Can we get up the stairs?"

Bernstein nodded. "If we go quickly." He motioned for the group to go through. Harris was first and Bernstein held the door open for him. The stairwell was completely full of smoke. "Keep your hand on the railing, there. The bulkhead door isn't locked."

Max and the girls were last to the door. Bernstein leaned down and picked up Mimi. He cradled her in and spoke to Henrietta. "You hold on to your father's arm, dear. All right?"

Henrietta nodded and Bernstein looked at Max. "Are you ready?" he asked.

Max was frozen and silent. After a second, he said: "This isn't it, you know."

"Come again, Max?" asked Bernstein sharply.

"What you were thinking last night. The business with Schlansky. This isn't it. He only comes after closing, you know!"

Bernstein nodded. "It started in a cutter's bin. The idiot was probably smoking."

For a split second, Max felt vindicated. But Henrietta squeezed his arm and brought him back to the present.

"But God help anyone on the ninth floor when those crates of overstock catch fire," Bernstein added.

Max's hands shook as he reached through the suffocating darkness for the handrail.

∞

HELL'S HUNDRED ACRES

Esther and Rachel crouched under a table between the burning partition outside the Greene Street stairwell and the crates of old stock that had just lit up. Esther looked over to the elevator doors, a group of women just piled onto one of the cars. "Come on," she told Rachel between coughs, and she crawled toward the passenger elevator doors. Forty seamstresses or so were crowded against the two hoistway doors. The elevator on the right rose up and the operator heaved the accordion-style open gate back. Esther saw it was Gaspar. His white shirt was soaked with sweat and blackened. His face was covered in soot. No sooner was the gate pulled back than the women began pushing inside. Twenty seamstresses piled into a car built for twelve. More were trying to get on and Gaspar had to push them out and yell to get back as he worked the gate shut. Esther and Rachel moved closer, twenty or so remained and more were coming over from the Greene Street side. Once Gaspar's elevator car descended, a couple of women forced the hoistway door open. There was now a little space for Esther to get closer, and she held on to the wall and peaked her head into the shaft. Smoke was rising quickly and venting somewhere from the machine room above, but Esther could clearly see flames coming through the doors on the eighth floor below. Her heart sunk further. *How had Gaspar made it through the fire?* She could see the thick, grease covered cables moving down in the center of the shaft as Gaspar's car dropped to the lobby. Someone was pushed up against her back, and Esther nearly fell into the shaft. She managed to squeeze through the throng and found Rachel.

"I don't think the elevators will come back up," Esther said.

Rachel went to the stairwell door. Those who had been trying to open it before had given up. Rachel tried turning the knob and pulling. It didn't budge. Esther put her hand on her shoulder and leaned into her hear. "We need to get down the other stairs."

The flames coming from the crates of overstock were now reaching the ceiling. They hurried past. Esther grabbed a blouse from a tabletop and bunched it up to her nose and mouth to keep out the thick smoke, and Rachel followed suit. They got down on their knees and found a group huddled by the Greene Street stairs. The partition was still burning, and Esther was shocked to see one of the women get off her knees and run straight through the flames toward the stairs. She heard the women let out a scream but then the scream faded. *Did she make it to the stairs?* Another woman ran in, then another. "We have to make it to those stairs," Esther told Rachel. She partially stood and tugged her sister's arm.

Rachel would not budge.

"Rach... Come on—there's no more time."

Rachel was frozen. Esther leaned closer to see her holding the crumpled shirtwaist to her face. Tears streamed down her cheeks, and she shook her head. "I can't go. I can't go."

"It will only burn for a second. Look—more are going in. If there was no way through, they'd be bunched up and stopped."

Another woman running through let out a scream. Rachel gasped.

"Esther began crying. "Rachel—this is our last chance. We need to go."

There was a loud cracking sound and the partition fell in on itself. The flames erupted higher. There would be no getting through now. The flames were coming toward them. The heat was intense. Esther felt her face, ears, even her hair burning. She backed away until she hit a table. Rachel was with her. They kept backing away, untangling themselves from sewing machine pistons under the tables. They were close to windows now and from her crawling position she saw people climbing up onto the windowsills. She pulled herself up and stuck her head out a window. It was Greene Street; she saw people down in the street pointing up. She looked to her right and saw three women standing on the edge of the wide sill. The closest one turned, made eye contact with Esther and jumped. Out into the open air, out into nothingness, she leapt.

A bolt of dread struck Esther and she pulled her head inside. The choking black smoke again stuck in her throat, and she put the blouse up to her face.

"Gaspar will come back," Rachel said. "I know it, Est. He'll come back."

Esther thought of the look in that woman's eyes as she jumped and nodded. She tried to look across the open space to the Washington Place elevator doors, but there was no visibility through the smoke. "Let's go," she said. "We'll crawl under the tables."

※

"Get up the Washington side," Edward told Assistant Foreman Woll of Hook and Ladder 20. "Seventy-two Engine is operating on Eight. I need you to get the remaining workers from Eight out." Woll was a solid fire officer, and Edward was certain he knew what to do, but felt the need to tell him anyway. He needed to assure himself that all that could be done was being done. Hook and Ladder 20 should have already been up on the eighth floor. They were the first-due ladder company, and the eighth floor was the original fire floor—the first due truck company's primary position. But 20 had arrived to find multiple victims about to jump. They needed to act quickly. They had to try something. They tried their ladder. They tried the life net.

Another body crashed down. The three horses harnessed into Hook and Ladder 20's truck decided they'd had enough. The sound of bodies hitting pavement was unnerving for all, and what's more, Edward could smell blood in the air. It was all around, splattered across the cobble stones. The horses were now frenzied, and each's panic only fed the others. They reared, and neighed, and pushed forward into their harnesses. Only the ladder truck's stabilizers—planted firmly on the cobble stones—prevented the beasts from charging down the street with the rig.

Edward called his new aide, William, over. "Help Twenty Truck's chauffeur unharness these horses and walk them down the street."

"Right away, Chief."

"Is Three Truck in yet?"

"Don't know, Chief."

"Mr. Worth," Edward called out to the battalion chief who was conferring with his own aide. Worth looked over to Edward.

"Where's Truck Three?"

"They must have been out on another box," said Worth. "The second alarm companies are arriving now. I'm sending the next truck company up the Greene Street side to operate with Eighteen Engine on the ninth floor."

"Good man," said Edward. He looked up. Flames were still blowing out of the eighth-floor window. The ninth-floor windows were full of people—some standing on the ledge of the sill, some waving their arms from within. He looked for Chief Worth again and found him directing the engineer of Engine 13. Worth was pointing up to the ninth floor. Edward went over just as the engineer opened a valve and a thick stream of water blasted up into the sky.

Anticipating a question, Worth explained to Edward. "If we can create a water curtain, perhaps cool those people off—maybe they can hold out. Maybe they won't jump."

"Anything's worth a try, Mr. Worth," Edward replied. The stream shot up to the bricks just above the ninth-floor windows. The engineer worked the tip of the water cannon side to side. The pressure was just strong enough to put a heavy mist inside the windows. Edward watched a man, standing on the ledge and clinging to the side of the window frame. The water washed over him. Edward held his breath. *This has got to work! This has got to help!*

Edward waited. Seconds felt like hours. Then, the man jumped. Two others seemed encouraged by the man's leap and followed him down to the ground. *We've got to get to that ninth floor faster.* Edward turned and saw Engine 33's foreman and called him over.

"Mr. Dunn, where is your company?"

"They had to wet down some of the bodies that landed, Chief. They were on fire. I've just sent them now to get the hose roll-ups."

"Good man," Edward answered. "I want you to come with me."

Edward stepped over criss-crossed hoselines. In some spots, fallen bodies lay over the hose. None of this prevented onlookers from filling the street, by now numbering in the hundreds. "Get back, goddamnit, get back," Edward yelled. He held out his arms and was trying to herd the people back onto the far sidewalk. "Back—get back," he directed, and then he saw a familiar face. "You too, Mr. Shepherd—please."

William Gunn Shepherd was silent and visibly shaken by what he was witnessing. Edward looked him dead in the eye. "We'll all take this day to our graves."

Shepherd nodded. "God help them," he answered, looking up to the ninth-floor windowsills and the desperate souls teetering on the ledge.

Edward turned and scanned the street for the Engine 33 men he'd been waiting for. They were coming down the street with hose roll-ups on their shoulders.

∞

CHARLIE CAME OUT OF the Washington Place entrance. The palm of his right hand was throbbing. The scolding doorknob had seared the skin of his hand and now the fresh air stung. His coat, hair, and face were blackened by soot. As he was making his way around, to get to the Greene Street entrance he knocked into Floyd Mance, who was carrying an axe and a claw tool and heading toward the Washington Place door. Mance stared at Charlie for a long second, then stepped around him and went in. Charlie continued. He heard a loud smash; something had fallen from above. There was a burning lump of rags, half on the sidewalk, half on the street about ten feet ahead. He went past and felt the metallic taste of vomit rising into his throat when he realized what it was.

The Greene Street stairs were now empty and he ran straight up to the sixth-floor landing, where a fireman from Engine 18 was disconnecting the building's firehose from the standpipe outlet and attaching F.D.N.Y. hose. Charlie stepped over and continued up. The company's foreman and three firemen were gathered on the stairs between the seventh and eight floors.

"I need to get to the ninth floor," Charlie told the foreman.

The engine company officer looked down the steps. His eyes were hard. Sweat beaded up on his temples. "You need to evacuate, son—we'll get there as soon as we can."

"I'm a fireman—Twenty Truck. I need to get to Nine."

"We can't get past the eighth-floor landing," the foreman said, nodding his head upward. Charlie saw the fireball blowing out into the stairwell. "We have to knock down the fire here on Eight before we can head up. We're waiting for our engineer to charge the standpipe. People were jumping all around—he and the probie had a hard time getting hose into the siamese."

From below, the man at the outlet yelled up: "Here comes your water, Mr. Ruch."

"Let's flake it out good," the foreman told his men. Charlie bent down and grabbed the hose. Water flowed in and filled out the hose and Charlie made a wide loop up the stairs. The nozzleman opened the valve and a thick and forceful stream shot up and turned the orange flame at the top of the landing into a cloud of gray smoke and mist. Charlie fed hoseline up the stairs as the firemen lay on their bellies and crawled into the hellish depths of the eighth floor. They beat the flames back into the doorway and moved the hose in further. Charlie tried to climb to the ninth floor, but the heat and smoke still pouring out the eighth-floor door and up the stairs made it impossible.

※

Esther and Rachel made it to the last table. Before them was a group of women at the elevators, behind them they saw only fire. They heard screams. Esther saw the elevator on the left with the gate open. The operator—not Gaspar, but the other one—was trying to close the gate, but there were too many women pressed in. She watched him push a woman back and slam the gate shut.

Esther tried to shout out. *Wait! Wait!* But the crumpled shirtwaist she held to her mouth muffled her cries. The elevator car descended. She put her hand on Rachel's arm and crawled out from under the table toward the elevator. The hoistway doors were open. There were still two dozen or more women waiting. Esther went to the right shaft, Gaspar's elevator, and looked in. She couldn't see anything—not the cables, not the car below, nothing. There was too much smoke. "Three girls fell in," another seamstress said from behind Esther. She turned and saw the young woman pointing at the shaft. She was crying. "The last time he came up. He filled the car and went down. There was so much pushing from the crowd—three girls fell in. That elevator hasn't been back since."

Esther went to the other open shaft and looked in. She could see just enough to make out the car down in the lobby. *Will he come back again?* She turned to find Rachel. The fire was practically on top of them. The heat was so intense, Esther's hair was hot and burning her scalp. A woman ran past Esther and jumped into the open elevator shaft. Esther watched her fly out and grab onto the cables. The woman was suspended mid-shaft and began sliding her body down the thick metal cables. Another women reached into the shaft and grabbed the rolling mechanism for the hoistway doors. Then a third young women leapt. What she was trying to grab onto, if anything, Esther couldn't tell. But the woman screamed and plummeted. There was a loud, crumpling, crash. Another woman jumped for the cables and missed. Another crash. Through the thin fabric of the blouse, Esther yelled for Rachel until finally her sister grabbed onto her arm.

"The elevators can't come back. We're going to have to climb down." Esther thought she'd need to convince her sister that there was no choice. Climbing down was their only hope. But Rachel didn't argue. They knew they were about to burn. Anything else was better.

Esther watched the woman clinging onto the cables. She slowly shimmied her way downward. Esther was nearly knocked into the shaft by two women who jumped. Without hope or a plan of any kind, the two hurled themselves to certain death. They too smashed into the roof of the elevator car below. As soon as there was room on the cables, Esther jumped and grabbed, and made it. Nine stories up an elevator shaft, Esther Greenberg of Essex Street, born in Bialystok, Poland, daughter of Ezra and Romena, squeezed her legs and her hands around two thick steel cables smothered in black grease.

She dared not looking down. Instead, she stared across to Rachel, frozen at the opening. "You can make it Rach," she called across. "It's not as far as it looks. Once I slide down, just reach out and jump. You can do it." Esther slid her body down as fast as possible. The grease stuck to her fingers. The cable itself had tiny metallic splinters sticking out and the pain was horrific as she slid her hands down the wire rope. She made it down four or five feet. "Now Rachel," she yelled up. "Now!"

Esther was looking up. Right before she leapt, Rachel looked down and made eye contact. Esther was instantly back at the train station in Bialystok. She was in her mother's arms on the moving train's step. Her father had a hand on the rail trying to pull himself aboard. She looked into Rachel's eyes. She saw her father's eyes. Rachel jumped.

※

MAX SAT ON THE roof of Joseph Asch's building. He was ten stories above the city. He was safely out of the inferno below. Black smoke surrounded the parapets from three directions. He sat with his back against a brick wall and cradled his daughters in each arm. Tears rolled down his cheeks. He hugged the girls in tightly and kissed the tops of their heads. Bernstein came over. "There's a university professor on the neighboring roof," he said. "We can climb onto there. There's a ladder that connects—and we'll get down to the street through the university building."

Max said nothing. He just stared ahead, still holding onto his daughters tightly.

※

ANDREW WAS CARRYING A six-foot hook and a ten-foot hook. He knew there would be high ceilings to open up at some point and figured it'd be better to have options and not have to come all the way back down to the street later on. Overhauling ceilings, however, was not his priority at the moment. If he got upstairs, he could maybe grab some of those poor people before they jumped. He followed the other Twenty Truck members into the Washington Place entrance. The scene in the lobby was utter chaos. There was a young man, in a white shirt and bell cap, face covered in soot. He was standing on a chair in front of the open elevator door and pulling the ceiling of the elevator car. The entire roof of the car was destroyed, with the ornamental tin ceiling panels hanging loose and support beams bent and ripped from their fastening bolts. There was fire on top of the elevator car.

Assistant Foreman Woll stepped closer to inspect, and Andrew peeked his head in the car.

"*Io non ci credo... Io non ci credo...*" the young man on the chair kept saying.

"Anyone speak Italian?" Woll asked the members of Hook and Ladder 20. No one answered, but the young man turned and looked at Woll. Tears ran down his cheeks. "I speak English," he whispered.

"What happened?" asked Woll.

"Right after I made the last pick-up—they started falling on top of the car."

"What started falling?" asked Woll. Andrew already knew the answer.

"The girls—they jumped. Help me," the elevator operator continued. "They're up here—they're burning up here."

Andrew ripped back a section of the tin ceiling panel. He could see a mangled body with its clothing on fire. He looked at several crumpled bodies, searching for any movement. "There's a bunch of 'em," he called back. "Can't tell if any are alive."

"Ott—you and Mance help this man get those people down," Woll directed. "Any chance we can get these elevators moving again?"

Andrew pulled back another section. The main beam, which was attached to the cables and the guide rails on either side, had taken the full force of a falling body and come dislodged from the guide rail. "It's off the rail, Skip," he answered. "I'll have to check the other car, but doesn't look good."

Another group of firemen entered the lobby. Andrew saw Chief Croker with Foreman Dunn from Engine 33 and a handful of men carrying hose roll-ups.

"What happened here, Mr. Ott?" said Croker.

"Chief, it looks like this man," he turned to the elevator operator. "What's your name, Mack?"

"Joe—Zito, I'm Joseph Zito."

"Joe Zito here saved a lot of girls from burning before his car took one too many hits."

"Good man," said Croker. "Is Mr. Woll on the eighth floor?"

Andrew looked to the stairs. "Yeah, Chief—they just went up."

"Come, Mr. Dunn," Croker called out as he went to the stairs. "We've got to get to the ninth."

The men of Engine 33 followed the chief. Andrew helped the elevator operator down from the chair. "Pull the chair back, Joe," he said. "Let's get some of the ceiling out of the way and get to these people."

Floyd Mance was standing half in, half out, of the other elevator car, looking up between the wall and the door of the car. "There's fire in the shaft," he said.

"How many trips did you make?" Andrew asked Zito but didn't wait for an answer. "How the hell did you make it past the fire?"

Zito shrugged. "I don't know how many times—the fire was coming through the gates each time. Gaspar had the other car—he made a lot of trips too. His car was damaged first, and he helped the girls get outside."

∞

ESTHER CONTINUED HER PAINFUL descent. The bruises on her legs all burned with a searing intensity as she squeezed her thighs against the greasy cables. Her hands felt like little more than bloody stumps of raw meat—the tiny shards of steel rope splinters had destroyed her palms and fingers. But still she clung for dear life. She looked up to check on her sister. Rachel was about six feet above her, screaming for the pain being inflicted on her poor hands. She looked down to the top of the elevator car at the base of the shaft.

She had made it about halfway. From above there was a sickening bout of screams and Esther saw a young woman drop past her in an instant. She crashed loudly below. Esther looked up. Out the open hoistway door, from the ninth floor she and Rachel had just escaped, another seamstress jumped. The woman screamed and hurdled down right toward Rachel.

Esther screamed with horror as the falling woman collided with Rachel. Then both women fell onto Esther. The grip of her greased and bleeding hands was no match for the force of two plummeting bodies.

※

ANDREW PULLED DOWN THE tin ceiling panels from the elevator's roof, while Joe Zito piled the debris in the lobby. Mance had gone up to the second floor to try opening the hoistway doors and see if they could access the top of the elevator car from there. If Andrew could open enough space he could use the chair, or a small ladder, to get up there and reach the bodies atop the car. He was working as fast as he could. He wasn't sure if he'd seen movement, but if there was any chance to save someone—it wouldn't last long.

Without warning, there was a tremendous crash. A whole section of ceiling came down on Andrew and knocked him to the floor. He could hear screaming above. He tried to get to his feet, but then there was a second crash—bigger than the first.

Andrew thought he'd blacked out for a moment, because the next thing he knew, Joe Zito was pulling pieces of the elevator off him.

"You all right?" Zito asked.

"I uh…" Andrew mumbled. "What the hell was that?"

※

CHARLIE KNELT OUTSIDE THE stairwell door on the eighth-floor landing. The men of Engine 18 had pushed deep into the burning loft space, and a great deal of the fire had been knocked down. Thick, hot smoke still hung in the air and Charlie couldn't see much past the heavy bend of two-and-a-half-inch cotton jacket hose he was holding on to. He tried to keep a loop, chest high, so the engine men would be able to move in deeper with less hose drag. He had to get to the ninth floor. Maybe he could tough out the heat and smoke long enough. He went over the configuration in his head. He was in the Greene Street stairwell. The stairway landing in the lobby faced the door and then wrapped upward floor by floor, with a newel post at the start of each set of stairs. This doorway in which he was kneeling must face southward, and there should be windows facing Greene Street to his left. Charlie lay down on his belly and crawled in. There was a partition door a few feet in and then the space opened. He slid ahead, making a sharp left turn into the room. He kept a hand on the wall. His eyes burned and he was choking. He went forward—six feet, twenty feet, he was not sure—until he hit the wall and saw daylight through the rolling gray smoke. He put up his hand and felt openness—a window. He stood and leaned out. He was eight stories up, looking down on Greene Street. The other eighth-floor windows on this side all had gray smoke seeping outward. But the ninth-floor windows right above had fire showing, with the other ninth-floor windows pushing heavy black smoke. He crawled back to the stairwell. On the floor was a roll of cloth and he pulled it along.

No matter how bad it was above, he now knew how to find the windows. He ripped a length of cloth from the roll and tied it around his head, covering his nose and mouth, and went up the stairs.

IN THE WASHINGTON PLACE stairwell, Edward was kneeling on the ninth-floor landing, trying to see through the smoke enough to decipher what kind of lock was holding the door shut. Engine 72 had knocked down enough fire below that the landing above was now tenable. Foreman Dunn came up the stairs. "Twenty Truck left this at the doorway below," said Dunn.

Edward leaned closer and reached out his hand. He felt the heavy, iron claw tool and grabbed hold. Feeling ahead with one hand, He lined up his target and then used two hands to jam the prying end of the tool in between the door and the jamb. The tool went cleanly into the space as the wood jamb splintered away. Edward pushed forward, but the thick door resisted. "Give me a hand, Dunn," he said, and the engine officer pushed on the tool as well. The door gave way and swung in. They were met by a wall of flame.

"Reinhart, Meehan," Dunn called out. "Get that line up here."

"Coming, sir."

Edward grabbed the knob to pull the door back while they waited for the nozzle team, burning his hand. He then tried pulling on the door itself, but the men of Engine 33 had the nozzle ready to move in. He pushed the door fully inward and got out of the way.

∞

ANDREW AND MANCE REACHED the bodies on top of Joe Zito's elevator car. The force of the last women falling had opened up enough space to access them from below, with the help of Zito and the chair. They pulled them down—one by one—with their smoldering skirts and dresses and their deformed limbs and bloodied, sooty faces. They were all young women, one a teenager. Andrew checked them all carefully for signs of life. Nothing. Mance had now climbed up atop the elevator car and was maneuvering the victims to hand them down to Andrew.

"This one's alive," Mance called out.

Andrew looked at Zito, whose somber demeanor softened at the news.

"Can you free her without hurtin' er?" Andrew asked.

There was a loud, ominous screech from high up in the shaft. Andrew couldn't see up into the shaft to know what it was. "Something's getting' ready to let go," he told Mance. "You gotta get outta there."

He couldn't see Mance's face, only the underside of his boots as he kept working. "I'll leave when she leaves," Mance said calmly.

There was another screech, louder and longer. Andrew looked at Zito. "Joey—pull those others to the other side of the lobby for me. Let's keep this space clear." He wanted to get Zito out of harm's way, in case whatever was making that noise came down. Andrew, however, stayed in the elevator car so he could take hold of the victim as soon as Mance had her out.

Mance passed her down feet first and Andrew cradled the unconscious, but breathing, woman into his hulking frame and stepped back. "Can ya' get down, Floyd?"

"I got it, Ott—get her outside. See if there's a doctor."

Andrew ran outside, carrying the injured woman with little difficulty. He looked around frantically, searching for some means of getting medical help. He could see Chief Worth directing the stream of an engine-mounted water cannon. The chief seemed too preoccupied to know where a doctor might be. Hoses ran all across the cobble-stoned street. Water sprayed from brass fittings. He stepped over the hoses and into the crowd of people on the opposite sidewalk.

"I need a doctor!" he yelled into the crowd. "Doctor—any doctors here?"

A middle-aged woman stepped forward. "I'm a nurse."

Andrew lay the victim on the sidewalk. "Gimme some room," he bellowed. The people quickly cleared out an opening.

The nurse knelt beside the injured woman. "Water? Is there any water?" she called back, while looking over the victim.

Andrew stooped down and ripped a strip of fabric from the bottom of the victim's skirt. He went over to a hoseline coupling and held the strip in the spraying water.

"Is this good?" he asked, offering the wet cloth to the nurse.

"Yes." The nurse wiped away soot from under the injured woman's nose and then held the dripping strip against her forehead. The victim coughed. "Can you hear me, dear," the nurse said. "Are you able to speak?"

The woman nodded, ever so slightly. Andrew knelt on one knee. He needed this poor girl to be all right. The countless horrors happening across the street, he put aside, and focused all the hope he had left inside him on this one frail young woman.

"What's your name, dear?" the nurse asked tenderly.

The poor victim opened her eyes and looked up, first at the nurse, then directly at Andrew. When she spoke. Her voice was scratchy, but soft and barely audible.

"Esther Greenberg."

∞

CHARLIE FELT AS IF he were coming out of a dream. He sensed there would be daylight if he opened his eyes, but kept them closed as he felt cool water wash over his face. An involuntary inhalation overtook his chest causing a coughing fit. Someone was cradling him and a raspy, concerned voiced coaxed him to consciousness.

"Nice and easy, boy," said the familiar voice. "There you are. Nice and easy."

Charlie eased his eyes open and groggily tried to make sense of what he was seeing. *Floyd Mance?* The fireman was holding

Charlie's head on his thighs as he knelt and cradled him. He held a cup of water and poured it gently on Charlie's forehead. "Mance," Charlie said between two coughs. "How'd I get here?"

Charlie was lying in the street on the outboard side of Hook and Ladder 20's truck. He could see smoke high up in the air over Mance's shoulders. The Triangle factory building loomed over.

"I was helping the elevator boy carry the dead girls out to the street—I saw a couple of guys from Engine Eighteen carrying you over to the rig here. They said they found you, knocked out on the ninth-floor landing, over on the Greene Street side."

Charlie noticed Mance was bleeding from his ear and neck. "What happened to you?"

"Ott and I was takin' the girls down from the top of the elevator—some stuff started fallin'. After the last girls was out—I climbed down just as a beam or somethin' let go. Came down on top of the elevator. A piece of ceiling tin hit the side of my head here. It's just a scratch."

Charlie tried to sit up. Mance helped him gently while supporting his shoulders. "You all right, kid?"

Charlie nodded. "Did they get up to Nine?"

"Think so, the Engine Eighteen guys said they were knockin' down fire up there. Ott headed up the Washington side to find our guys. I was goin' up too when I saw you bein' carried out."

"Thank you," said Charlie weakly.

"The guys from Eighteen said you made a push up to the ninth floor—that's where they found'ya."

Charlie nodded. Mance helped him sit up and lean against the truck's stabilizer.

"Ya know..." Mance said. "During the Draft Riots, when half the city was burning, there was a volunteer engine company that found themselves fightin' a fire in a four-story orphanage all by themselves. Six men to fight four floors of fire. One of the orphans, just a kid, helped them with the hose stretch. The kid was flakin' out line and pushin' hose up the stairs and around bends. The men took a beating, but they put the fire out—with the help of that orphan. The kid took some beating too—finally passed out from the smoke. He died—right there in front of the building with the firemen around him. The kid died, and after, they found out his name. Ya know what it was?"

Charlie shook his head.

"Johnny!" Mance smiled. "The kid was Johnny."

It took a second, but then it dawned on Charlie. He smiled.

Mance smiled. "So we call our new guys—the kids—Johnnies." He patted Charlie's shoulder, then stood and buckled his denim coat. "Ya good, Johnny?"

Charlie nodded and Mance took his helmet, which had been set on the truck's running board, placed it on his sweaty head, grabbed his axe and claw tool and headed toward the Washington Place entrance. Charlie stared at the back of Mance's coat and helmet as he disappeared into the building.

※

BY THE TIME ANDREW reached the eighth floor, Assistant Foreman Woll and the rest of Twenty Truck was coming back out to the stairwell. "Seventy-two has it knocked down," said Woll. "It looks like all the workers on Eight got out. Let's head up to Nine."

Andrew followed his company up. There was a haze of smoke that hung in the air, but he was able to see well enough. The stairwell door on the ninth floor was in bad shaped; the top part had started to burn away. Andrew noticed the work of a claw tool where the door jamb was splintered. It had clearly been forced open. Andrew put his hand on the door and looked at the locking mechanism. It was still intact—still locked.

Andrew entered the ninth floor. The smell of smoke and charred wet wood hung in the air. Black water was pooled up several inches deep on the floor and Engine 33's hoseline snaked across the open space to where the engine men were hosing down hot spots near the front windows. He was not even ten feet in from the stairs when he saw them. Charred bodies were strewn across the clearing before the open elevator shafts. There must have been a dozen right there. Laid out on the wet floor in grotesque positions, the burnt figures each betrayed a last hopeless gasp for a salvation that would not come. Andrew reverently stepped over the bodies and walked between a row of long sewing machine tables and a line of crates that had served as so much fuel for the angry inferno.

"You got that ten-foot hook, Ott," Woll called out. He was standing next to Engine 33's foreman. "We need this ceiling opened up."

"Aye-aye, sir," Andrew yelled across and started to make his way over. The long tables complicated his route, and when he was nearer to the Greene Street side, the magnitude of the horror that was the ninth floor came into full view. There had to have been at least thirty scorched bodies, some laid atop one, or even two, others, gathered here, not far from the stairs where a collapsed pile of charred wooden studs blocked the stairwell door. The men of Engine 18 were on the other side of the pile, sporadically hosing down the debris and picking through it.

"They never had a chance," someone said.

Andrew turned to see Chief Croker. His eyes were glassy. His white helmet, face, and slicker coat were covered in wet, black soot.

"They didn't die for nuthin'," Andrew said.

"How so."

"What you said to the aldermen—they'll sure as hell pass that law now."

Chief Croker looked around at the dead young women. He reached under his slicker and from his pocket took out a watch. After a moment he spoke: "Ten minutes past five. All this happened in less than half an hour's time." The chief shook his head and tucked the watch away. "First there'll be shock and grief. Then there'll be outrage and blame. Then there'll be a committee. And long after the public has forgotten—nothing will change."

Andrew felt sick in his stomach. "They can't have died for nuthin'."

"No, Mr. Ott," Croker's voice was low but steely calm. "By the gods I swear it."

***

Esther felt pain throughout her body. Her head pounded. Her throat was horrifically sore—she found it difficult to take a deep breath or speak anything other than short phrases. The bruises on her legs, still sore, felt oddly nostalgic—a reminder of the time before. Her hands, however, were nothing but agony. Thin slices cut across the flesh of her palms and fingers, and each hand was slimy with thick black grease and blood. There was a woman tending her hands. Esther thought the woman had said she was a nurse. She had whispered her name and was trying to say more, but it hurt. Her throat burned, but still she mouthed the only thing that mattered:

"Rachel."

The nurse was wiping Esther's hands and stopped to look up. "What is it, dear?"

"Rachel," Esther repeated, slightly louder. "Where's Rachel."

The nurse lowered her head for a moment, then looked Esther in the eye. "I don't know, dear. They're taking other girls out now."

Esther began to rise. The nurse put a hand on her shoulder and tried to keep her lying down, but Esther pushed back and somehow got on her feet. The crowd of people was overwhelming, spilling out onto the cobble-stoned street. There were hoselines everywhere. She glanced up. Light gray smoke seeped out of the upper-floor windows of the tall factory.

The nurse was undeterred by Esther's rising and kept tending to her hands. There was a fire truck not far away with its tall wooden ladder reaching up and resting against the building, much lower than where the fire had been, Esther noticed. Leaning against the truck was Charlie.

"Charlie," she called out. It was a low-pitched cry and her voice cracked. Not even the nurse beside her was able to hear. Esther tried again to no avail.

"What is it, dear?" said the nurse.

Esther pointed. "Charlie," she said with tears running down her face.

The nurse turned to look, but the street was full of people.

"Charlie—on the fire truck. Charlie."

"Charlie?" said the nurse. "You know that boy?"

Esther nodded. The nurse held both Esther's hands and walked her through the crowd toward the truck. As they got closer, Esther was nearly overcome with emotion. Charlie was looking around the crowd nervously, and when he saw Esther his eyes softened and he exhaled.

He stepped closer, saw the nurse holding Esther's hands and put his own hands on her shoulders. "Are you all right?" he asked.

Tears ran anew down her cheeks, and she shook her head. "I can't find Rachel," she managed to scratch out in a whisper.

Charlie looked to the nurse and the woman let go of Esther's wounded hands. He then wrapped his arms around her and hugged tightly while she sobbed.

ONE CENT

✳ Evening Edition ✳

SPECIAL EDITION

VOL. 11.   SUNDAY, MARCH 26, 1911   NO. 85.

EYEWITNESS AT THE TRIANGLE

WILLIAM G. SHEPHERD

New York, NY., Mar. 25— I was walking through Washington Square Park when a puff of smoke issuing from the factory building caught my eye. I reached the building before the alarm was turned in. I saw every feature of the tragedy visible from outside the building. I learned a new sound—a more horrible sound than description can picture. It was the thud of a speeding, living body on a stone sidewalk.

Thud—dead, thud—dead, thud—dead, thud—dead. Sixty-two thud—deads. I call them that, because the sound and the thought of death came to me each time, at the same instant. There was plenty of chance to watch them as they came down. The height was eighty feet. The first ten thud—deads shocked me. I looked up—saw that there were scores of girls at the windows. The flames from the floor below were beating in their faces. Somehow I knew that they too must come down, and something within me—something that I didn't know was there—steeled me. I even watched one girl falling. Waving her arms, trying to keep her body upright until the very instant she struck the sidewalk, she was trying to balance herself. Then came the thud—then a silent, unmoving pile of clothing and twisted, broken limbs.

As I reached the scene of the fire, a cloud of smoke hung over the building... I looked up to the ninth floor. There was a living picture in each window—four screaming heads of girls waving their arms.

"Call the firemen," they screamed—scores of them. "Get a ladder," cried others. They were all as alive and whole and sound as were we who stood on the sidewalk. I couldn't help thinking of that. We cried to them not to jump. We heard the siren of a fire engine in the distance. The other sirens sounded from several directions.

"Here they come," we yelled. "Don't jump, stay there."

One girl climbed onto the window sash. Those behind her tried to hold her back. Then she dropped into space. I didn't notice whether those above watched her drop because I had turned away. Then came that first thud. I looked up, another was climbing onto the window sill; others were crowding behind her. She dropped. I watched her fall, and again the dreadful sound. Two windows away two girls were climbing onto the sill; they were fighting each other and crowding for air. Behind them I saw many screaming heads. They fell almost together, but I heard two distinct thuds. Then the flames burst out through the windows on the floor below them, and curled up into their faces.

The firemen began to raise a ladder. Others took out a life net and, while they were rushing to one side of the sidewalk with it, two more girls shot down. The firemen held it under them; the bodies broke it; the grotesque smile of a dog jumping through a hoop struck me. Before they could move the net another girl's body flashed through it.

(continued on page 2)

KRUGER WAREHOUSE
Piano Sale
All Models
25% Discount
THIS WEEK ONLY
Kruger Brothers Sellers of Fine Instruments Since 1853
Fulton Street & Hoyt St. Brooklyn

WILLIAM'S TENNESSEE RYE

Great Whiskey at a Great Price
Frances Jay   Pier 13
& Co.   New York
NY Agents   City

TO-DAY

Born on March 26th

Emanuel Kania
1827

John Rogers Thomas
1830

Historical Events

President Thomas Jefferson is presented with a "mammoth" loaf of bread, March 26, 1804.

Ludwig van Beethoven died March 26, 1827.

EYEWITNESS AT THE TRIANGLE (CONT.)

The thuds were just as loud, it seemed, as if there had been no net there. It seemed to me that the thuds were so loud that they might have been heard all over the city.

I had counted ten. Then my dulled senses began to work automatically. I noticed things that it had not occurred to me before to notice. Little details that the first shock had blinded me to. I looked up to see whether those above watched those who fell. I noticed that they did; they watched them every inch of the way down and probably heard the roaring thuds that we heard. As I looked up I saw a love affair in the midst of all the horror. A young man helped a girl to the windowsill. Then he held her out, deliberately away from the building and let her drop. He seemed cool and calculating. He held out a second girl the same way and let her drop. Then he held out a third girl who did not resist. I noticed that. They were as unresisting as if he were helping them onto a streetcar instead of into eternity. Undoubtedly he saw that a terrible death awaited them in the flames, and his was only a terrible chivalry.

Then came the love amid the flames. He brought another girl to the window. Those of us who were looking saw her put her arms about him and kiss him. Then he held her out into space and dropped her. But quick as a flash he was out on the windowsill himself. His coat fluttered upward—the air filled his trouser legs. I could see that he wore tan shoes and hose. His hat remained on his head.

Thud—dead, thud—dead—together they went into eternity. I saw his face before they covered it. You could see in it that he was a real man. He had done his best. We found out later that, in the room in which he stood, many girls were being burned to death by the flames and were screaming in an inferno of flames and heat. He chose the easiest way and was brave enough to even help the girl he loved to a quicker death, after she had given him a good-bye kiss. He leaped with an energy as if to arrive first in that mysterious land of eternity, but her thud—dead came first.

The firemen raised the longest ladder. It reached only to the sixth floor. I saw the last girl jump at it and miss it. And then the faces disappeared from the window. But now the crowd was enormous, though all this had occurred in less than seven minutes, the start of the fire and the thuds and the deaths.

I heard screams around the corner and hurried there. What I had seen before was not so terrible as what had followed. Up in the ninth floor girls were burning to death before our very eyes. They were jammed in the windows. No one was lucky enough to be able to jump, it seemed. But, one by one, the jams broke. Down came the bodies in a shower, burning, smoking-flaming bodies, with disheveled hair trailing upward. They had fought each other to die by jumping instead of fire.

The whole, sound, unharmed girls who had jumped on the other side of the building had tried to fall feet down. But these fire torches, suffering ones, fell inertly, only intent that death should come to them on the sidewalk instead of in the furnace behind them.

On the sidewalk lay heaps of broken bodies. A policeman later went about with tags, which he fastened with wires to the wrists of the dead girls, numbering each with a lead pencil, and I saw him fasten tag no. 54 to the wrist of a girl who wore an engagement ring. A fireman who came downstairs from the building told me that there were at least fifty bodies in the big room on the ninth floor. Another fireman told me that more girls had jumped down an air shaft in the rear of the building. I went back there, into the narrow court, and saw a heap of dead girls... The floods of water from the firemen's hose that ran into the gutter were actually stained red with blood. I looked upon the heap of dead bodies and I remembered these girls were the shirtwaist makers. I remembered their great strike of last year in which these same girls had demanded more sanitary conditions and more safety precautions in the shops. These dead bodies were the answer.

DISTRICT ATTORNEY ANNOUNCES INQUIRY

GRAND JURY TO INVESTIGATE FIRE SAFETY IN FACTORY LOFT BUILDINGS

SAMUEL WORTH

New York, NY., Mar. 26—After a preliminary investigation at the scene of yesterday's fire, District Attorney Charles Whitman announced plans to open a grand jury inquiry to investigate the conditions that led to such a devastating loss of life.

The grand jury will determine if existing laws are adequate for the protection of life in loft factories, as well as whether the laws are being followed, said Whitman.

When asked about witness reports that exit doors on the factory floor had been locked at the time of the fire, the district attorney said, "I will be speaking, in the coming days, with Chief Croker as well as the fire marshal to determine exactly what conditions led to such a fateful disaster."

MCGOVERN SALES CO.
LUXURY MOTOR CARS
LATEST MODELS
998 E. 141 ST ST.
BRONX, NY

Part Five

36

SUNDAY, MARCH 26, 1911

ON THE SHORE OF the East River, near 26th Street, sat the Charities Pier. The dock itself was an enclosed metal-frame structure with just a row of narrow windows on each of the four walls. Due to the large number of victims at the fire, the city coroner commandeered the pier as a makeshift morgue. A line of people, hundreds deep, waited along the fence line trying to find their missing loved ones. Charlie stood with Esther and her mother. The line moved slowly—they'd been standing out in the windy morning air for two hours. Waves broke against the rocky shoreline and sea gulls crowed overhead. Esther spoke sporadically to her mother in Yiddish, and Charlie looked on, wanting to be helpful but unsure how.

He looked at Esther, with her hands wrapped in bandages and her voice still hoarse. She had limped all the way along Houston Street and up First Avenue. Though she'd sobbed into his shoulder when he hugged her beside the fire truck, he hadn't seen her cry since. She displayed nothing but resolve—determination to bring her sister home and give her a proper Jewish funeral. When Charlie had offered to assist with the arrangements, Esther said that this was her responsibility. "I've never forgiven myself for not giving my father a funeral," she told him. "And I won't let that happen again."

That was the most Esther had ever shared with him about her past. So they'd both lost a father. Now was not the time, however, to dig deeper. The best he could do today was help her find Rachel and bring her body home. There would be time later to learn more about Esther's father and to share his own past. Today Esther had much to do. Tomorrow, Charlie was resuming his job at the firehouse. He'd have liked another day or two to stay by Esther's side, but he was happy to be a fireman again. He'd come so close to losing it—to throwing it away. Chief Croker looked out for him—almost as a father would have. He wasn't sure why the chief did it. But he took something away from the whole affair—something intangible.

ESTHER WAITED IN LINE with her mother and Charlie. She was exhausted. Her legs ached and her hands throbbed beneath the bandages. She hadn't returned home the night before until well after dark. She'd been desperate to find Rachel. Her sister was not among the survivors; she would have seen her. She'd accepted that, and wanted to look at the bodies lined up on Washington Place, but the policeman wouldn't let her near the blanket-covered corpses. Finally, the coroner began transporting the dead by horse wagon to the pier. She went home, but didn't really sleep, having sat up late with her mother, aunt, and uncle. Right before dawn, on her bed, alone in her room staring at Rachel's side of the bed, she drifted off to sleep for a short time.

They said very little to each other as they inched forward ever so slowly. She was looking up to the open bay door where there was a table and some policemen. Esther saw Clara Lemlich come out the door heading back toward the street. She noticed Esther and came straight over. "Esther—hello. What are…" Clara's words trailed off. She looked at the bandages on Esther's hands, and then at Esther's mom and Charlie. She held her hand to her mouth and tears formed in her eyes. "Rachel?"

Esther felt her own eyes watering up. She nodded, without speaking.

"Oh—I'm so sorry," Clara said. She put her hand on Esther's shoulder.

"Why are you here?" Esther asked softly. Her throat burned.

"You remember my cousin, Lena."

Esther nodded. She remembered Clara's cousin was also a seamstress at Triangle, though didn't know her personally. "Is she here?" Esther asked, motioning her head toward the pier.

"No, I looked at every coffin." Clara paused and became very emotional. "Some are burned so bad they're hard to recognize. But my aunt said Lena was wearing gray stockings and brown leather boots. I didn't see any of the burnt girls wearing those."

"So now what?" Charlie asked.

"Clara, this is Charlie."

Clara offered a hand. "Clara Lemlich."

"I remember you from the union hall," Charlie said while shaking her hand.

"The policeman said if Lena wasn't here," Clara said. "I should go check at Bellevue. There are some injured survivors in the hospital."

Esther felt butterflies in her stomach. Her thinking brain knew it was impossible, but still there was a sliver of hope, impossible to ignore. "They never said anything about survivors at Bellevue," she rasped out. "They said we had to come here."

The line moved forward a bit. Esther felt her head spinning. She wondered if she should translate what Clara had just said for her mother. The poor woman was clutching a handbag with both hands and staring down at her feet. Perhaps reading her mind, Charlie leaned toward Esther and spoke quietly: "We're almost inside. Let's check in there first and then I'll go with you to Bellevue."

Esther nodded.

"They're interrogating every visitor," said Clara. "The police at the table there. They said they found crooks who showed up to go through the pockets of the dead girls. So now they're asking questions to make sure only family members get in."

"How awful," said Charlie. But Esther couldn't stop thinking about the survivors at Bellevue.

"Altsding lozt zich ois mit a gevain," Clara said in Yiddish. Everything ends in weeping. Esther's mother looked up and began to cry. Charlie looked on silently.

Clara rubbed Esther's shoulder, bowed her head to her mother, and said goodbye to Charlie. For Esther, the waiting now became unbearable. She needed to get inside. Perhaps… perhaps… After all, the firemen had found Esther alive atop the elevator and carried her out. They may have done the same for Rachel… brought her to a different spot…

INSIDE THE PIER STRUCTURE, two long rows of plain wooden coffins had been laid out. Once screened at the entrance, family members walked along the two rows trying to identify their loved one. Many of the bodies were horribly burned, others simply had soot covered faces, and some looked relatively clean if perhaps somewhat swollen and stiff. Mothers removed shoes to look for sewn holes in socks to identify their daughters, children sifted braids looking for their mothers' hairpins. Through teary eyes, fathers stared at blackened faces trying to decide if they really were their daughters.

With every coffin they passed, Esther fought the urge to raise her hopes. Rachel couldn't be here. These bodies were empty vestiges of something that *was*. Rachel was so *full*. Full of hopes and dreams, full of love. Full of history—she'd escaped the horrors of Bialystok. She was supposed to have been dancing—maybe with

Gaspar—at the dance that Saturday night. She had her first kiss to look forward to, someday. She wasn't lying here lifeless in one of these macabre boxes, Esther knew it. She felt it.

Esther walked with her bandaged hands wrapped around her mother's arm. Charlie followed. Some bodies were too big, and they passed those coffins without stopping. The younger victims got closer scrutiny, but—one by one—they were able to rule them out. Not the right dress. Hair too long. Not Rachel. Not Rachel.

They'd made it down the entire length of the first row and then walked around and started back up the second. Not Rachel. Not Rachel. Wailing spouses rummaged through the dead's pockets for trinkets and heirlooms. Some just huddled around a coffin and prayed. Esther, her mother, and Charlie moved down the line. Esther had let go of her mother's arm as they shuffled through a small grouping. She turned to see if Charlie was following and when she came back around to her mother, found her stopped in front of the next coffin, staring down at the dead girl's shoes. Esther looked and felt the wind leave her chest. She knew the shoes at once: scuffed brown leather, just above the ankle, and the front of the right-foot sole flapping apart.

Esther knelt down and brushed hair away from the face. One side of the head had been gashed open and dried blood stiffened the hair in clumps. But save for some soot around the mouth and nose, the face was not damaged at all. It was Rachel. Esther's eyes teared up and she stood and hugged her mother—still frozen at the foot of the coffin.

─────

WHEN ESTHER HUGGED HER mother and the two began crying aloud, Charlie stepped back. They needed their moment. He had been nine-years old when his father died. Much of that day was just blurry bits of memory, but he remembered how his mother hugged him, how she sobbed and squeezed his body tight against hers. He could still remember how her chest heaved with deep cries of grief.

And Cousin Charlie had swooped in. Maybe it was guilt. Maybe it was to keep up appearances—Silent Charlie the beneficent. Perhaps it was genuine concern. He wasn't sure of the motive, but he resented his cousin nonetheless. The last thing Esther needed was for Charlie to step in and try to fix the situation. Esther had her own strength—she'd experienced tragedy before. And this couldn't be fixed anyhow. He would just love her. That's all Esther needed. Love didn't fix grief, but it gave you something to cling to as you went forward.

※

THROUGH TEARY EYES, ESTHER looked up from her mother's shoulder to Charlie. He stood off to the side, quietly waiting. She made eye contact and found compassion in those honest eyes. It wasn't like when her father died. Back then, she felt completely lost—not knowing where they'd go or what she would do. Now was different. Charlie was there. He would hold her if she wanted.

She was grief-stricken for sure. But Esther wasn't scared about where she'd end up. She'd worked hard in America. New York was her home. The Lower East Side was where she belonged. She knew exactly what to do. The world would not be allowed to forget Rachel, the way it had forgotten her father. No longer would Esther's fingers stitch garments. From now on they would stitch sentences. She would tell the world what she knew.

She broke from her mother's embrace and stepped toward Charlie. He said nothing as he wrapped his arms around her. She did not cry as he squeezed her tightly. She tucked her head into his shoulder and looked up. The late-morning sun beamed long lines of light through the high windows at the eastern end of the pier.

The steel roof of the building was supported by an open-webbed system of iron trusses suspended fifty feet overhead. From just beneath the line of windows, a small bird jumped off the thin ledge. It swooped down through the bright rays of sunlight and gave a flutter of elegant flaps, before settling into an easy glide over the twin rows of coffins below. Esther watched the heavenly creature sail effortlessly through the dank air and land perfectly on the cross section of a far truss beam.

Epilogue

1913

Joseph Morgan had hoped to become a fireman. At the firehouse near his home, he'd inquired about applying. He was told the Civil Service Commission had yet to open up new applications for probationary fireman positions, but there were openings for inspectors with the new Bureau of Fire Prevention.

He liked his job well enough. Most of the day he was on his own, walking from factory to factory checking for fire safety violations. The owners and managers of these businesses rarely gave him a hard time. If Joseph found an infraction, he usually allowed them to correct it on the spot. Not enough water pails? *Fill four more and properly display them before I finish my inspection.* No record of a fire drill? *Fill out this here card with dates and times and mount it in a prominent place.* He had a certain amount of leeway in enforcing the fire code and his supervisors were more interested in compliance than punishment. There was, however, one infraction that Joseph was never allowed to overlook. It required an immediate court summons to the owners.

Joseph stood at the stairwell exit door on the fifth floor of a five-story loft factory. As soon as he saw it, Joseph told the manager escorting him to go find his boss. Now he waited, hoping to see the manager return with an owner. It was a hassle if the owner wasn't on the premises. He would have to issue the court summons to the manager in the factory owner's name, both men would have to appear in court, and more than once the judge had thrown out the charges when the owner feigned ignorance. The manager returned with another man. He was stocky. His thick neck bulged out from his collar. "What's the problem here?" said the man impatiently.

"Are you the owner of this factory?" Joseph asked.

"Yes, I am. What's going on?"

"Sir, I'm an inspector with the Fire Department's Bureau of Fire Prevention. You have a locked exit door during business hours—while employees are working. That is a violation."

The man looked at the door. There was a slide bolt with a padlock. There was no arguing the fact. "What do you mean by violation?" he said angrily.

"I have to issue you a court summons."

The man looked as if he were about to explode. His face turned red and he balled his fists. But he said nothing. From his satchel, Joseph removed a pad of pre-printed violation forms. He fished around the bottom of the bag for a pen. "What is your name, sir?"

The man stared at him for a second, then said: "Blanck. Max Blanck."

LABOR LEADER WEEKLY

VOL. 26   MARCH 22, 1936   NO. 12

THE TRIANGLE FIRE, REVISITED WITH CHIEF EDWARD CROKER

ESTHER GREENBERG-PENDERGRASS

This Wednesday marks the twenty-fifth anniversary of the terrible fire at the Triangle Shirtwaist Factory. One hundred and forty-six perished that day, among them the sister of Labor Leader Weekly contributor, Esther Greenberg-Pendergrass. For those who lost loved ones that day and those who struggled for reform in the years that followed, March 25 th is a day to reflect on what was taken and what was gained.

The U.S. Secretary of Labor, Frances Perkins will be in New York, where at the corner of Washington Place and Greene Street she will lay a wreath to commemorate the victims of that tragedy. Former Governor Alfred E. Smith will also attend. Both Perkins and Smith served on Senator Robert F. Wagner's Fire Safety Committee in the aftermath of the fire. There have been many leaders in this fight for change regarding factory safety, but perhaps none more prominent than the former chief of the New York Fire Department, Edward F. Croker.

Croker stepped down from his post just one month after the Triangle fire and founded the Croker Fire Preventing and Engineering Company. He is widely considered the foremost authority on fire safety across the nation and has published several articles and books on the subject. From his home in Amityville, Long Island, Croker sat with Esther Greenberg-Pendergrass for an interview. (Disclosure: Greenberg-Pendergrass's husband, a battalion chief with the New York City Fire Department, is a former colleague and long-time friend of Croker.)

Greenberg-Pendergrass: Chief Croker, you have described the fire at the Triangle factory as the worst fire of your career. Along with the horror of such a large loss of lives, what is the memory that has stayed with you all these years?

Croker: Without a doubt it is the helplessness I felt that day. The officers and men I served along side with in the Fire Department were the finest in the world, but we still failed that day. I saw to it our department was the best equipped, but no tool at our disposal was effective at saving those girls. I had fought for preventative measures, almost none of which were adopted prior to the fire—the principal exception being the high-pressure water system. If nothing else the engine companies had water in their hoses—they put out the fire quickly. But it was still too late.

Greenberg-Pendergrass: Many were surprised when you decided to retire after the fire. Despite the blame being aimed at many city officials, you were widely praised for your leadership. Even the *Times*, which had once criticized your appointment as chief, lauded your tenure when you left. Do you still feel it was the right decision?

Croker: Often I have heard that it was the terrible sight of those poor girls jumping to their deaths that led me to retire. Other's have blamed it on my relationship with the fire commissioner at the time, Waldo. But neither is true. First and foremost, I wanted to spend time with my family. For too long I had given the demands of my post priority over the demands of a husband and father. And secondly, I wanted to use my knowledge and experience to shape the reforms that the fire's notoriety made inevitable. I had seen too many unscrupulous actors step in to corrupt and profit unfairly from measures that began for the public good. Sprinklers are

(CONTINUED FROM PAGE 1)

a fine example. I was pretty sure the legislature would finally move on automatic sprinklers in factories. What I could not abide, was to see the installation of sprinklers become a racket. It was too important. I wanted to be at the forefront, and my conscience would never allow me to work both sides. The chief of department must be pure of any conflicts of interest.

Greenberg-Pendergrass: Has enough been done, in your opinion? Are the laws at present sufficient to keep factory workers safe from fire?

Croker: The unprecedented growth of cities in this country at the end of the nineteenth century brought with it a menace from fire never seen before. It has taken us a generation to come to terms with this modern phenomenon. In strict financial terms, the insurance underwriters agree that we've made steady progress from the losses to fire of thirty years ago. Automatic sprinklers have saved many millions of dollars more than they cost to install. But the loss of lives by fire is one that cannot be measured in dollars nor expressed in words save by those unfortunates whose relatives and friends have succumbed in many deplorable calamities. Regular fire drills and unencumbered exits have saved hundreds, if not thousands of lives. These two measures, sprinklers and fire drills, were the key reforms and yes, I do believe highly sufficient reforms at that.

Greenberg-Pendergrass: Are there any measures you would have liked to see taken that weren't?

Croker: The new laws, as well as the Bureau of Fire Prevention created after the fire, were good. But I would have stiffened the penalties for non-compliance. The owners of the Triangle Company, Misters Blanck and Harris, were acquitted of manslaughter. They had the fanciest lawyer money could buy and they beat the charges. I'm sure the legal fees were considerable because the penalties for manslaughter are considerable. The penalties for fire code infractions, at first, were minimal. The legislature may have been pushed to action by the public outcry after the Triangle fire, but they still caved to pressure by the owners when it came to punishment. The new laws gave the Fire Prevention Bureau a means to require safer practices, but I feel changes would have come at a quicker pace if infractions brought higher penalties or even jail time to the owners. As it was, many owners found it easier to continue business as usual and simply pay the fines as they arose. Slowly, however, things have changed. The inspectors have done their job.

Greenberg-Pendergrass: You've had a long and distinguished career in the fire service...

Croker: Over fifty years!

Greenberg-Pendergrass: Extraordinary. As you look back, what is it that you're most proud of?

Croker: It has, without question, been my honor to work along side with the people I have along the way. The men I served with in the fire department are the finest and most dedicated in the world. I demanded much of them, professionalism and discipline, and they in return gave a level of loyalty and respect unequaled elsewhere. After the Triangle fire I worked with many advocates for the public good, from Al Smith and Miss Perkins, to the women, in particular, the women, such as yourself who so eloquently led the way forward. The tragedy that was the Triangle fire was the convergence of decades of growth and indifference. It was the moment those two forces met, with terrible results. But it was also the moment when all the people I've just mentioned came together. It was the end of one era and the start of another. I am most proud of what I was able to bring to that moment.

SOURCES

As the reader will no doubt know, many of the characters in this book are based on real-life people. I have used both primary and secondary sources, as well as interviews to compile a wealth of information on these lives. In some cases, as with Edward Croker, the subjects' own words were the source of much important dialogue. *Fire Prevention* was first published by Croker in 1912 and sections of this informative text became the fire chief's speech to the garment workers in my story (which I place in 1911). Similarly, Croker's famous *I have no ambition... but one* speech—so ingrained in fire academy curricula across the country—is widely available in both printed and web-based sources.

William Gunn Shepherd's article detailing what he witnessed at the fire first appeared in the *Milwaukee Journal* on March 27, 1911. The other articles in this book attributed to Shepherd are my own fictional creations based on real articles from the time. Esther's interview with Croker is entirely fictional.

Details of Max Blanck's life, descriptions of working conditions at the Triangle factory, as well as the timeline of events on March 25, 1911 were informed by sources including David Von Drehle's *Triangle,* compilations of survivor accounts on Cornell University's Triangle Fire website, and Fire Chief Jay Jonas's *Division 7 Training and Safety Newsletter,* as well as documentation preserved at the F.D.N.Y. Academy's Mand Library and the New York City Fire Museum.

I am extremely grateful to the writers and historians listed below for the hard work they put into documenting this important historical event and era.

Selected Bibliography:
Benin, Leigh et al., *Images of America: The New York City Triangle Factory Fire,* (Charleston: Arcadia Publishing 2011).

Coe, Andrew ed., *F.D.N.Y. An Illustrated History of the Fire Department of the City of New York,* (New York: W. W. Norton & Co. 2003).

Cornell University School of I.L.R., "Remembering the 1911 Triangle Factory Fire," https://trianglefire.ilr.cornell.edu/index.html.

Edward Croker Papers/Files, F.D.N.Y. Mand Library, New York.

Golway, Terry, *So Others Might Live,* (New York: Basic Books 2002).

Johnson, Gus, *F.D.N.Y.: The Fire Buff's Handbook of the New York Fire Department 1900-1975,* (Boston: Western Islands, 1977).

Jonas, Jay, "The Triangle Shirtwaist Factory Fire & the F.D.N.Y.," *Division 7 Training and Safety Newsletter,* (May/June 2019).

Kogos, Fred, *Dictionary of Popular Yiddish Words, Phrases, and Proverbs,* (New York: Citadel Press, 1997).

Scher, Steven, *Images of America: New York City Firefighting 1901-2001,* (Charleston: Arcadia Publishing 2002).

Triangle: Remembering the Fire, directed by Daphne Pinkerson, 40 min., HBO Films, 2011.

Von Drehle, David, *Triangle: The Fire that Changed America,* (New York: Grove Press, 2003).

Quotations:
p. 32 *I'm going to throw you out...* adapted from Edward Croker [Public Domain], from Mand Library collection.

p. 42 *Gentlemen... This is Smokey Joe Martin...* Edward Croker [Public Domain], as recounted by Golway, and Mand Library collection.

p. 65 *Most of the troubles of the world...* Charles Murphy [Public Domain], as recounted by Von Drehle.

p. 89 *Get the hell out of here...* Edward Croker [Public Domain], from Mand Library collection.

p. 100 *This city may have a fire as deadly...* Edward Croker [Public Domain], as recounted by Cornell University School of I.L.R.

pp. 100-101 Croker's speech to garment workers adapted from *Fire Prevention* (Dodd Mead & Co., 1912), [Public Domain].

p. 172 *I've no ambition...* Edward Croker, [Public Domain].

p. 236 *Every little movement,* lyrics by Otto Harbach from the musical *Madame Sherry,* 1910, [Public Domain].

pp. 275-276 "Eyewitness at the Triangle," William Gunn Shepherd, *Milwaukee Journal,* March 27, 1911, [Public Domain].

p. 282 "*Altsding lozt zich...*" Yiddish proverb, [Public Domain].

Acknowledgments

There are many I'd like to thank for their help along the way. My starting point in learning about the Triangle Shirtwaist Factory Fire was a training article written by Deputy Chief Jay Jonas—a great overview of the tragedy, as well as a timeline of the fire department's actions fighting the blaze. Chief Jonas was also kind enough to speak with me and make helpful suggestions focusing my research.

There has been much written about the Triangle fire, and as the bibliography shows, I made ample use of these excellent resources. None stands out more than David Von Drehle's *Triangle: The Fire That Changed America*. Von Drehle's narrative is richly detailed and, above all, a fitting tribute to the victims.

Don Maye, Eric Smith, and Frederick Melahn, at the F.D.N.Y. Mand Library were friendly and eager to help. The library's collection of documents and manuscripts relating to Chief Edward Croker were an invaluable tool. And Sandra Chiritescu was extremely helpful in reviewing my Yiddish phrases.

I would like to thank Raymond Ott for sharing with me the family stories of his grandfather, Andrew Ott. Rita Perretta, Richie Portello, and Jamie Kirkpatrick were kind enough to read early manuscripts and offer advice. And I also want to thank my cousin, Christie Derrico, for her guidance.

I am deeply thankful to my editor, Amber Hatch. Not only were her edits perfect and her observations astute, but her emotional investment in the story was a great encouragement.

And I am extremely grateful for all the survivors of the Triangle fire who told their story—the real life Esthers. Most were young women who had recently immigrated to America. They kept the memory of the victims alive and fought for change.

I want to thank Sofia and Luca for making me smile every day.

And, of course, my wife Teresa deserves my heartfelt thanks for resuming her role as first reader of all my books. Her belief in me makes writing possible.

A.S.

About the Artist

The cover art and interior illustrations for *Hell's Hundred Acres* are by **Chris Burke**. He was a firefighter with Ladder 20 for twenty-two years. In addition to his work as a graphic artist, Burke is a painter and specializes in tattoos. He lives in Warwick, New York with his wife and two sons.

@gooddaystattoo
gooddaystattoo@gmail.com

Also by Andrew Serra

The Dead Florentines
At the heart of the Italian Renaissance lies the city of Florence and the dominant force of the city's life are the trade guilds. When Lorenzo has the good fortune of securing an apprenticeship in a lucrative guild, his destiny is imperiled by the factious rivalries of a city as dangerous as it is beautiful. *The Dead Florentines* is the story of a young man's Dantesque journey through hell and back in which he is drawn to a love that is unattainable and protected by a guide who must battle his own demons. When dark secrets from the past and his love for a powerful guild master's daughter threaten Lorenzo's life, his hope for salvation lies with an unconventional Catholic priest.

La Petite Parisienne
The French Revolution has brought young Jacques and Olivie together even as the world around them erupts in violent upheaval. The children become fascinated with a popular street singer and his song about the infamous chevalier Armand Dourienne. As Jacques and Olivie discover more secrets behind the legend of Dourienne, revolutionary fervor and their own family histories endanger them both. The danger that descends upon them leads to the birth of a new legend, the legend of La Petite Parisienne.

Finding John
In the aftermath of 9/11, life for firefighters became a whirlwind of searching for human remains, staffing firehouses, caring for the families of the fallen, and attending hundreds of funerals—all performed in the spotlight of new-found national media attention. In March of 2002, Firefighter Andrew Serra and a team of rescue workers uncovered the remains of a fallen firefighter. Later that year, a story would be published which accused that deceased fireman of a terrible breach of duty and honor. Like all firefighters, Andrew Serra passed the months and years after the attacks putting the pieces of the Fire Department—and life in general—back together again. He would spend many more years, however, searching for the truth.

Zuccotti Park

In the fall of 2011, protestors gathered in an open plaza set between high-rise office towers in lower Manhattan. The Occupy Wall Street movement was underway. Following his wife's death, Frank Scala decides to retire from the police force. As the protests heat up, Frank sees a world changing before his eyes and struggles to hold on to the things he holds dear. Jen Scala is mourning the loss of her mother but finds solace in a budding relationship with a classmate. She sees her father as a painful reminder of the past and wants to move forward. The protests provide a perfect place to start. *Zuccotti Park* is a moving story of ordinary New Yorkers caught up in social upheaval, personal grief, and the search for renewal.

The Tenement Series

Millions of immigrants arrived in America in the late nineteenth century. In New York City, tenements were built to house the tens of thousands of new arrivals. One such building, an ornate, red-bricked tenement stands at 56 ½ Mulberry Street. Known as Mulberry Bend, the block is notoriously deadly. For Patrick Monaghan, however, it is the only home he has ever known. His family is beset with hardships, and he dreams of a better life. But sinister forces, led by the dreaded gang leader Spots McCavish, make getting out impossible. In the name of progress, authorities clear the gangs out of the alleys of the Bend—leading to what is, for Patrick, the greatest crime of all. He would spend decades searching, never imagining the truth lay where it all began.

www.ingramcontent.com/pod-product-compliance
Lightning Source LLC
LaVergne TN
LVHW091209160125
801453LV00019B/120/J